STRAY CAT

A NOVEL BY

Don Matheson

SUMMIT BOOKS

NEW YORK · LONDON · TORONTO · SYDNEY · TOKYO

This book is a work of fiction. Names, characters, places, and incidents are either the product of the author's imagination or are used fictitiously. Any resemblance to actual events or locales or persons, living or dead, is entirely coincidental.

PUBLISHED BY SUMMIT BOOKS
A DIVISION OF SIMON & SCHUSTER, INC.
SIMON & SCHUSTER BUILDING
ROCKEFELLER CENTER
1230 AVENUE OF THE AMERICAS
NEW YORK, NY 10020
SUMMIT BOOKS AND COLOPHON ARE TRADEMARKS OF
SIMON & SCHUSTER, INC.
DESIGNED BY EVE METZ
MANUFACTURED IN THE UNITED STATES OF AMERICA

1   3   5   7   9   10   8   6   4   2

LIBRARY OF CONGRESS CATALOGING IN PUBLICATION DATA
MATHESON, DON.
STRAY CAT.

I. TITLE.
PS3563.A83545S7   1987   813'.54   87-10013
ISBN 0-671-64112-3

FOR VICKIE

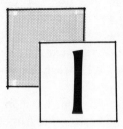

Kneeling on the weathered wood of the dock, Charlie Gamble stretched to retrieve a floating yellow plastic roller skate from Boston Harbor. Plastic skate; not enough ball bearings to make the damn thing sink, he mused. He used the skate to dip for a condom that bobbed like the ghost of a cucumber along with the tide. He put both into the white garbage bag he carried. As he tied its corners together, he admired the June sun glinting from the glass of the jagged bar-graph cityscape across the water.

"Hey, Gamble, here's another jewel for yer crown!" He turned and saw Lew Faucet, his beer belly swelling over a baggy paisley swimming suit, draining the last gulp of a Pabst Blue Ribbon. Lew was silhouetted on the stern of his boxy cabin cruiser, *Lew-Sea*, in improbable foreground to the standing rigging of *Old Ironsides*. The forty-four-gun frigate was mothballed to ignominious servitude; a lure for Charlestown tourism; reminder of an age when a wooden boat could be built to last two hundred years. Lew tossed the beer can in Charlie's direction, and he snatched it out of the air, slipped it through the open corner of his bag.

He continued his barefoot walk along the dock, under the peeling sign that read "Charlestown Marina." He could hear

Lew laughing and telling his wife, Lucy, that "this mornin' Gamble done 'is duty on a rubber an' a roller skate."

On a cool starlit evening the previous spring, his intellectual discrimination dimmed by a rare indulgence in Colombian marijuana, Charlie had tried to explain to Lew that stooping once daily, on his way to the dumpster, was a gesture calculated to cleanse his soul, not the harbor. On the mornings Lew was up early enough to catch him at it, Lew usually repeated his comment that taking one piece of garbage a day out of that cesspool was like spraying Bactine on Asian gonorrhea.

Charlie didn't mind Lew's derisive attitude about his morning routine of token marine sanitation. The trash in the harbor disgusted him. One morning he grabbed some random garbage on the way to the dumpster, and it made him feel good. It got to be a habit. It wasn't a bad habit. He came to think of it as a ritual. It was as close as he came to religion anymore, and the fact that it evoked the scorn of the tattooed retired petty officer did not shake his esoteric faith. It was sort of like kissing the Blarney stone: ya did it, and it was no less fulfilling for being futile. On the other hand, he had to admit that the harbor seemed to be no less filthy than it had been before he started.

It was a windless day, the sort on which the heat accumulated, making June seem like August. The asphalt was already hot in the parking lot. It made him hip-hop his way to the dumpster with his offering. He noticed a flashy red sports car that he hadn't seen at the marina before. On the way back, he saw a dark shape in the driver's seat. Regaining the cooler wood of the dock, he looked back to confirm it. It was a Ferrari. The windows were up tight. Someone was inside. He scurried to the driver's side, where shadow kept the pavement cool, and peered in.

The woman was sleeping, head back, mouth open, rivulets of sweat running into her dark hair like a face emerging from a pool. He tapped on the glass, and she started, hugged herself protectively, worked at getting her bearings.

"You better roll the windows down, miss, or you're going to bake in there."

Shoulders slumping, suddenly aware of the stifling heat, she seemed to realize he wasn't a threat. When she opened the door, the superheated air hit him in a wave. She half rolled out of the low seat, steadied herself with a hand on the door as she stood. "Wh-where . . . ?" The rich tone of her skin went sallow before his eyes as her knees buckled.

Charlie caught her by one limp and sweat-slippery arm. He got her under the armpits, then awkwardly up across his chest, her neck stretched so far back, it seemed broken. For a second he stood there wondering what to do, then got the idea to fight heat with cold, carried her to the wooden hut where the marina's showers were, hesitated a moment on the silly consideration of whether to go into the one marked "Buoys" or the one marked "Gulls." Hearing no noise from either, he walked into the men's shower, spun the cold-water knob, and stood there as it ran over both of them.

She came to, sputtering and flailing at the water, eyes closed. He put her down on the step outside. He pushed her head toward her knees and held it there until enough blood got to her brain that he could feel some strength fighting back. When he let her up, she looked at him uncomprehending, head swiveling around as she struggled to focus on something familiar.

He spoke softly. "You're okay, miss. Everything's all right. You were asleep in your car, and it got very hot. When I woke you, you got out and fainted. I ran the shower on you to cool you down, bring you around." He kept on like that until she began to compose herself; issued a few "ohs" and "ahs" to indicate she was remembering how she got there.

Finally, she looked down at herself. Her white duck trousers and salmon-colored blouse clung to her and made it rather obvious that she'd made a hasty job of dressing . . . either that, or she didn't believe in underwear. She did a thing with her elbows and knees, covering up.

Charlie noticed a green beach towel hanging on the rail behind her. It occurred to him to drape it around her. But that impulse was checked easily on the rationalization that one could be chivalrous to a fault. While the woman's body language was

9

circling the wagons around her ample endowments, her head was unbowed and unabashed as it took in the surroundings.

"Did you have to try to drown me?"

Right about then he realized that she was one of those women who take the breath away, even soaking like a wharf rat. Her teeth were as white and even as Chiclets; the blue eyes had those fancy radial lines in the irises; these set in angular cheekbones that changed the look from Sears catalog to haute couture. He realized she had the kind of looks guys like him saw in movies, then didn't bother to dream about, they were so far out of reach.

"If I'd wanted to drown you, I could have tossed you in the harbor."

"A cool rag would have been sufficient, I think."

"Look, lady, nobody said to wake you up before your brains baked or catch you before you broke your face on the asphalt, either, but that's what I did, and the water seemed like a good idea at the time!"

He reached over and grabbed the towel, tossed it at her. She caught it, surprised. He turned and started down the dock, thinking this was a good example of why he'd never strained himself chasing face-heavy women. They got so much attention they became spoiled. People put up with their being peckish, so they forgot their manners.

"Wait!"

He turned and saw her getting unsteadily to her feet, pulling the towel around her like a shawl. "I'm sorry. Of course you're right. I was just upset."

"Right," he said, "and bitchy, too."

She smiled a little. "Okay, and bitchy."

"And stupid to be sleeping in a hundred-and-twenty-degree car."

"Let's not get carried away. 'Careless' would be strong enough, I think. With your penchant for overkill, I hope I never have a fly on my nose when you're standing by with a shovel."

He smiled without meaning to. She looked around again, at Boston across the water, then up at the crosshatch of bridges spanning the Charles River. She was probably in her mid-twenties, tall, her brunette hair cut short, to let the facial structure show, Charlie thought.

"I admit it isn't the first time I've been accused of intemperance," he said. "Are you meeting somebody here?"

A guarded look. "Why, is this your marina or something?"

"I meant to help you find your friends, if you're looking for someone. I know most of the boats around here."

Maybe it was the way her hair was slicked back from the water . . . maybe the bright sunshine on a face awakened to crisis. Anyway, he'd never seen emotion appear that way, out of nowhere, and take over a face so quickly, her mouth hanging open, eyes beginning to blink back salty tears, then the grimace. There was nothing theatrical or pretty about it.

It made Charlie forget how beautiful she was. He thought maybe the heat had done more damage to the lady than he'd realized. "I don't know much about heat stroke. Maybe I should take you over to the emergency room at Mass General."

She didn't answer or look back at him. She shook her head, stamped her foot, and cursed. Charlie took it for exasperation at her own display of unbridled emotion. Then she started walking toward her car. She looked back briefly, gave a little wave and a wan smile from ten feet away. "Thanks," she said, and kept going. When she got to the Ferrari, she looked around again, as though the world had been rearranged since she'd seen it last.

Charlie called out to her. "I have some coffee on my sailboat. Would you like a cup?" She hesitated, hand on the car door. "You could change to some dry clothes if you like."

The look she gave him, Charlie thought, didn't flow from the usual feminine concerns one might expect in such a situation: Was he an oddball of some kind, or a bore, or a rapist? The look was suddenly level and sure, like maybe she was appraising a pair of shoes in a window.

Charlie was aware that his looks tended to polarize women into two groups: those who found him unremarkable and those who found him terribly attractive. He didn't understand why, unless it had to do with a leanness that was a quirk of metabolism. He could and did indulge in rich food and drink without visible effect on his slightly-over-six-foot frame. More than one woman had told him it had to do with the way he looked at her, a stillness in his gaze that showed interest without affront. He discounted it partly to his belief that women like to believe that their lovers are gorgeous whether it's true or not. He had never been called handsome by anyone.

She shrugged, the towel falling open, she noticing but not caring, just going with it, running a hand through the wet hair, grabbing a soft leather shoulder bag from among several similar ones he could see in the car. She activated the Chapman lock and alarm of the car, followed him down the ramp to the dock. Along the way, he said I'm Charlie Gamble, and she said I'm Rosemary Marlette, call me Rosy.

While Charlie heated the coffee in the dripolator, Rosy said she'd like to shower. This meant he had to give her the routine on the idiosyncrasies of marine plumbing. He always felt ridiculous giving adults instructions on the use of a toilet. Not nearly as ridiculous, however, as he did taking stopped-up pipes apart, the inevitable result without a little orientation sermon on the incompatibility of paper and one-way valves.

What the hell. The lady's in no position to put on airs herself. Sleeping in a car packed with luggage. Some kind of runaway, maybe? Fight with her husband? A lush, too drunk to remember arriving the night before? The car showed no signs of sloppy driving. More likely just saw the superbright lights of the marina lot from the interstate, pulled off to sleep in the security they afforded. Logical but wrong.

There was a huge government housing project five blocks away. The fancy cars around the marinas were prime targets. Chapman locks and burglar alarms were de rigueur if the car had any style at all. When they had put up the lights and a case-hardened steel chain across the opening in the chain-link fence, given all the slip-holders keys, Charlie decided to save the money he paid to garage his RX-7. Two nights later some enterprising thief cut a ten-foot-wide hole in the chain-link fence itself and drove the damn thing through it. The marina management repaired the fence, kept the lights, for what they were worth, and admitted defeat by dispensing with the chain and installing a sign that said "Boston, car theft capital of the world. Park at your own risk."

Charlie put the insurance money in the bank. His life-style had changed such that he didn't need a car anymore. The realization gave him a certain amount of pleasure . . . trimming the fat from his life: first the house, then the car, then the job. Well, the house was second, really, after the wife. They sold the house and split the money down the middle with the marriage.

He'd married his wife for many of the same qualities that later carried her to an anchor desk at a Boston TV station. He'd been thirty when he married her, and she was still defensive about a recent change from print to television journalism. She thought she could make a difference in the depth and focus of reporting.

The marriage suited him pretty well for four years. Their schedules hadn't left them a lot of time. His was a daytime career, but hers fluctuated with the news. For him, it was good time, though. They were moved to sneers and laughter by the same things; in bed they achieved excitement, exhaustion, and sleep in unison; and he admired her self-possession, the dispassionate candor that came across so well on the tube. Fawning women made him uncomfortable.

When a major New York station called, she couldn't say no. Charlie decided he could. It seemed like a city that took a long time to get out of. She said it was exposure that could lead to a network job. He pointed out that they already made plenty of money. She snorted at that, said, "Charlie, grow up!" From there it degenerated into name-calling.

He was surprised when she chose the job over him; thought she'd blown it. After a while, he realized there'd been a lot of stuff about her he'd never recognized. A year later, trying to rid himself of a lingering sense of desertion, he decided, feminism and chauvinism and all the platitudes about balance aside, given the way things worked, most marriages needed either a follower or a lot of damn fortunate coincidences, and they had lacked both. He bought her a Christmas card but realized before he mailed it that it was a wimpy move. It wouldn't change anything; would only feed his regret, to correspond with her. He wasn't above hoping his silence reaped small revenge. Her self-possession be damned.

He guessed that a Ferrari would go for around sixty thousand bucks. Why would anybody with that kind of dough not stay in a hotel? The world's sexiest car thief? Too much luggage.

Rosy emerged from the head in a cotton shift, very appropriate boat attire, and something colorful underneath. Probably a bikini, he thought. Her hair was in towel-dried curls. She smiled and accepted the coffee he poured for her.

"Thank you. What a strange shape this cup is!"

It was a heavy mug, wide at the base, narrow top, rubber pad on the bottom. "So it won't spill when the boat's in a seaway," Charlie explained.

She nodded slowly and moved about the large open cabin, frankly inspecting the premises as she drank the coffee. By the navigation station she asked, "What are all these electronic gadgets?"

"Loran, Sat Nav, they're both things that tell you where you are . . . very accurate; within fifty feet, usually. That's a radar screen, shows you where things are if the weather fogs up."

She was wearing perfume that smelled like something more expensive than flowers. Up close he could see a fine white down on her skin. She wore no rings. "VHF radio, and this is the important one." He pressed a button, and speakers in the aft bulkhead began to spill riffs from John Klemmer's saxophone.

She slipped past him, sat at the teak salon table. Thinking she'd taken the stereo as a lounge-lizard move, he turned it off, sat across from her, gave her plenty of room.

"You live here, or is this boat your toy?"

"I live here," he said. "Have for the last year and a half."

"Alone?"

He'd moved from marriage to the marina. He had owned the

14

boat. There were a lot of people around in the warm months. In winter, the company was sparse but interesting. One had to be a little odd to live on a boat in Boston in the wintertime. Lately he'd been feeling odd, and enjoying the sensation. He had a growing conviction that most people were missing the point.

He wasn't sure what the point was, either, and he knew this insight to be a classic symptom of madness. But he also knew the average American worked eight hours at a job he hated and watched about six or seven hours of television. About all that was left went into caring for the basic bodily functions. He had to go with his instincts on the issue.

"Alone, except for Rogers, the bane of unwary seagulls," he said, remembering to open the aft cabin door. Rogers, a twelve-pound neutered cat, black with white feet and nose, strutted out as though to fanfare. He stopped when he saw Rosy, then jumped onto the table in front of her, sat down, and stared at her. She got the message, scratched his chin, and said in a deep voice, "Pleased to meetcha, Rog. Not very shy, are you?"

Reminded that cats are supposed to be standoffish, Rogers shot from the table out the companionway in one athletic bound. Rosy laughed, stuck her head out to see him leap to the dock and trot off.

"Where's he going?" she asked.

"He never tells me. He just showed up one day last winter and bawled at me until I fed him some leftover bluefish. He comes and goes by his own lights, prefers leftovers, but will eat most anything from a can that smells bad. He's named after Will Rogers, who never met a man he didn't like."

She cocked an eyebrow at that as though about to respond, but she thought better of it. His wife had had the same restraint, and he'd admired it until the stuff she'd left unsaid crept up and blindsided him all at once.

"Where are you from?"

"Boston," she said, put her hand on the handle of the aft cabin door, and looked over her shoulder at him questioningly. When he nodded, she opened it, saw the large berth that filled

15

the stern, dark blue double sleeping bag rolled up on one side, the aft head. "You're certainly neat for a single man," she said.

"Anything left out flies around when she heels over. After a while, I got tired of things getting broken and tangled up, started putting them away. I've gotten addicted to it. Can't stand to have stuff lying around; the space gets to feel crowded."

"I know what you mean. I've been traveling for a while, in my car. Just got back into town. At first, I could never remember which things were in which suitcase. Now I have it down to a science."

"Where were you traveling?"

A flutter of the eyes, then level at him. "California and points in between, here and there, visited a few old friends."

"Now you're back and looking for a job and apartment?"

"Right," she said, "as a matter of fact." She held a lot back from the smile she gave him then—not like she was conning him, really, more like she was enjoying watching his wheels turn, didn't plan to help him out very much.

"What do you do for a living, Rosy?"

"I've done some modeling. I have a degree in philosophy, but there aren't many jobs as resident philosopher around," she said without smiling. Charlie noted that she was quick to put the degree on record, even though it wasn't being used; defensive about the modeling, maybe. "I think I'm supposed to go back for a graduate degree or something, but I can't seem to get motivated for it."

"Why not?"

She looked at him and didn't hurry the answer. No fidgeting, maybe using her face to try to disconcert him. He thought she might have been working out what he wanted to hear. "I don't know."

So maybe she hadn't pegged him yet, either. "Why philosophy?"

"It seemed like the ultimate liberal art to me. Figure out what's right and wrong, then you're ready to do life."

"You make it sound like a sentence."

"Oh?"

16

"Did you figure it out?"

"Not the way I thought I would. I didn't realize until after I graduated that I had the chicken and the egg mixed up. People decide how they're going to live, then make up philosophies to justify what they're going to do regardless."

A confused look on his face, Charlie said, "Well, that covers the wisdom of civilization. . . . I think we skipped about seven pages of the small-talk syllabus."

Only a little snort of air got through her mouth, but Charlie knew a laugh when he saw one, thought maybe it constituted a regular giggling jag for this one.

She shrugged. "You asked."

"Yes, and I'm glad I did. I've decided to live on a sailboat, avoid traffic jams, especially on hot days, and spend as little time as possible doing what other people tell me to do. Maybe you could help me figure out how to justify that."

"You're offering me a job of philosophy, huh?"

He nodded slowly. "Ship's philosopher. That's what this navy needs."

"I didn't realize I was being interviewed."

Charlie thought, Like hell you didn't, honey. The way you look, your whole life's an interview, and that's what's got you jumpy, but he said, "If you can start right away, your first assignment will be to justify a little cruise to the islands just outside the harbor. It's going to be a scorcher today, and I thought I'd motor out and anchor, take a swim, maybe comb a beach, sip something tall and cold to beat the heat."

From the unsettled expression he saw on her face, he thought he'd gone too fast, said, "If you have to be back at some particular time, I can be flexible."

She shook her magnificent head, said, "No, it isn't that." Blurted it out, embarrassed, "I can't swim."

A short while later, Rogers having returned from his morning constitutional and lapped up a disgusting concoction of liver and egg, Charlie dropped the docking lines of his forty-two-foot sloop, *Squareknot*, and guided her down the harbor. As he steered, he puzzled over the foolhardiness of Rosy going out on a vast and friendless ocean with a stranger when she couldn't even swim. She didn't seem a fool, so he concluded that she must enjoy the adrenaline jolt one gets from taking a risk with open eyes. Either that, or she carried concealed weapons that gave her confidence.

The man who'd been watching them from the bridge ground his teeth. He walked to the Boston side and got into a black Ferrari similar to the one in which Rosy had been sleeping. The engine roared to life, and tires screamed on the hot pavement. Within the hurtling soundproof envelope of smoked glass and steel, the driver shrieked, "Bloody bastard, bleeding bitch!"

2

Wilbur Coughlin might have seen the man getting serious rubber in the Ferrari, or *Squareknot* headed seaward, as the Dodge van in which he rode sullen shotgun crossed the bridge headed north, pulling a tar baby in its wake. But he wouldn't have cared. Wilbur was being carted to work.

For two months he'd been tarring roofs in downtown Boston. Jablonsky Roofing did a lot of flat stuff in the city. Today Wilbur and Jim, the other half of the two-man crew, were doing the rare suburban job. Wilbur had already tired of the hundred-and-twenty-degree heat of a blacktop roof on days like this one. He'd also tired of Jim. He'd told Jim a week before that if he said, "Jablonsky Roofing, where ya start at the top," one more time, he was going to drown him in a bucket of hot tar. His parole officer had said the same damn thing when he got him the job. "Ya don't deserve it, Coughlin, but I got you a job where you'll start at the top." Frigging comics.

Some twenty years before, Wilbur had narrowly missed being saved from juvenile delinquency and subsequent criminal recidivism by athletics. At sixteen, he could bench press three hundred pounds and run the hundred in ten seconds flat, the kind of kid that a coach likes to help transcend his socioeconomic background. That was the year his stepfather gave him a halfhearted cuff for smarting off, then found himself spitting out bloody pieces of his broken dentures after Wilbur hit him back. Thenceforth, Wilbur had felt invincible.

So when the football coach at his high school told him to quit jaking on the sit-ups, Wilbur told him to stick it and giggled as he looked around for the reaction of his peers. The coach, who was suffering from a brain-racking 7 Crown hangover, was in the mood for making an example of somebody. A former lineman himself, who believed that all backs were expendable, he yanked Wilbur to his feet, slapped him three times before Wilbur knew what was happening, and kicked his butt off the field. That was the end of a promising career in athletics. Thereafter, Wilbur bolstered his feeling of invincibility by carrying a gun.

He carried it into a 7-Eleven in suburban Buffalo that happened to be staked out by two police officers. It cost him a shattered femur that still ached from time to time, twenty years later. When he got out of jail, he tried to sue the state for a million bucks for poor medical care during his incarceration. He used a cane going into court, but the idealistic young Legal Aid attorney was laughed out of the courtroom when a very fit young cop testified that it had taken him seven blocks to catch up with Wilbur in a foot race leading to a subsequent arrest, for which he'd beaten the rap. What pissed Wilbur off was that the cop'd never have touched him if he still had two good legs.

A few years later, he left the motor of a hot-wired Oldsmobile running outside a bank in Brookline, Mass., and carried another gun inside; he came out to find the alligator-clipped wire gone and two officers screaming, "Freeze, asshole!" and threatening to do it to him again. He dropped the gun and the paper bag. Twenty- and fifty- and hundred-dollar bills started blowing all over the damn street like so many chewing-gum wrappers. Cuffed in the squad car, he laughed, watching three female bank employees scurrying around the street picking them up while the cops tried to minimize shrinkage from a finders-keepers crowd of onlookers.

That is not to say he was particularly inept, or that law

enforcement is foolproof. Even a stopped clock is right twice a day, and Wilbur was giving them plenty of chances. He never was connected with any of the four people he'd killed in armed-robberies-turned-shootouts. He just got away and spent the money, those and many other times. These were the times he remembered, and it kept him feeling invincible . . . especially in combination with various pills manufactured ostensibly to help fat women take off unneeded pounds.

When the confines of the city had given way to open country, he began to look around. By the time they got to Beverly Farms, he'd noted that one couldn't even see the houses from the road, and the cars coming out of the driveways were usually Mercedeses or Cadillacs or Porsches or Jaguars.

The ultramodern box-type house was sitting on a ridgetop overlooking the seaway into Manchester Harbor, and as Wilbur sloshed hot tar about with his brush, he counted eight mansions poking their heads above the trees along the craggy, curving coastline. Looking down, next to a black marble rectangular swimming pool, he saw a lady with leathery wrinkled skin, wearing a blindfold, drinking a Bloody Mary that she placed on a silver tray between sips. Her ring finger sparkled sunlight. The bored-looking teenage girl on the lounge chair beside her had a thin gold chain around her slightly pudgy left ankle.

Wilbur had to drive the van on the way home. By afternoon, as usual, Jim was well on his way to oblivion. As they passed through Salem, Jim got real maudlin about the fact that two years before, he'd had a good job in that town as a cop. After twelve years they'd just kicked him out on the street, saying he was an alcoholic. He swore it was politics; proved it by pointing out it was a nephew of the mayor who filled his spot.

A little while later, Wilbur looked at his watch, said, "Hell, don't you live in Revere? No sense going back into town just to fight the traffic getting back out. I'll drop you off on the way in and punch you out when I clock out." At the next liquor store, he pulled in and bought a pint of Jim Beam, took one swig, and passed it across the cab.

The traffic was thick and slow as cold tar. By the time they got to Jim's house, Wilbur had to help him inside. They turned on the TV; Jim made drinks, and passed out five minutes later.

The cop uniform was hanging in the closet in a mothproof bag. It was all there but the shield. Wilbur took the coat off the hanger and tried it on, looked at himself in the mirror, drew an imaginary gun, said, "Boom!"

3

Charlie and Rosy anchored in the lee of a small tree-covered island and dinghied ashore with a cooler of beer and wine and finger food.

Charlie made an effort to give her a free swimming lesson. He tried to convince her she was denying herself one of life's great natural pleasures. He realized just how deep-seated the resistance was when Rosy claimed a congenital abnormality of her "nose or larynx or something"; something that hampered her ability to prevent water going down her nose the way most people could. Her mother couldn't swim, either, and this she interpreted as evidence that she had inherited it from her.

Charlie said it sounded to him as though she'd inherited from her mother a perfect nose and a phobia of swimming. She met that with a frosty look that didn't give him the feeling pestering would help. He swam alone.

When she got hot, she'd go in up to her ankles, sort of swoop down, dip water with her hand, splash it over her skin, pat herself with it as though it were expensive perfume. Charlie felt uneasy when he caught himself thinking the move looked feminine instead of candy-assed.

Lying on the blanket, she asked what he did for a living.

"I'm a Nopey," he said. She waited for a definition, raised

an eyebrow. People with great voices love to talk. Rosy used her face a lot. Made you look at it to get a response. "The antithesis of a Yuppie . . . yup, nope, get it?"

"Barely. How are you the opposite of a young urban professional?"

"I'm still working on the acronym: Not On the Program; Not Obsessed with Profits; Nary One Pressed suit, maybe—something like that. I'm a few years from forty, I prefer a beer on the waterfront to power-partying, and I make my living fixing boats."

It felt like a confession. Here it is, lady. If you thought I was rich, you screwed up. She seemed puzzled, asked if he'd gone to college. Yes, he told her, he'd done that. Isn't this boat of yours worth a lot of money? About three hundred thousand.

"Where does a . . . Nopey get that kind of money?"

He hesitated before saying, "Think of it as a carryover from a past life. I might ask you how a sometime model gets the money for a Ferrari, or how someone with the money for a Ferrari ends up sleeping in a parking lot."

She let her lashes fall over her eyes, doled out a smile that Charlie took for friendly conspiracy, said, "That wouldn't be the gentlemanly thing to do, would it?"

To Charlie, it felt like a truce with honor; an agreement to stop at the line beyond which they weren't prepared to tell the truth. If his confession bothered her, she handled it gracefully.

She did everything gracefully; slow, full movements punctuated by dramatic pauses that gave you time to watch and record. Charlie decided it was a way of coping with the knowledge that people were looking at you. Like a deer being still to go unseen? Or a cobra waiting for you to come an inch closer? It was hard to tell.

When they got back to the dock, she gathered up her stuff while he was securing the boat. She thanked him for the trip and said she'd better be on her way.

"Your way to where?" he asked. She said she would stay with a cousin while she looked for a place, but Charlie didn't believe her, wondered if he was being led through a verbal minuet. "There are extra berths here."

"Thanks, Charlie, but I don't want to impose."

"What impose? You make up your berth, you pick up your clothes, you don't leave bottles of goop all over the head, you don't impose."

The couple of beats of hesitation told him he was making headway before she began, "My cousin will be glad to—"

"Come on, Rosy," he interrupted. "I don't know where you're going or where you've been, but one place you ain't going is a cousin's house. You slept in your car last night because you have no place to go. We both know that. Maybe you can afford a hotel, and if that's your pleasure, I enjoyed the day. But don't tell me that so you can go sleep in your car, okay?"

She didn't blanch at the aggressive tone, said, "Maybe I don't want to pay the rent."

"What rent? I'm offering you a free place to stay."

She snorted, "One way or the other, you'll expect me to pay."

Charlie stared at her for a moment, then had to smile, shake his head. "You are a cynic, you know that?"

"You're saying I'm wrong?"

"What, that I'm going to expect you to put out to pay the rent?"

"Right."

"Yes, you're wrong."

"Are you gay?"

"No, I'm not! I didn't say I wouldn't enjoy it, I said I wouldn't expect it, and I wouldn't consider it due."

"On the other hand, you wouldn't turn it down."

"Probably not, but I'd give as good as I got."

"You're a real stud, are you?"

Charlie stood up, raised his arms in a shrugging gesture, said, "Hey, I don't need this. You want to sleep in your car, sleep in your car." He went below.

He heard her footsteps receding on the dock; told himself the woman was extremely uptight. A few minutes later, he heard her returning, admitted he was relieved. She came below, a leather bag in each hand, said, "Long as we have that settled, I'll take you up on your offer. Where should I sleep?"

He pointed to the forward stateroom, hoping he wouldn't regret it.

That negotiation set the tone for a strange two days during which they came and went separately from *Squareknot*.

Charlie worked on various boats around the marina. He had a reputation as a good general mechanic, informally for hire—"informally" in this case meaning, "IRS-immune cash, no checks, no records."

He had limited experience, mostly on his own boats and what one picks up kibitzing in a boatyard. He enjoyed the work as an unequivocal exercise in putting right; in contrast with his years in business, where his vested interest overshadowed the common weal. As a mechanic, when he started a job, something was broken. When he finished, it worked. After a day of mechanics, he could wash the stains from his hands. Business stains were less accessible. He didn't charge for work that wasn't successful, but that was unusual, as his friend Lew, a retired navy mechanic, could outline the steps of diagnosis and repair for the most apoplectic of machines.

Lew preferred that the only screwdrivers he actually touched be in tall glasses with ice and orange juice, but he took great delight in listening to a problem, then taunting Charlie, "Oh, my boy, that is a starter problem," a gleeful expression animating his face, a thick finger pointing into some contortionists-only crevasse in the bowel of the bilge. "The starter is that cylinder on the bottom of the engine. That sucker's gonna be an eight-knuckle buster to get off . . . if you can reach it at all. Wait while I go bleed my lizard and freshen my beer! I don't want to miss a one of your colorful words for Mr. Volvo."

Charlie looked at it as an independent apprenticeship, on-the-job training. Retraining, really, for his mid-thirties career change. His background was in sales, computer-related items, but that had ended abruptly. His new plan, loosely defined, was to work around boats. Since he'd always loved them, it seemed a logical direction in the absence of professional goals. Maybe he'd take *Squareknot* south, do some chartering; maybe run a small boatyard, if he could find one for lease. For the short term, the cash-basis sideline paid surprisingly well. Yards charged thirty-five an hour. He charged twenty-five and didn't add tax, so he stayed as busy as he wanted.

He spent a lot of time thinking about Rosy. There was something stray cat about her quiet combination of wariness and grace. Sleep didn't come easily with her outlandishly ripe body alone a few feet away, and Rogers's penchant for crawling onto his abdomen during the night didn't help. He wondered what she'd been through to become so cynical while still so young, how she'd ended up sleeping in her car at a marina, and where she went when she left the marina during the day.

The first morning she was aboard, he looked up from the shroud turnbuckles he was turning on an old Pearson and saw her walk past her car, leave it in the lot, and cross the bridge on foot. She didn't carry one of those big portfolio things that models carried to job interviews. She didn't have a newspaper with circled ads under her arm. He smiled at a squalid impulse to follow her, had a feeling it would be interesting. But his instincts told him to be patient. If he didn't bother her, she might stay awhile; and if she stayed, anything was possible.

Rosy walked across the bridge from Charlestown to Boston, through Quincy Market and the financial district to the central shopping area on Washington Street. Above the more conspicuous shops on the ground level, the sedate gem merchants of the city had their offices. She paused at a small, chest-high display window.

Looking back through the square of bulletproof glass was a black marble bust of a woman nestled in loosely draped black velvet. Around its graceful Hellenic neck was a gold chain that supported ten one-carat diamonds in an elegantly straightforward row. A concealed light refracted through the matched cut, color, and clarity of the stones. Each diamond was cantilevered on its own delicate, curving gold stem, as though it had grown there, a daffodil diamond from burnished black soil. Rosy felt a slight shudder run through her as she looked at the necklace.

She stepped to the door beside the window, pressed a button beside the brass plate engraved "Michael Barkum, Fine Gems and Handmade Jewelry." She waited for the electronic pulse that unlocked it. She climbed the poorly lit and narrow stairs, pressed another button, and, when an answering buzzer sounded, stepped into a room no larger than fifteen feet square.

The room was bordered on three sides by waist-high beveled glass display cases containing jewelry, with loose gems seemingly strewn among the set pieces on the velvet. She knew the scattered, unset stones to be nothing more precious than zircons, but it created a mood she found amusingly excessive . . . and flattering, as she had suggested the decorative touch herself.

A bent, bald, and thickly built man of some sixty-five years and scant more inches emerged through the doorway in the center of the rear wall. The brow over his right eye drooped bushily into his line of vision, so that he appeared to see you only with his left. Rosy had puzzled over whether it was a congenital deformity, one that suggested his calling to spend most of his life with a jeweler's glass gripped in the permanently squinted socket, or if it had grown that way from years in the position.

When he saw her, his mouth formed an "O" like that of a child who spies a butterfly and stoops breathlessly to catch it. He pulled the door to the back office closed behind him and leaned over the counter toward Rosy. "We'll have lunch, of course, as usual?"

"Thank you, Michael. I'd love to."

He nodded quickly, unrolled his sleeves before donning the coat to his charcoal worsted suit. Rosy reached out and ran her hand along his sleeve. "You always wear such beautiful classic fabrics."

He looked closely at the sleeve, ran his own hand over it, and looked up. "Thank you. I happen to know that you're right. I hope that doesn't sound puffed up. It shouldn't. I didn't make the fabric, I'm only privileged to wear it . . . so few young people notice, you know. Just a drab old man in a drab old suit." A trace of a smile belied the self-pity; a less-than-innocent old man polishing a new compliment before putting it away.

He left a sign on the street-level door, "Out to Lunch." Once she'd asked why he didn't have one with a clock face that indicated when he'd return. He said, "At my age one shouldn't make rash predictions. Besides, my customers take pride in the fact that I'm irresponsible . . . artistic temperament."

She took his arm. They walked around to the taxi stand on Franklin, and he opened the door of the front cab for her. "The Ritz Carlton, please, driver," he said.

They both ordered gin and tonic with lime after the warm taxi.

Michael used the linen napkin to pat the perspiration from his forehead, lips, cheeks in a pattern like a small sign of the cross.

"I've been worried about you," he said. "I was afraid my warnings had proven prophetic."

"You're sweet to worry, but I'm in less danger than you imagine."

"Any possible event, given enough time, will occur, unless the probabilities decrease over time."

"You're so sure of these pronouncements you make, Michael."

Her patronizing if affectionate tone didn't elude him. "That was an accepted law of statistics, not an oracular pronouncement. Not that I expect you to heed my warning, despite the fact that I know your scheme was not profitable this time."

"I noticed that my necklace is still in your window," she said. As she spoke, she pulled a necklace from her purse and placed it on the table between them. To any but the most acute observer, it could have substituted for the one in Michael's street display. "So this must be a toy."

He produced a jeweler's glass, as though from his sleeve, and examined the stones in the necklace quickly, his face bouncing along its length like a hungry man at corn on the cob. "Has your eye become so good you can tell at a glance?"

"No. I noticed the clasp was different. Given the man's personality, I suspect the stones are fake."

Michael smiled slightly as he continued to examine the piece. Rosy went on, "To make it worse, he turned creepy on me. He had a violent streak." Michael looked up from the necklace, studied her as she continued. "I had to carefully play his game until he fell asleep. Then I slipped out and ended up sleeping in a marina parking lot, of all places. How about it . . . are they diamonds?"

"Your instincts were right about the stones . . . man-made. But the craftsmanship, I must say, is superb."

After studying his face a moment, she said, "You old rascal. You made the copy yourself."

He shrugged. "I performed a service for a customer. Your Doctor . . ." She supplied the name. "Yes, of course, Regar. He came into the shop, asked if I could make an accurate duplicate of the piece in the window, using zircons instead of real diamonds, a minimum of precious metal. A rather nice commission for me, as it turned out. I didn't undercharge for what is really a very nice piece of custom costume jewelry. In his mind, I think what he bought was the moral victory in his game with you."

"It isn't necessary to gloat."

"He wasn't the least bit swayed by my attempt to sell the real thing. He came right out and said they were for a woman who imagined him a sucker, and he had no intent of playing it her way. He said if I don't do it, he'd find someone else. I put a different clasp on it, so you'd see that it was a copy."

"Don't look so smug, Michael. Just because one man sees through my scam doesn't make it obsolete. That's the first time it hasn't worked."

His teasing tone hardened. "Yes, but it sounds as though it came close to being worse than mere business failure. You obviously emerged unharmed, but it could have been . . . a disaster."

She didn't contradict him.

30

"Maybe now you'll stop this nonsense. You should find a regular job and a nice man and get married."

"A nice man . . . maybe a college professor? Someone with refined tastes who takes his wife to museums . . . to the Pops and Philharmonic . . . would even buy her a Ferrari? . . ."

"Don't mock me," he said sharply.

The waiter delivered the drinks. It was a tribute to Ritz Carlton breeding that he didn't bat an eye at the necklace sitting on the tablecloth. His bearing made it easy to imagine that he could tell they were fake but was too polite to say so.

They accepted his offer of more time to read the menu. Michael sipped his drink daintily, then took several gulps of the ice water. "I didn't say marry someone you barely know, someone who fits some fairy-tale image. I said find a nice man."

She looked down, toyed with the spoon in front of her. "I'm sorry, Michael. I shouldn't make fun of your concern. I should be glad that you care . . . even though most women these days would also say I should be mad at you for suggesting what I need is a man to take care of me."

"Rosy, this thing will ruin you. You've got to stop it."

She squirmed under his intense scrutiny, said, "I don't know what I'm going to do, Michael. I fell into this scam when I was hitting bottom, at a time when it seemed every man I met wanted a piece of me, and I decided to turn the tables. I never expected to live this way forever. Maybe I've played the game too long. My luck may be running low."

He looked at her for a moment. "This Regar must have been bad."

She shrugged. "The thing is, with the delay he caused me, stiffing me with this paste, I'm practically broke. I need a grubstake. I think I have to do it once more."

"Once, and once, and once! When does it become never again? When one of these men strangles you for a whore?"

Rosy shifted in her seat, looked around, realized that the placement of the tables had kept his angry words private. Her even response was clearly under tight rein. "I'm not a whore.

31

A whore is someone who sacrifices self-respect for money. I withhold what they really want. I keep myself. I take their money."

"You sleep with them."

She threw something imaginary over her shoulder. "This is not the big deal it once was, Michael. The important thing is that they try to buy me and fail. . . . I control them. I screw them."

The lid of Michael's visible eye dropped closed before he bowed his head. She reached across the table and touched his hand.

"I'm sorry, darling, I know these things upset you."

The waiter took their order and left. They sipped their drinks, looked around at the other diners eating and talking in the quiet tones called for in opulent surroundings.

Michael said, "There's another way."

"To sell the necklace?"

"Yes. I'd do it for you, give you the full retail price . . . or the car. It must still be quite valuable."

"I thought of it. . . . A few years ago, it's what I'd have done, as when I banked everything on my college professor. But I found out I was wrong about him, didn't I? I don't want to leave myself without resources."

"There's another way still."

"What's that?"

"I can give you some money."

"No."

"Why not?"

She thought before speaking. "You've been my only real friend these last years, Michael. I don't want to risk that by taking money from you. You've helped me enough. You might begin to feel that I used you . . . like the others. I can get the money easily."

"Easily? I find that frightening, that it's become easy for you."

"I don't know if I can make you understand this, Michael. What these men get from me in bed they could get from any woman. My looks don't change the biological facts of life. If all they wanted was sex, they wouldn't pay thirty thousand for it.

"What they really want from me is something different . . . the same thing they try to buy at the Ferrari dealership. They see me, and they want to prove something to themselves, about themselves. Some of them, it's just to be seen in public so people will think them great lovers, or men of influence. Because of my looks, I'm a prize for them. Once I'm there, I know how to . . . comply with their wishes, but at the same time make them realize I'm not . . . overawed by their attentions, if you see what I mean. . . ."

He looked puzzled.

"Men today know that sex is not supposed to be just for their pleasure, but they don't necessarily know what to do about it. If I were to overtly tell them they're nowhere in bed, they'd just call me frigid or something. But if I don't complain, just drop inconclusive hints that I'm unimpressed, they stay at a level of insecurity that makes them suggestible. . . ."

"I don't think you need spell it out further."

She smiled at his propriety, but went on, wanting him to understand. "They can't stand that. They begin to panic in fear that I'll leave and they'll have to face their inadequacy. I suggest dinner at the Parker House, walk them by your window, admire the necklace. Usually, that's all it takes. They come back alone and buy it for me. Of course, my prospects are carefully selected . . . from men who buy outrageously expensive sports cars. Their capitulation comes from the same reliance on flash that bought the Ferrari."

"And this trick of bringing rich old men to their knees . . . you get pleasure from this?"

"No. I get money from it. And the freedom to work only about four weeks a year."

"Because you are lazy?"

Her patience broke. "Because wherever I go the same game is played. All I've done is refine the steps to eliminate wasted motion."

33

Their crab legs arrived, and they allowed a truce to settle over the meal. Rosy told him about her encounter with Charlie Gamble and the fact that she'd been sailing with him, was staying aboard his boat.

"What's he like?" Michael asked. "Is he a boat bum, or a playboy, or what?"

She toyed with a gold earring in the shape of a scallop shell, said, "It's hard to say. He works on boats around the dock in Charlestown, but he lives on a three-hundred-thousand dollar boat. He certainly could be a playboy, if that's what he wanted; he's a very attractive man, in a rawboned kind of way.

"He has an edge to him; but something . . . whimsical as well." She noticed Michael's pointed look, smiled, said, "Chew your food, Michael. We're staying in separate cabins, and I assure you, I'm not the type for canvas shoes and faded denim."

Over coffee, Rosy said she'd be in touch with her friend at the Ferrari dealership; she'd call Michael when she knew who the next mark would be.

"The last mark," he said in a tone that reflected his displeasure. He told her he'd do it one more time, and this time he meant it. If she ever asked again, he'd know that he'd been wrong about her; she wasn't worth protecting.

He said, "Rosy, you're playing with people's lives, telling yourself it's a game. What's worse, I think you're starting to enjoy it."

Coming from him, the words chilled her to the bone. Walking back through town toward the marina, she told herself he couldn't be expected to understand. He'd never been a woman, never felt the unrelenting measurement of the eyes of men.

Her mind began to work on the problem of finding another mark. Usually she relied on a contact at the Ferrari dealership to point her in the direction of very wealthy men who weren't above spending their money frivolously. She remembered that she still didn't know where Charlie got the money for the sailboat, whether there was more where that came from. Maybe it was worth investigating. She toyed with the idea of letting him make his advances. "I'll be damned," she said in mild surprise as she crossed the bridge. She'd realized she was looking forward to it. Nothing wrong with enjoying one's work, she mused.

It irritated her that Charlie was as good as his word. Her first night on board, he'd completely ignored her. The second night, when she returned from visiting Michael, he boiled some lobsters bought cheaply from a fisherman he knew on the dock, threw together a salad, and heated some hard rolls. He made light conversation about the marine environment, the sense of freedom he derived from the constant possibility of setting sail at any moment. After doing the dishes, he retired to his cabin with a book without so much as a good night.

When he still had made no advances by the third night, she walked into his cabin wearing a T-shirt he'd lent to her. It hung halfway to her knees, draped nicely on nipples reacting to cool sea air. She sat beside him on the berth, said, "Charlie, if you don't like women, I'll leave you alone."

He thought of several smart-ass remarks about who was paying rent to whom, but since saying nothing had gotten her there, he left well enough alone. He joined her in an exploratory embrace, kissing and twisting and soft tugging that improved positions, confirmed the supple fitness of her, and quickly eliminated any doubt about whether he liked women.

Rosy's perfume matched her worldly style, but the clumsiness with which she attacked him reminded him of fold-down seats in a Nash Rambler. Her eagerness seemed too much too soon, and he decided he didn't believe it. With an effort of will, he shifted gears.

Alert for an unguarded response, he tested her every inch from the hair on her head to the paint on her toes, supplemented his natural enthusiasm with wily deployment of lips, fingers, and fantasies. In due course, he coaxed from her noises that no sane person would counterfeit. Welcome to the land of bareback stunt comets and electric volcanoes. Once you're in, the rides are free.

Later, he thought he might have overreacted to her opening remark by spending so much of the night devising ways to make

35

her shudder and hop around like a runaway machine gun. Part of him was embarrassed at being suckered into such a sophomoric display. Maybe it was her, and maybe it was just the thought of the Nash Rambler. On the brighter side, at least nobody said, "I love you," so nobody had to say, "I love you, too."

Sometime during the night, her head resting on his shoulder, her leg over him, she said, "I've always hated letting men think they seduced me. I hate to be a notch on anybody's belt."

"Don't be ridiculous," Charlie said. "You seduced me."

"You interrupted me. What I was going to say is that I never would have minded if the others had made me feel the way you just did."

"You mean you don't feel like you've just paid the rent?"

"Rent? You want rent? Okay, I'll give you my Ferrari, but not a penny more."

Stretching out the next morning, sharing with Rogers the warmth of sun coming through an open hatch onto their berth, Rosy said, "Mmmmm, this is luxu-u-u-urious. You don't feel the motion unless you think about it, but it rocks you like a cradle. You never did tell me where you got the money for this boat."

Surprised that he was telling her the truth, he heard himself say, "Part-time, I've dabbled in blackmail." He expected her to take it as a joke; if not that, then to be a little bit horrified. But there ya go, ya can't figure people.

She paused in midstretch, still as a reclining marble nude, said, "Now we're getting somewhere."

Seeing the unprotected midriff, Rogers stepped onto her like a miniature stalking panther. Her composure held. Bemused, she watched him settle there. He flattened himself against her and began to purr. She flinched when she felt his claws.

4

After mentioning blackmail, Charlie found himself the object of Rosy's persistent and charming inquisition. It being a Sunday, they lolled around over *The New York Times*, Bloody Marys, and brunch, Charlie teasing her with the secret at first. But before the day was out, he'd given her the flavor of his career working for Continental Computer Corp., "C Cube," as it was nicknamed in an industry of mathematicians.

Charlie had been one of the first salespeople the two founders, long since sold out and gone fishing, had hired. C Cube made computer disks, marketed them blank and with licensed programs. They developed and sold a broad array of software, sold direct under brand names, also did private labeling for some of the major marketers in the business.

Though he was a very competent salesman, Charlie was no superstar by industry standards. He never had a piece of the action and wasn't motivated enough to bother, though he knew people who'd made fortunes around him. He used his competence to work smart, did his job without time-consuming false steps, used the saved time to work on his house or his boat, hobbies he enjoyed. Fact was, a campus radical in the late sixties, he still felt a little guilty about the amount of money he earned. Going on his own would have meant a huge change in life-style and mind-set, changes he wasn't willing to make. Instead he drifted along, feeling he was in it, but not of it.

It began to sour, ironically enough, when his business went through the roof. One of his customers was the first to hit the street with an integrated data-base, spread-sheet, word-processing program at an affordable cost. Their package got rave reviews, became a runaway best-seller, Charlie getting a commission on every one they sold, since C Cube did all their manufacturing.

He got a call from Wendell (Wendy) Rust, the president of the division. Wendy took Charlie to the Harvard Club for lunch, told him he was well pleased with his performance, and he needed people like him inside; his climb to the top had begun. Distinctly unthrilled by the prospect of being in an office so much, Charlie listened to the pitch. He politely declined the offer, however, when he heard the salary and calculated that he'd be losing a couple of hundred thousand bucks versus what he already had on the books in the next two years.

Rust got huffy about it . . . said Charlie was making a big mistake, that anybody with sense realized sales was a burnout career; an older man couldn't do it. When Charlie continued to decline, Rust got madder still, told Charlie he didn't want deadwood in the organization; that if he didn't have any more ambition than that, he didn't want him around in sales, either. He made the decision easier by telling Charlie he intended to rearrange the account assignments if he stayed in sales, so that Charlie would lose his big accounts, wouldn't make shit in commissions. In short, take the management job at a stable but reduced income, or take a walk.

He took the job, but understanding didn't hit until a couple of weeks later, when Rust's son turned up in Charlie's old territory, fresh out of business school with built-in commissions of three hundred grand a year: commissions on a business Charlie had built.

The next couple of years, Charlie freely admitted, were a textbook case of the Peter Principle, the business phenomenon of people being promoted to their level of incompetence. He found that he lacked the ability to keep his attention focused in the meetings that he attended for hours on end.

His penchant for appearing at work with brown socks and blue suit, or vice versa, was noted and frowned upon. One of his fellow managers, in a show of goodwill, confided a management secret: he instructed his wife to put the blue ones and the brown ones in different drawers, so he didn't have to take them out in the morning to tell the difference. When Charlie admitted, apropos of nothing except what was on his mind, that he and his wife were having problems . . . in fact, she was moving to New York without him, the guy was horrified.

"Don't let Rust hear that, Charlie . . . he's a real nut on family . . . thinks sloppy personal lives are the gestation place of executive failures."

"No shit," Charlie said, thinking he was probably right, and that secrecy would be impossible since his wife's TV news job was very visible and announcement of her move to New York would be on the streets momentarily.

What really got to him, however, was the adversary attitude he found he was forced to take toward the salespeople he was supposed to be managing. His own experience wasn't unique. People would work for years to develop business; then when they hit something big; management would swoop down on them and pick their bones in various underhanded ways. As regional sales manager, it was Charlie's job to force-feed the arbitrary policy and commission changes that trickled down with depressing regularity whenever somebody started doing exceptionally well.

It hadn't always been that way. From his new perspective inside, Charlie could see that the foundation of advantageous technology that had built the company was being slowly eroded by overtaking competition. While the research and development department had swollen with more scientists than ever, the geniuses were gone, and innovation was lagging. Market share and dividends were being kept up by price cutting, so management was squeezing whatever cost savings it could from the commission checks, as well as other areas that were beginning to cause problems in product quality and supply. Rust's underhanded style was trickling down the line.

A typical but extreme example came up with a salesman named Talbot. Rust burst into Charlie's office with a sheet that showed the monthly commission payments.

"Who the hell is this Talbot guy?" he demanded.

"The other major Boston territory besides your son. He's come up with a gambit that the people in his territory love, as far as the way he structures agreements. It works well for us, too; helps with manufacturing scheduling. You may have seen my memo to the field on it last week. It's brilliant! What he does is—"

"Okay, I get it, he's a hotshot, but I've been looking over these commission payments, and he's way out of line."

"Sure he is, but so's his business; nobody's even close to him in new accounts."

Rust smiled. "Charlie, a commission plan should be generous enough to motivate, but not so lavish ya give 'em a windfall. That can be demotivating to the rest of the force. Ya end up with one guy getting spoiled and fifty sales people feeling like they aren't being taken care of. We gotta be fair to everyone."

"Wendy, they all have the same plan. If they sell as much, they make as much, it's that simple. It's where the juice comes from to keep them going hard."

"That's what you want to happen, Charlie, but this guy is so far out, he'll break their competitive spirit." He stood and dropped some papers on Charlie's desk. "I've taken a look at the account responsibility as far as how the two Boston territories are split up. Talbot has gotten the growth accounts while the other territory is on a downswing. I've made some notes on which accounts should be traded. You take a look at it and get back to me." Exit Wendy.

The notes made Wendy's real goal clear. They instructed Charlie to trade four of Talbot's strong accounts for four of Wendy Jr.'s losers. Wendy Jr.'s sales curve was as sharply downward as Talbot's was upward. In short, make the plan more "equitable" by screwing the producer out of fifty thousand bucks and giving it to the guy who is running business off at an unprecedented rate. Nasty work. And it was Charlie's job to make Talbot live with it.

Charlie fought it and lost; it was the last straw. He was working on his résumé when Talbot showed up in his office.

Like most good salespeople, Talbot didn't look like a salesperson. He looked more like a guy somebody kept in a basement to stoke a boiler: thick hands poking out of a suit that's too tight, heavy brows, and almost no hair on top of his head, the kind of guy that the customers aren't afraid of because he doesn't look too slick. By the time they realize he's the equal of Satan himself for pure shrewdness, it's too late.

He and Charlie had met for breakfast to exchange information and ideas twice a month for the five years they'd split the Boston market. He'd never seen the man smile.

"I got Rust in a box," Talbot said. He dropped a file on the desk. "He's got an accomplice in quality control. They're declaring product bad before the logo goes on, taking it out the back door, and selling it to fly-by-night mail-order houses in generic packaging through a dummy manufacturer, Digidisk.

"Industry figures show this thing at a two-percent market share in floppy fives. Not enough to worry about or attract attention in the industry . . . just enough to do about eight hundred thousand a year. My guess is six is going straight into his back pocket. I discovered it a few months ago . . . been waiting for him to screw me on the commissions. He did it to me once before. This time I'm ready for him."

"How'd you learn all this?" Charlie asked.

"I been selling these things since they were invented. I saw one of the disks in an account, recognized some of our proprietary technology. Thought I was just doing my job to find out who was ripping us off. When the trail got fuzzy, I got suspicious, had a lawyer friend of mine pursue it. He came back with Rust's name as the hidden wizard behind it.

"I don't give a rat's ass what you do with it, Gamble, but I know it wasn't you got into my pocket, so I'm giving you a shot at being the exposer rather than the exposee. I'd rather not waste my own time on it, to tell you the truth. All I want is what's coming to me. Are you with me?"

"With you? I could kiss you."

"No thanks," he said, poker-faced.

The next day Charlie was in Rust's office, showing him a copy of the file. Rust looked up and said, "Who else knows?"

"I'm not at liberty to say . . . consider it my information."

"Okay, I do business with you. You could use thirty grand a year, couldn't you? That'd buy a helluva sailboat."

That was Rust's idea of the personal touch. He learned one thing about you and beat it to death. "How's the sailboat?" he'd asked Charlie about fifty times. He never waited for an answer.

Charlie shook his head. "Forget it, Wendy. Your speeches have motivated me so much that I'm a true believer. I love this company. Digidisk is a competitor that I intend to bury."

Rust stared at him, then began again, "Okay, okay, I get it, you want a full share, but look, I got partners. Takes so many people to make it work, it's really hardly worth it. We been thinking of closing down. I think I can get them to go thirty-five cash; that makes you a full partner . . . any more, we're working for you."

"I'm not negotiating, Wendy. Digidisk is out of business. You'll send the customers a letter to that effect in the next few days . . . say, Friday of this week."

He handed Rust a piece of paper on which were the names of five of the twenty-five salespeople who reported to Charlie. Each name had a number next to it. Talbot's name topped the list. "These are some debts you've incurred in my name. They will receive cash payments from you and your part- ners . . . something low-key like a plain brown box in the mail will suffice . . . no sense involving the IRS in our dirty laundry, right?

"On the bottom of the page are some territory and policy changes that are being reversed to better reflect what my people have done."

After looking at the page, Rust snorted, "You're crazy, Gamble! We haven't got the cash to make payments like that!"

Charlie's tone was ironic. "Knowing your ability to run a business, I almost believe you. I figured your capability by dividing what I could have made on your scam in half, then figuring half your team would have sense enough not to expose themselves by spending it all, so we're talking lowest common denominator already. If I've given you more credit than you deserve, that's your problem. Get the money, pay your debts, or I go public next week."

Rust came back at him like a pit bull with bees on his balls. "You wanna play chicken, huh, Gamble? You say you know the figures, okay. Think I'm gonna let a snot like you put a stop to that? Give me that file, burn the copies, or you are a dead man. I lose my job? Big fucking deal. I'll never go to jail. The company will hush it up and never press charges. Adverse publicity is bad for the stock. I got enough cash to splurge and have you killed. Then I retire to Miami Beach. How's that grab ya, smart guy?"

Charlie could hear his own heart beating. The guy was not a good enough poker player to fool him. He meant it. He would have him killed. Sweet Jesus.

Charley reached in his pocket and pulled out his company-issue Dictaphone. He flipped the rewind button for half a second, played Rust his own voice saying, "How's that grab ya, smart guy?"

"You realize that my notarized testimony, along with the file and this tape, would reach out from the grave and squeeze your balls into so much pudding. It'd go to the D.A. and the newspapers, not the company. You might go to jail for murder. At the very least, with the story already out, the company would sue you for any assets you had to recover its money."

Charlie could feel a little quaver in his voice, but, judging by the sick look on Rust's face, he was taking it for anger rather than fear. "Now, one other thing. . . . Digidisk will be good enough to give me a list of the accounts they are abandoning. I'll see that our salespeople arrive before our competition and

43

soak up the business. C Cube should make a nice piece of change on that in the next couple years, and since I'm responsible, I'm sure you'll want to reward me. . . . You'll send an announcement to the organization that I'm being promoted to a new position as your assistant in charge of strategic planning."

"You gotta be on something, Gamble. You butt-fuck me, then say you wanna work for me."

"Not exactly. You'll hire a consultant to do a quarterly report on industry trends and what our appropriate response should be. You'll mail it to me. I'll come to the quarterly management meeting and present the findings as my own work. Maybe it'll get this company moving out of the dark ages, if you have sense enough to implement the findings. I'll drop by the office to pick up my check every couple weeks, say hello around the office so people don't forget what I look like."

"And how long do you expect this scam to last?"

"Long as I want it to, Wendy. Or as long as you can keep your job, which probably won't be long, at the rate you're going. That's why I included the plan to get you some management advice before you run the thing into the ground. In the meantime, I should have time to plan a new career."

"Yeah, doing what?"

Charlie smiled. "First, I'll put about a year's work into that sailboat you're always asking about. If you'd ever waited for an answer, I'd have told you it was a beat-up classic I bought for seventy-five grand, but with a year's work, a few bucks in materials, it'll be worth a quarter million easy . . . not a bad year, if you ask me . . . especially with the two hundred thousand salary from C Cube as your assistant.

"That, by the way, is the salary we'll agree on. A year's worth ought to about cover the differential between my current salary and what I lost to your son when you 'promoted' me."

"A goddamned grease monkey. I'm being fucked by a goddamned grease monkey."

"With a sandpaper condom, Rust, and no foreplay, the same way you've been getting yours around here for years. . . . How's it feel to be catching rather than throwing?"

44

Rust didn't answer.

Charlie left him that way. Back at his own office, he found Wendy Rust, Jr. Earlier, Charlie had called him in for a meeting without explaining what it was about. Wendy Jr. was sitting at Charlie's desk whispering into the phone. As Charlie walked in, he stood, switched to a bluff salesman's tone, said, "Okay, well! I appreciate the business and I'll get back to you soon." The twinkle in his eye told Charlie some broad was probably on the other end saying, "Oh, I get it, you can't talk. You're a sly one, you are, Wendy. I'll see you tonight, and don't forget to stock up on you know what."

"You finally get a piece of new business?" Charlie asked, ignoring the extended hand.

"I beg your pardon?" he said.

"Never mind . . . if you did, it's a little too late." He took his seat, handed Junior a piece of paper on which were listed about fifteen accounts, next to which were categories in which the company did business.

"What's this?"

"The reason I called you in here, Junior, is to tell you it ain't working out."

After a moment's surprise, he smirked. "It isn't, huh?"

"Right. It ain't. That list shows the business you've run off in my territory since I turned it over to you. From what I hear from my old customers, you're too lazy to take care of what you have, and so arrogant you couldn't peddle penicillin in a syphilis epidemic. Someday you'll thank me for helping you realize you're in the wrong line. You're fired."

Junior had the gall to laugh. "Gamble, that business was shaky because you hadn't taken care of it. If it weren't for me, we'd have lost twice as much."

Charlie stared at him. "Don't make yourself look foolish, Junior. Some of those people still send me cards on my birthday and Christmas. My secretary has the paperwork. You'll get two weeks' pay when you sign the forms. You might as well leave quietly."

He stood, stepped toward the door, turned to fire the shot

Charlie was expecting: "When my father hears about this, we'll see who doesn't work here anymore."

Charlie softened his voice. "I hate to tell you this, Wendy, but it was your father's decision. You think I'm naive enough to do it without his approval?" He paused to let that insidious worm of an idea crawl between his ears.

"It's a tribute to his integrity, really. You should be proud of him. He said to me, 'Gamble, I hate to do it, but we cannot expose ourselves to charges of nepotism. The boy ain't cutting it, we gotta get rid of him.'"

Charlie stood and offered his hand. "Hey, really, Junior, I hope you find your niche. No hard feelings, huh?"

The idiot took his hand, said, "Sure," through trembling lips. It made Charlie feel like a shit in his moment of glory.

When Rosy had learned all of that, she asked, "What have you done with the money?"

"Some of it's in mutual funds and municipal bonds . . . a little grubstake for getting a business started. The rest I put into the boat."

She leaned into him and kissed him playfully. Charlie still felt the rush of surprise, like a first kiss, that such a creature was with him. He was willing to take her obvious interest in his financial affairs in stride.

"So now you spend the rest of your life luring young girls onto your fancy sailboat for a ride?"

He didn't think he deserved that one. "Now I take the nest egg I earned and start a business . . . something physical that doesn't require a huge corporation."

"And make your quarterly presentations," she said.

He was surprised. She'd misinterpreted something. "No, that's over. After a year, I'd gotten back what they owed me. I couldn't see just setting Rust free on the organization again. Some of them are good people. I told him if he'd retire, I'd give him the whole bundle. He took me up on it. In the end, he was rather tragic . . . told me he hadn't seen his son in a year . . . like it was my fault."

"You mean you just let him go?"

"Yeah, a couple of weeks ago, in fact."

"Why? He deserved everything he got."

Charlie was aware of a new intensity straining her voice, like it was personal with her. "I figured if I took a dollar more than he owed me, I was stepping into the slime with him. I'd have to admit I was no better than him. I wasn't that bad off."

There was more on her mind, but she turned away. He'd been aware that she'd been gently prodding him through his story all day. He'd tried to turn the conversation to her several times, but she'd slipped through the questions gracefully, revealing nothing but generalities . . . she'd been married, she had no siblings, she "traveled, mostly." Now he felt entitled to a quid pro quo.

"That's my story. What's yours? Is your travel aimless wandering, or are you looking for something?"

"What should I be looking for?"

"Something over your shoulder gaining on you, maybe?"

She didn't answer, left him in the cockpit, where he sat in a terry-cloth robe, dark blue to match the boat's hull, *Square-knot* embroidered on the pocket. A lady had given it to him, along with a smaller one like it. He'd avoided her since. Rosy'd found them in the hanging locker, and they'd lounged in them all day. Now she dropped hers to the cabin sole before stepping into the head. He heard the water pump start and then water running in the shower.

Intrigued more than ever by the bold-faced and bare-assed evasion, he savored his first daylight view of the stern end of her svelte nakedness until it faded to the memory of Burt Bacharach, a well-known composer who'd written a string of hits in the sixties with Hal David for Dionne Warwick.

Charlie had been on an Eastern shuttle to New York with him years before, sometime after Burt and Angie Dickinson split up. It was summer. The young woman with Burt wore white jeans and an unadorned white T-shirt, both snugly fitted and unmarked by the unsightly lines of underwear; no jewelry; just her and her whites. He'd stood in the taxi line seven or

47

eight feet from where they got into a limousine. Looking at her made him want to cry. She was flawless. Charlie couldn't get her out of his mind for weeks.

For all he knew, it was his daughter, or just a friend, maybe, but he doubted it. Charlie hated Burt forever after, with deep green envy so undiluted he didn't even kid himself about its origins. If the unidentified girl wasn't enough, the clincher was that Angie D. had been a favorite fantasy for years. It wasn't fair.

Just as it wasn't fair that Rosy, with the capriciousness to which she was entitled by being as flawless as Burt's girl, had literally stumbled into his life and decided to inhabit it for a while. Just as it wouldn't be fair when she made her equally unexplained exit, a part of the future he felt he could predict with certainty equal to a description of yesterday. He didn't know what she was after, but he was pretty sure it wasn't him.

It dawned on him why he'd made her the first person other than Lew Faucet to hear about the blackmail scheme he'd milked for a year. After thirty-seven years, it was all that made him stand out from the crowd. He wanted her to remember him after she left. Because she was beautiful, yes, but also because she brought something intangible to that beauty that almost made her glow in the dark.

It made him feel grasping and ridiculous. For the first time in his life, he felt himself growing old. What had he done with the years when he could have been practicing the piano?

His gaze drifted upward to the bridge spanning the water. A pedestrian stood at the railing looking in his direction with a pair of binoculars. Goddamned tourists. Charlie shot him a bird, watched him recoil from his lenses in surprise.

48

5

Rosy had left Charlie in the cockpit because she was confused. She was confused because little pieces of Charlie kept sticking to her mind. For some time, as far as men went, she'd prided herself on her nonstick mind.

Like the morning before, when she'd climbed into the cockpit after she'd woken up, had seen him picking up floating debris as he'd carried the trash to the dumpster; his catch of the day had included a plastic wrapper from a bag of ice, a couple of Styrofoam cups, and one blown-out flip-flop, perhaps jetsam from Jimmy Buffett's Margaritaville.

"Are you some kind of crackpot?" she'd asked. "Picking up garbage while the rest of the world throws it out?"

He'd actually blushed, said, "It's symbolic. A fly's breath of resuscitation for a brain-dead-elephant world. I do it to earn the luxury of calling myself part of the solution instead of part of the problem."

He saw the futility, made fun of himself for doing it . . . but he still did it.

Or coming in from the sail on the day she'd met him, she'd been bummed out by the buildings of the city looming over them, had said, "Those crisp neat rows of windows look so logical and innocent from here. It's almost more terrible, the

49

innocent look, when you know the squalor and filth and evil that permeates this town."

He'd looked at her long and hard, hadn't jumped on it. Both of them had watched a train they could see moving across a bridge. When he had spoken, it was, "Maybe so. Kind of tempting now and then, though, to just settle for the view, the crisp and neat. Pretend we're a couple of cute little painted sailors on a train-set sea, put here by a friendly giant wearing a bill cap that says Lionel." Then he'd grinned, and she could tell he'd been wishing the train would blow its whistle.

Next I invade his bed to play with his mind, and what happens? He takes his time. After a while I realize I've thrown Br'er Rabbit in the briar patch. He's so gentle and sure that before I know what's going on he's got me doing the scales like a mad soprano. He's lean and he's quiet and he's mean when he needs to be, but disdainful of guile. . . . All he wants is what's his.

Rosy's next thought made her laugh into the shower: I can't swim, and he's a boat freak; how typical is that? What's the plan, Lord? Whisper in my ear. Make him love me, then make him watch me drown? Or make me love him, then let him find out how I've lived, so he'll find me repulsive? Who's the big loser in this love affair? Sorry, O Great One, but I'm going to sit this one out.

Maybe I should tell Charlie how I spent the night before we met. That would put a halter on his ardor, keep him from harm. That should get his hormones back in line.

She pulled her soap-slippery arms into her sides to quell the shiver that shot through her as she remembered. . . .

The night Dr. Regar came through with the fake diamond choker, he felt entitled to let the serpents crawl out of his ears, and perform for Rosy.

There had been warnings . . . both that his perfunctory performance in bed was only the tip of his emotional iceberg, and that the man was not generous about money.

Several days before, they'd gone to a staff party, a farewell for the chief resident, who was taking his hot-stuff Boston education to practice in rural Arkansas, where good surgeons were needed. The reactions of his peers to this self-imposed martyrdom ran the gamut from amusement to outrage. Regar said he felt as though he'd wasted his time teaching him.

The resident got mildly smashed, asked her to dance, despite the fact that John Regar was not a convivial man, not a man whom anyone would expect to be sanguine about a younger man moving in on his date, even if it were done in fun. Regar never laughed at the jokes about doctors thinking they were gods. They seemed only to puzzle him.

"Where in the world did Johnny Cash find you?" the resident asked her.

He had a wry smile, a tousled insouciance. She'd heard Regar say he was irresponsible about his peripheral duties, but his best protégé in "the arena," which is what he called surgery. "Why do you call him Johnny Cash?" she asked.

"Probably the same reason you're with him . . . the man likes money in very large quantities."

The insult hit so close to the bone that it didn't even make her mad. Somehow, she preferred being pegged for a golddigger to having this man actually believe she liked John Regar. The music was a slow rock thing that one could have danced to separately or together . . . the resident was almost doing a mash number, his arm across the small of her back, pulling her groin into his, but leaning back so he could watch her as she spoke, giving her that smile that said, Hey, it's just pretend.

She could see Dr. Regar staring at them, making no pretense of taking the performance lightly. Rosy realized that she was being used for an oblique insult aimed at Regar. The look on Regar's face intrigued her, so she resisted a passing impulse to cool the guy's jets with a knee jerk to the balls on a base beat; instead she waited to see what would happen. "Is that news? . . . I suppose you chose surgery out of humanitarian ideals."

"I intend to be comfortable, and I make no apology. We commit ourselves to spending our lives *mano a mano* with sickness and death . . . it ought to carry some recompense. But Regar is in a class by himself."

"How so?"

"All the other teaching surgeons at least write 'accept insurance only' on the patients' charts. That way those who can't afford it still get taken care of without being ruined. I mean, why not? Regar gets four teams of interns and residents going on four different bodies . . . then just pops from room to room giving advice. Since he's the surgeon of record, he gets the fee. He's making about twenty thousand an hour, for chrissake. What's the difference if one or two can't pay?"

"Sounds reasonable."

"Not to Johnny Cash. He takes it all the way to the collection agency . . . the guys who want to know what your car is worth."

Rosy was sorry she couldn't tell him what her intent was, why she was with Regar to begin with. She let it pass and went back to the original question. "He found me at his garage. We drive the same kind of car."

"The famous Ferrari."

Regar put his hand on the younger man's shoulder and wrenched him away from Rosy. Then a tight voice said, "Thank you, Doctor, I'll take it from here."

The two men faced each other with the naked animosity of strung-out heroin addicts over the last Oreo, but Rosy could tell their enmity had little to do with her. It was no contest. The resident's eyes fell before Regar's, and Rosy herself felt a comet of fear flash through her at the look in his face. Prior to that, she had thought of John Regar as a very repressed, uptight guy who made a bold front of taking himself very seriously. It was the first time she saw the volatile stuff seething behind the façade. The resident left the party before the dance ended. His school days were over, and he'd flinched on his last chance to remember them proudly.

But that night Regar had been his usual perfunctory self in bed. So far, he was the kind of guy you wouldn't know he'd gotten off except for the mess he made.

After she'd worked on him for another week, kept him anxious doing her number on his insecurity, the night he gave her the diamond choker, he must have decided it was payment enough for the real thing. He'd been in the bathroom an unusually long time. When he came out, she'd looked at him and laughed quickly, then stifled it, as he wasn't smiling.

He wore a leather mask that covered the top half of his face, wide leather wristbands; chrome studs decorated both of them. She thought he looked like something out of an old Kirk Douglas movie.

She didn't know how to act. Was she supposed to swoon or something? Fall down and hug his loins? The tattered leather loincloth was doing a poor job of hiding, or a fine job of displaying, maybe, the fact that Johnny Cash himself found his own performance enormously engrossing.

She didn't want to blow her role, because the only thing he was wearing that hadn't once covered a cow was the diamond choker. That was her reason for being there. It was stretched so taut against the flexed muscles of his neck, she was afraid it would pop the fine gold chain that linked the daffodil settings together.

He made her role painfully clear then. He slapped her hard enough to raise her up and land her on the bed.

Dazed, confused, she thought the joke wasn't funny. He straddled her, standing with his feet next to her ears. Her vision was blurred, and it accentuated the strange perspective that felt like looking up at a giant from a hole in the ground. He removed the necklace and hung it on the obvious, where it danced in the light from the bedside table. "There it is, bitch. Your hints were childishly transparent. Just how badly do you want those stones? Are you willing to pay the price? Reach up and take it, if you dare."

That was when her vision cleared and she noticed that the clasp on the choker was different.

He didn't hit her any more. The big entrance got him started. After that it was all playtime. When he finished, he turned away from her, lay there a moment, then turned off the light. She heard snaps being undone, his paraphernalia landing in the darkness against the far wall. Her fear had begun to subside when she felt his hands slipping around her neck. Deftly, his surgeon's fingers fastened the clasp, putting the diamonds he'd taunted her with about her throat. Then she felt his breath on her face, so controlled it was silent.

"We can't pick our dreams. We just find ourselves in them. Do you understand that, Rosemary?"

"Yes," she said, and she did. But the remorse in his voice was bottomless, and she felt that the next layer of this man's libidinous onion could be more violent than the last. She wondered whether he ever dreamed about using his scalpels outside of surgery. She wanted to get out of there but was afraid to move until she heard the regular breathing give way to the odd snuffling noises she'd heard other nights when he slept.

In darkness, she found her purse and her overnight bag with her clothes still draped over it, and she crept down the stairs. On the first floor, realizing what her flight would mean to him, her fear turned to terror, and she didn't stop to dress as she'd planned. She went out the door into the yard surrounded by trees that cast filigreed shadows in the moonlight, climbed naked into her Ferrari. She used the light from the open car door to find her keys. She heard her name called inside the house.

The temperamental fuel-injection system needed adjustment. It sputtered before surging into a roar that John Regar had to hear, then stalled. She turned the key, and the grinding noise was like hysteria choking in the dark. Light erupted from the windows of the ground floor of the house. The car started. John Regar's body was silhouetted in the doorway as she slammed the gearshift into first, shot across the cobblestones of the drive.

Only after five miles did she realize that her knuckles were white on the wheel, that it was safe to pull over for a moment. She dressed herself in the dim light from the dashboard. She didn't stop again until she saw the marina's brightly lit parking lot from the Interstate and pulled off and parked.

As she sat in the car trying to calm herself, the scene with

Regar kept coming back into her mind. Was it something he'd done before with other women? Or was it the emergence of a long-harbored secret? She decided it was the latter. She'd given him an excuse to do what he'd long suppressed.

She told herself she'd overreacted . . . panicked. John Regar was trapped in his nasty playacting, but he wouldn't really have hurt her. She could have waited until the next day to leave. Now, in any case, it was over.

She listened to the tapping of the halyards on the masts in the marina, took comfort in the bright anticrime lights that illuminated the lot, and fell asleep finally with the windows up tight and the doors locked. The red, red, Ferrari-red car stood out in the parking lot like a gypsy at an Amish wake.

Charlie was never one to let the threat of future losses poison present victories. He had pushed the pessimistic thoughts out of his mind by the time Rosy emerged from her shower and had invited her to town for drinks and dinner. He said, "I'm usually too sensible for this kind of crap, but being with a girl as beautiful as you makes me want to spend a day's pay on luxury. Where would you like to go?"

They were still vacillating between Francesca's and Jimmy's as they crossed Commercial Street, when something loomed in his peripheral vision. Charlie turned his head in time to see a big green Mercury crossing the center line toward them.

He'd always thought the key to survival of a run-down would be getting up high, so the legs wouldn't snap like wheat in a combine and pull the body under the wheels. His lurching twist may have been an attempt to throw Rosy clear; it may have been only a reflex. The movement flowed upward in one continuous rolling motion, half discus throw, half spinning tailback. Up in the air, it was quiet; no noise of squealing tires, just an instant of silent wonder, before the car came through him with a hard and heavy slamming in a dark and empty hall.

6

Rolling a joint, Darrell Bead balanced the steering wheel of the mold-green '73 Chevy Impala with his knee. He was driving north from Boston on U.S. 1. It's the type of road that's half speedway, half milk route, six lanes of hurtling commuters vying for right of way over those pulling on and off at restaurants, shopping centers, and office parks; strip and clip joints to suit every taste except good taste.

He sucked on the joint, drove carefully, and tried to forget about the deafening roar caused by a hole in his exhaust pipe. The damn thing had blown on the Tobin Bridge, and he didn't have time to fix it. It made him nervous. Anything to do with waving flags at cops made him nervous. He'd had his share of police attention in his twenty-seven years, six of them on hold in one or another of the country's free flops with bars.

He realized with some chagrin that the junker Impala was no worse than he deserved, in light of the fact that he'd trusted stupid Doris to make the purchase. He'd given her a grand to get something that would roll without attracting attention. She'd come back with five hundred dollars' worth of "Hey, coppers, here we are" puke-green Impala. What had happened to the other five hundred was no mystery: stupid Doris had had enough leftover cocaine around her nostrils to look like she'd been snorting sugar doughnuts.

When he'd seen it, he'd told her, "Doris, you are one stupid broad, and that nose candy don't make you no smarter. You could eat fish all day for a month and still be stupid." She'd gone on grinning like he'd told her she was queen for a day.

The man he was driving to rendezvous with, Wilbur "Crazo" Coughlin, was another one. Trying to go ninety in a fifty-five world . . . with a brain rated for school zones. And Darrell was none too proud of himself, headed out of town, where he didn't know his way around, to meet the guy for some scheme so crazy even Crazo wouldn't tell him what it was. Every exit, he thought about turning around. But he didn't.

Darrell turned on the staticky AM radio, tuned it to WCOW, Boston's answer to country and western. Blaring exhaust and wind-tunnel radio: that's what the nose candy queen got for his thousand bucks. Sounded like Linda Ronstadt singing in a popcorn popper. He made the decision he had to haul ass soon. He'd fallen in with bad company again.

The story of his life. Some dumb broad who spends his money like he's a millionaire and some idiot sidekick who knows a million ways to get rich . . . long as you don't mind going to jail on every third or fourth "deal." Could he ever find anybody who stayed cool, did things reasonable, smoked a little weed, maybe, but didn't go overheating their brains on every pill and powder the street doctors prescribed? Hell, no. And sure as cartoons on Saturday morning, if he stayed where he was, he was going down for another vacation in La Cage aux Folles (Darrell, mistakenly believing he could translate French, interpreted this title of a popular play, which he'd never seen, as "the cage of folly" and believed the play to be about prison life).

Bead pulled off at Cantaloupes, a maxi strip joint just south of 128, continuing to the far corner of the parking lot, where Coughlin had said he'd meet him. The marquee read "Last Night!! Juanita Jalapeño!!! Hot Stuff!!!!"

Bead lit a Marlboro and thought about going back home. Coughlin said they were going to horse country, where the gentry lived. It made him nervous.

"Freeze, scumbucket!"

Darrell's head spun left toward the voice, his hand halfway to his mouth with the smoke from the Marlboro drifting into his right eye. The dark shape gave off those flashes of light from badges and buttons that spelled cop. The figure was crouched behind his gun, holding it with both hands. When he saw Darrell was staying cool, one hand went to his waist and came up shining one of those long, chrome flashlights in his face.

Fuckin' A, Darrell thought, Coughlin got hisself busted before I even got here.

"Keep those hands visible there, Darrell babe. Reach out the window and open the door from the outside; get out real slow."

Darrell did as he was told, thinking, Shit, the cop knows my name from Coughlin telling him I'm the one. I'm going to jail, and I don't even know what crime I'm here to commit. The cop kept the light in his eyes, spun him around, and pushed him up against the car, hands on the roof. He felt the muzzle of the gun on the base of his skull, then heard giggling and a voice saying, "Boom!"

"Shit, Coughlin, that you?"

"Of course it's me, anal pore!" The giggle again, high-pitched and silly like a teenage girl's.

Coughlin spun him around, still pointing the gun at him. Bead didn't know for sure if it was a joke until Coughlin holstered it and did a little pirouette so Darrell could admire the get-up. "That was a little demonstration of the power of the uniform. Pretty convincing, huh, Bead-brain?"

"Not bad," Darrell said, trying to regain his cool, standing his five nine straight up against Coughlin's hulking six four. "Good enough to get you arrested for impersonating a cop, I'd say."

"Beady baby, you got no imagination! This ain't like our

neighborhood. There ain't no cops out here at eleven o'clock at night." He held his hands up, gesturing around. "You see any cops?"

He didn't, but he also had sense enough to know that if there was a place likely to attract one that far from the city, it was probably the parking lot of Cantaloupes. "No place to hide, either. It ain't like the city, where you can dive in a hole that lets out four places in ten seconds."

Coughlin shook his head. "You ain't list'nin', Bead-brain. I said, you see any cops?"

"They don't need street cops here. Everything's wired to bring 'em as soon as ya touch it."

"Ah, ya been readin' the burglar alarm ads. Ain't half these places wired. Besides, we don't have to break into nothin' the way I got it planned." He grinned, proud to have secret knowledge and dying for Darrell to ask him what it was.

Darrell was afraid to hear the rest of it. The thought of Coughlin planning a big deal terrified him.

Look at the guy, standing here in the middle of the parking lot in a cop suit under a streetlight wasting time with faked-up arrest games. The only one Coughlin ever fooled was the shrink let him out of the horse pistol for the criminally insane. That fact is too plain when you listen to him giggle and look backwards over that forty-five he's always pointing and saying "Boom!" over. The freak thinks he's Jesse James.

Bead realized he must have been crazy himself to come out here off his turf to play games. Then he remembered the line that had lured him: he'd told Coughlin he was more sure in the city, and Coughlin had said, "Yeah, you're comfortable staying in here with the losers; none of 'em a pot to piss in; all of 'em rippin' each other off, stealin' each other's nothing. Hell, Bead-brain, ya wanna steal somethin', ya gotta go where they got somethin'.'"

"Okay, Crazo, I'm here. What's this big deal you were talking about?"

The grin froze on Coughlin's face. His voice was almost

gentle. "First, let's get something straight. I went along with the Crazo bit in the joint because it bought me some space. Out here I'm Wilbur, got it?"

"Well, what's the difference between that and you calling me Bead-brain?"

"The difference?" Coughlin leaned closer to him as he spoke. "The difference is that if you call me Crazo, I'm gonna stick my gun down your throat and take your tonsils out the back door."

Bead bobbed around like a courting pigeon, ducking the words. "Fuckin' A, who cares, you want Wilbur, I'll call you Wilbur. Now what're we doin' here?"

"I'll give you a hint. It's easy as highway robbery."

"Hint, shit. I didn't drive all the way out here to play no games."

Coughlin laughed at Bead's little show of toughness. He put an arm around him, like a big brother, and walked him across the lot to his car. He opened the trunk and told Bead to get the map of metropolitan Boston out of the paper bag.

Also in the bag, Bead noticed, were three battery-operated warning lights, flashers, still in the bubble wrap from K mart. There was also a pair of hand-held radios—kid stuff, the words "Space Mates" on the box with a picture of two kids floating in the air having a conversation. "What the hell *is* this deal we got planned tonight?"

Coughlin took off the cop regalia and pulled on a sleeveless white T-shirt and a kelly-green nylon windbreaker that said "CELTICS" on the back. He craned his neck around, then took off the cop pants and stepped into a pair of black Levi's jeans that fit him like skin. "Tonight?" He gave Bead another smile filled with hidden meaning. "Tonight, Bead-brain, we rehearse. That's the way I do things, see? A careful plan, to foil the man, you dig? That's why I checked out how that cop suit worked on you. . . . See this?" He showed Bead that the badge was actually just a flattened wad of aluminum foil. "It wouldn't work in daylight, but I figured it'd be fine at night.

I mean, if *you* bought it, you having so much experience at being busted, it's cool."

He took the map from Bead, draped an arm around him again, said, "Come on. I'll stand you a bourbon and Coke while I tell you the plan. You ain't gonna believe what Juanita Jalapeño can do with a couple a flaming torches! Boom pa-pa boom boom! Hot stuff!"

7

In the emergency room, Charlie asked the nurse working on him whether Rosy had been hit, too. She twisted her mouth up, said, "The tall lady? Looks like a model?"

"Yes."

"I wouldn't worry about her if I were you. She's got three interns out in the hall fighting over which one's gonna put a Band-Aid on her elbow, while I'm in here checking to see if you're gonna die."

He had been disoriented at first from the good shot at the windshield he'd taken with his head, but he'd been conscious in the ambulance. After various pokings and proddings, X-rays, having his blood pressure taken numerous times, being told he had three cracked ribs and a minor concussion, to go with contusions over his entire left side, Charlie convinced the people at Mass General that he didn't need to stay in the hospital overnight for observation. They were horrified at his intention of leaving until he told them he had neither insurance nor the willingness to pay them a dime of his own money if they made him stay. It wasn't true, but after that, the pressure to stay abated considerably. Rosy helped him outside and into a taxi.

She fussed over him with some canned soup and crackers once she got him in the berth. Charlie thought she seemed distracted, almost angry, thought it was some kind of delayed reaction to the near miss. He groaned and fell asleep with a hand pressed against his ribs.

When Charlie woke up, Rosy made breakfast for him. She told him over coffee that a witness had said the driver of the Mercury was a white male with red hair and had given the cops a license number. She heard one cop tell another that the car had been stolen from the street in Charlestown moments before it hit him.

"Must have been some junkie in too much of a hurry to see his pusher," Charlie said.

She gave him a pointed look. "You think it was an accident?"

"Jesus," he said. "Don't you?"

"You said that man, Rust, would have killed you. You gave him the stuff you had on him."

"Come on, isn't that a little dramatic? In Boston, cars get stolen, people get run over. It doesn't need a murderer."

"He hadn't seen his son in a year . . . blamed you."

He thought about it awhile, shook his head. "Where does the young guy with red hair come from? Rust doesn't travel in circles where one can find a hit man." She stared at him without comment. "I'm sure it wasn't Rust," he said.

He was able to move haltingly around the boat, a hand on his ribs, his left side feeling very much run over.

He spent the morning sunbathing on deck with Rosy, thinking about his future. He decided it was inevitable that he'd end up sailing south. He'd been unable to find a boatyard around Boston up for lease, and if he was going to do that, it would be a better business at a latitude where it wasn't too cold to sail for half the year. He could explore the possibilities as he sailed down the coast; if nothing turned up on the way, he'd spend the winter in the charter business in the Caribbean.

He told Rosy all this in a ruminating way, looking for a reaction and getting cool stares. Neither of them had made any big deal over their time together in bed. It wasn't clear whether what they were doing might move from dalliance to incipient love affair. They were feeling each other out, he thought, like sparring in the early rounds of a boxing match. Patience was the key to finding out, though, of that he felt sure. Beneath the stray-cat cool, he felt sure there were also stray-cat claws, to be used when the exits were blocked. He had plenty of time. He wouldn't head south till September, and Rosy could disappear tomorrow.

For example, she told him she had a meeting and would be back before dinnertime; she went about making her preparations in a way that didn't invite inquiry about what kind of meeting it was. This time she took the Ferrari.

While she was gone, Lew Faucet saw him hobbling around, came over, and was told what happened. A little while later, he came back, said he and Lucy would fix dinner for them, to come over about seven for "bobbycued" chicken.

Rosy drove to a Ferrari dealership in Cambridge. Barely glancing at the Cabriolet sitting in the showroom, she walked briskly by a poster of a blurred racing machine and the words "Ferrari: Nine Times World Formula One Champion." She stopped at the doorway to Frank Singleton's office. She posed, a hand on the door jamb, waited for him to look up.

"Rosemary, darling!" Frank stood and straightened his blue blazer as he walked around the desk. He had the type of suntan that gave Rosy an image of him sitting inside a silver-lined reflector to intensify the rays. "To what do I owe the pleasure this time? Getting the Ferrari tuned, looking for more leads to sell insurance?"

Rosy almost asked what he was talking about. Then she remembered that the story she'd used to get information on his customers was that she was selling insurance, wanted to identify rich prospects. If he doubted it, the hundred dollars apiece quelled his suspicions. She'd visited him on a pretense about her car, had managed, through a combination of bribery and putting up with his sexual innuendo, to enlist his aid in meeting wealthy men.

"Leads, Frank." She brushed against him as she slipped through to the chair opposite the desk and took a cigarette from a package in her purse. He picked up a brass facsimile of a Porsche 911 from the desk and pressed the hood, and a flame shot out of the exhaust.

"How cute!" she said with sarcasm, lit the cigarette. "It's fortunate you're not into statues of small animals."

He mulled that over, came up empty, said, "I was just thinking about you today, Rosemary."

What a revolting revelation, she thought. Keep your filthy fantasies off me.

He held up two tickets. "I came upon a couple of tickets to a Bruce Springsteen concert."

"I hadn't heard he was coming to Boston."

He smiled. "He's not. New York, next Saturday. But hey, I have a friend who has a place there; great apartment, East Side, mid-sixties, balcony overlooking the city, first class all the way, kind of place you'd fit right in.

"No obligation, ya know what I mean? We take a demo, blow down there, take in dinner and the concert, anything else is up to you. A little outing for consenting adults, right?"

Rosy realized she was too tired and distracted to make the usual polite evasions. "What makes you think I'd cuckold my husband for you, Frank?"

He showed her a lot of teeth. "He seemed a little old and stodgy to me. I mean, I'm sure he's a great guy, but life's short. Maybe sometimes you wish you'd married someone a little less . . . wimpy."

She took three hundred-dollar bills out of her purse and held them up. "You're a salesman, Frank. I'm here to buy something. You want to sell it, or do we have to go round and round again?"

He shrugged, chuckled. "Sensitive today, huh? Well, these are the eighties, ya know what I mean, and . . ."

She tuned most of it out, seeing that he was still not giving up, wanted to retain the fantasy that someday she'd give in.

65

He picked up the lighter and flicked it as he talked, adjusted the gas flame up and then down. Eventually he got around to handing her a manila file folder.

Rosy opened it. Clipped to the first sheet was a snapshot of a fat man who looked short even standing next to the low-slung Ferrari. She wanted pictures so she could pick these men out of crowds in public places, meet them on neutral territory, make it look accidental. She'd given Frank a Polaroid, told him to say he kept a scrapbook of his sales. She figured anybody buying a Ferrari would go along with the idea that it might be an historic moment.

He already kept standard dossiers of his sales contacts, listed all manner of details picked up in casual conversation. It made subsequent contacts easier, more personal.

There was a business card clipped under the picture of the fat man: Jason Richards, Attorney at Law. The address was on Federal Street, a prestige address for a law firm. Apparently, most of their talk had been about food. Under lunch, three downtown restaurants were listed, the same for dinner. Next to hobbies he'd written gourmet chef and Rockland Park Race-track.

"What's this about Rockland Park?"

"He's a fan of horse races. Told me he's working on a system. I didn't tell him, but he's nuts to bet up there."

"Why's that?"

"They just rebuilt the track . . . had a fire. It's a slick facility, but no tradition to attract the big-stakes racers yet. Mostly three-thousand claimers run there."

"What's that mean?"

"Means they're losers . . . if a horse is entered in a claim race, you can walk up before the race, plop down the claim rate, and he's yours . . . it cuts down on the number of ringers. . . . Jason said he likes the ambiance better than Suffolk Downs. Said he feels like there's less chance of outright rigging up there than there is where the big-city money plays. Personally, I think he's got it backwards. . . ."

While Frank tried to impress her with how much he knew

about racing, she flipped through the folder quickly, seeing there were four more "contact" sheets with photos and info. She weeded out the two who were married, put them and the three bills on his desk, waited for a lull in Frank's monologue.

"Good-bye, Frank," she said, and left him still flicking his Porsche.

As she drove back to the marina, her thoughts picked up the two questions she'd been asking herself all day: first, was Charlie Gamble a good man or a damn fool; and second, what the hell difference did it make to her?

When Charlie told Rosy about the invitation to dinner aboard *Lew-Sea*, he said, "I think they've been peeking over here, dying to meet you. Lucy's sense of order is offended by orphans, lost dogs, and bachelors; thinks of them as members of the same category."

"How does her husband feel about her taking in bachelors?"

"Lew's retired navy; thinks officers are assholes, and that his money is safe in a Merrill Lynch Cash Management Account. Other than that, he'll agree with just about anything Lucy says."

"She's the power in the family?"

"He just agrees. Doesn't necessarily pay any attention after that."

"Retired navy, and he has money to invest?"

"He moonlighted a civilian job for the last five years he was in the navy. Through extreme tightfistedness and a natural disdain for conspicuous consumption in all its forms, he managed to save that and everything Lucy made as a secretary during the same period. Now he lives on his boat, works three days a week at a garage near here to supplement his retirement and investments, brags that he never touches the principal."

"Funny," Rosy said, "I wouldn't expect a retired navy guy to live on a boat. You'd think he would have had enough of the water."

"In a way, you're right. He doesn't go out much. Just kibitzes on the dock. He's paranoid about sinking, realized after he bought it that a fiberglass cabin cruiser is a lot more precarious than a navy ship. I think his living on a boat has more to do with never getting to be the captain while he was in the navy than it does with love of the water . . . that, and he got a better deal on the boat than anybody would give him on a house.

"Anyway, we were the only ones on this end of the dock toughing out the winter aboard this year, so we got to be friends. You'll like 'em," he said, but he was wondering how Rosy, fancy clothes, and icy reserve would mix with Lew and Lucy, Pabst Blue Ribbon, and redneck humor.

Before they left, *Squareknot* heaved crazily from the wake of a beefy sportfisherman coming in way over the five-knot limit; a couple of teenagers in Daddy's boat, headed for the gas dock. They heard Lew pounding down the dock after them, offering to tear off the helmsman's face. His practice was to embarrass hell out of such "shit-for-brains," as he called them. Lew went a bulky two twenty, sculpted like a TV wrestler, and none of his victims ever came by speeding twice. Occasionally, transients complained about the noise he made in the process, but the management treated him with the gratitude and respect one accords a rapacious guard dog who has solved an intractable problem with thieves. Charlie thought Rosy was a little wide-eyed when he told her that was her host for the evening.

It didn't inhibit her dressing. He whistled when she came on deck. She did a little spin to show off the billowing sleeves of a champagne-colored silk crepe blouse worn over matching satin silk pants with a delicate wheat-straw-pattern brocade. Her sandals were gold lamé. If the effect hadn't been so smashing, he might have overcome the lump in his throat to point out that it was a tad dressy for barbecued chicken aboard *Lew-Sea*. She stepped forward, enveloping him in some scent that succeeded in its purpose of addling his brain even further, gave him a little kiss, and said, "Shall we go?"

Lew was on the poop deck in a T-shirt that said "Sailors need blow jobs, motormen arrive full power."

"Come on aboard, if you ain't afraid of a real boat, Gamble. Here, let me help you."

Charlie, limping and happy to be coddled, put out his hand. Lew slapped it out of the way, said, "Not you, asshole!" He pulled Rosy aboard, said, "You're bound to be tired of that slow boat, honey. Thought you'd enjoy spending the evening on a boat that roars!"

He puffed up his chest at Charlie, making sure he read the sentiments there. "As usual, you're the avatar of subtlety, Lew."

"Yeah, so's your mother." He laughed and turned to Rosy. "First thing you gotta learn around the waterfront is stay off the boats with the telephone poles on 'em!"

Lucy came topside wiping her hands on a dishtowel. "Lew, I told you to take that shirt off before they came over here! You'll have this girl thinking her beau has Hottentots for friends."

"Oh, okay, dumplin'," he said, and whipped the shirt off to reveal another that read "I know I'm captain because my wife said I was." He gave Lucy a sheepish look, then grabbed her and squeezed her when she rolled her eyes.

"I hate to admit it," she said, "but I'm this fool's wife . . . Lucy." She untangled one of her arms from Lew's bear hug, shook Rosy's hand. As she did so, her eyes traveled up and down the silk outfit. Freeing herself, she gave a tug at the loose-fitting dress she wore, what Charlie would have called a muu-muu. "My, what a beautiful outfit you're wearing," she said.

"Thank you," Rosy said, giving Charlie a look that he interpreted correctly as Why didn't you tell me I was overdressed, you son of a bitch?

Lucy said to Charlie, "Honey, you got yourself a pretty one, didn't you?" Determined to break through her nervousness with Rosy, Lucy stepped up to her and took her hand again, just holding it instead of shaking it. "I seen you in that bikini the other day, wished you'd go away so's the rest of us wouldn't look so dumpy."

Rosy smiled, said, "Well, I know the magazines tell us men should love us for our minds, but I hate to take a chance." She took Charlie's arm and leaned into him seductively, making a joke of it. Lucy covered her mouth and giggled, then took charge of Rosy and led her below, beginning the inquisition with, "Where you from, honey?" Charlie, betting that Lucy would get more information in five minutes than he would in five days, wished he could have heard the answers.

Lew set about spraying charcoal lighter into the tripod grill that sat on the stern. He lit it and stood back as it flared up about six feet into the sky.

"Think you got enough juice on there, Lew?"

"We don't do nothing half-assed around here," he said. "Come on up to the bridge, I gotta show you my new loran, just installed it today."

Pushing any hope he had of being pampered out of his mind, Charlie managed to climb the ladder to *Lew-Sea*'s steering station with his one good arm. The ladies appeared back on deck with glasses of wine. Lew began punching buttons on the loran, the word an acronym for Long Range Navigation aid, a computerized device that triangulates position from timed electronic beacons on land. The older models, like the one Charlie had on *Squareknot*, just listed two coordinates, which one then looked up on a chart. The new ones like Lew's were programmed to accept waypoints, then figure position, course made good, and give continuously updated steering instructions to get where one wanted to go. This modern wonder wasn't much bigger than a pound of butter.

They jumped at the sound of a loud air horn. The sportfisherman that had rolled a wake under them earlier was headed back out. The two teenagers at the helm were waving at them. When Charlie and Lew looked their way, the engine howled and the screws dug deep, throwing a maximum wake under *Lew-Sea*. The laughing boys both dropped their swim trunks and mooned them on the way out. Lew was half smiling despite himself as he bellowed curses after them. His voice stopped short at the high-pitched scream behind them.

They turned to see Lucy frantically fanning at flames that leaped from the front of her dress as she backpedaled across the deck. In the instant they looked, Lucy's movement was checked as Rosy hit her from the side with a shoulder tackle that carried both of them over the side into the water with a hiss.

Charlie and Lew hit the water three seconds later from the bridge. Charlie reached Rosy, pulled her head above the water, and she climbed onto him, sputtering, pushing him under. He held his breath, kicked and pushed until he got her to the dock. He could hear Lew screaming beside him, "Did it burn you, did it burn you?!"

The four of them clawed their way onto the dock, where they lay wailing and sputtering like a detail from Dante's *Inferno*, the harbor slime all over their bodies, Lew ripping Lucy's dress open like flimsy paper to look for burns, as she was crying too hard to answer him. Rosy's golden silk clothes hung like gilded seaweed; her makeup ran down her cheeks as she vomited seawater. Charlie was holding the pain in his ribs, watching Rosy get her breath, when she started to laugh and point at Lucy, whose white belly crinkled in ripples as she heaved in hysterical laughter at the blackened tips of her bra, like she'd dipped them in soot. Still laughing Lucy rolled and crawled over to Rosy and hugged her, said, "Oh, your beau-u-u-tiful clothes!" She wiped at the running mascara on Rosy's cheeks with her fingers, and the two of them held each other until Lucy's hysteria ran its course.

One of the people who rushed up noticed the circle of fire on *Lew-Sea*'s stern, where the tumbling charcoal had landed after pouring liquid fire down Lucy's front. He jumped on board and put it out with a fire extinguisher.

They took showers and got stumbling drunk, Rosy in the closest thing she owned to blue jeans, the white ducks she'd been wearing when he found her. They cooked the chickens on *Squareknot*, on a grill that hung off the stern so that the fire couldn't fall on board.

As word of what happened spread around the docks, Charlie's friends, the winter people, drifted by and were welcomed aboard. More food was squeezed on the grill. A large bottle of rum was drained, and Rosy became acquainted with Gordon, a Legal Aid attorney who lived on a big decaying Chris-Craft that had no engine in it; Helen, an aging poetess who was famous around the dock for her daily nude showers on the deck of her small wooden sloop; and Carp, a fisherman from Baltimore who'd caught his wife cheating the year before, had steamed his rig north, and hadn't been home since. Rogers made a complete fool of himself going from lap to lap, doing push-push, sucking the buttons of people's clothes, and drooling. Helen said it was a sign he'd been weaned too early, and that she wished she could make her buttons give the poor dear milk. The word had spread about the car incident, too, and they fussed over Charlie in a way that Lew had failed to do.

Lew turned more maudlin the drunker he got, kissing Rosy more than once to thank her for saving his Lucy. Lucy finally told him that if he kissed Rosy again, they'd be pulling his ass out of the harbor, and everybody laughed.

Charlie thought Lew'd be talking about strangling the kids who had "waked" them, but he blamed himself for not replacing the tippy grill with one like Charlie's that was secured to the stern rail. He said he'd been wanting one for years, but the damn things cost a hundred and twenty-five bucks. He meandered into his favorite topic somehow, the twin dangers of piracy and sinking at sea, and made Charlie nervous when he went for his shotgun to show them they were protected.

After the guests had gone home, Rosy kissed him in a way he thought she'd never kissed him before. He felt that some gap had closed. She held his face and bet him that she could make love to him without touching his left side. They crawled naked into the berth, and she was well into proving her point when Charlie cheated, forgot the concept being tested, lost track of the pain behind a long, smooth wall of pleasure.

Later, she laughed at him when he moaned and asked her to get up for the bottle of wine. He had to get it himself, so he made a big show of being in horrible pain. She said he was a fraud. He said the pain came and went unpredictably.

Later still, when Rosy had been quiet so long that he thought she was asleep, she said, "Well, damn it, Gamble, you've got a lot of gall to paint this romantic picture of sailing south for the winter, then not even invite me to go along."

"I didn't think you'd be interested."

"You could have asked."

"Hell, you won't even tell me how you've spent the last two years of your life, and I'm just supposed to know you want to hit the high seas with me?"

"Who said I wanted to? I just said you could have asked."

"You want to go?"

"That's some romantic proposition."

"Don't blame me. You've already squeezed the romantic out of me tonight."

"Poor boy," she said.

"It wasn't a complaint. I know where to get more."

She snorted and put an arm across his chest. "You sure do."

"Is that a compliment or a call to arms?"

"Take your pick, Captain. You think that squealing I was doing earlier was complaining?"

"One never knows."

She tweaked his chest hair. "Bull. You know." Then she sat up and looked at his face. "You don't know, do you?"

He thought he knew, but he played dumb. "Know what?"

"That you make my ears flap every time we make love; that you're a lovable man, sweet, but tricky enough to keep one thinking."

"Please sail south with me!" he said.

"That's a little better, but it still needs work."

"Consider me your laboratory."

Eventually she conceded that maybe she'd go, as long as the trip included the island of Tortola. Why Tortola? She didn't know, but she'd always liked the name. It smacked of exotic mysteries and wormy wrecks ballasted with Inca gold.

The ringing of the telephone woke him the next morning. It was a detective with Boston's finest, Sergant Phillips. He asked after Charlie's health. Not seeing Rosy around anywhere, he said he was almost well.

"I have a patrolman's report on my desk, Mr. Gamble, about the incident night before last."

"Yes."

"I was surprised when I went to the hospital today to find you gone."

"I prefer recuperating at home. What's up, do I need to fill out a form?"

"My job is investigating crimes, Mr. Gamble. On this one I can't do much, unless you can give me something to go on."

"You already have a description of the car, right?"

"Sure, but it was stolen, later found abandoned. . . . What I want to talk to you about is something one of the witnesses said. A cabby waiting outside Polcari's. He said the car that ran you down was sitting halfway down the block for five minutes with the motor running before you came along. That doesn't make sense to me . . . guy steals a car, crosses the bridge, and hangs around for five minutes? Crazy.

"Then it occurred to me that the thief didn't steal the car to keep it. He only wanted to use it as a weapon. You know anybody who would want to kill you, Mr. Gamble?"

"Kill me? Hell, no." As wake-up calls went, it was effective but not smooth.

"Have you been involved in any angry disputes—money, women, anything—in recent months?"

That's the problem with blackmail, thought Charlie. When you say, Okay, I quit, and give the guy the thing he needs, and he starts trying to kill you, you can't even tell the police.

"Nothing, Sergeant. I think there must be some other explanation."

Sergeant Phillips made his skepticism clear but said he had a whole stack of open files on his desk, and he didn't intend to waste his time unless Charlie would be more forthcoming.

When he got off the phone, he climbed halfway up the companionway and squinted into ten-high sun. Rosy was nowhere

74

in sight. He went back below to make some coffee and found a note rolled up in the spout of the pot:

Good morning, my darling,
I didn't have the heart to wake you after the way I worked you over last night.
I have some business to attend to before we head for Tortola. If I don't get back tonight, I'll call you in the morning.
Don't even think about leaving without me. When you get it right, you get it right. Love, Rosy.

He was thinking he'd have to explain that nobody heads for the Caribbean in June when a sound in the cockpit made him look up. A pistol was being leveled at him in front of a grimacing face with purple hair. He dove to port as the gun went off with a deafening roar. He scrambled into the aft cabin, out of the line of fire.

The only heavy object at hand was a ten-pound mushroom anchor that he used in the dinghy. When a foot in a black running shoe appeared on the first step of the companionway, he slammed the anchor down on top of it. The foot disappeared to a scream of agony, and he felt the motion of the boat as the intruder jumped to the dock.

When he heard the syncopated steps receding, he looked through a port and saw the guy running and skipping off the dock. He got in a light blue Chrysler that waited with the door open, motor running, and drove off with a jerky motion. Not used to driving left-footed. He didn't bother trying for the license—no doubt stolen, like the Mercury.

He heard his name called and stuck his head out the companionway. Lew Faucet was standing on the poop deck of his cruiser with his shotgun. "Was that a shot I heard? Did that guy shoot at you?"

Aware that they'd have the attention of other boats, Charlie tried to laugh. "Hell, no, Lew. That's a goddamned fraternity brother of mine who's never grown up. Threw a cherry bomb at me and ran. Sorry about the noise."

Lew stared at him. "Sure looked like a gun in his hand."

"Probably was. He's into squirt guns, too. Fills 'em with gin so people think his victims are drunk."

"Well, he scared the crap right outa Lucy. You tell that son of a bitch he fools around like that around me, he's liable to get his ass shot."

"It'd serve him right, Lew, and I bet they'd give you a medal. Tell Lucy I'm sorry."

He went below and pulled on some jeans. Where the hell has Rosy gone? he wondered. He felt as though he'd had a full day before he'd even put on his pants. Jesus!

Then he heard the water rushing through the bullet hole into *Squareknot's* bilge. Sweet bleeding Jesus!

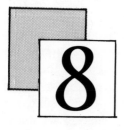

8

Rosy spent the morning down the street from the Meridian Hotel, at a salon called All of Me. Her brunette hair was cut short enough to live with a shower-and-shake technique, an expedience of her life-style. With her face, it created an effect on which a stylist would be hard-pressed to improve. The ritual performed at All of Me was more on the order of theatrical preparation of a psychological nature than a beauty treatment. It was a way she worked at building a wall between a role she intended to play and the personality she thought of as her own.

She began in the Nautilus room, working her muscles to a pump of swollen well-being. After a quarter hour in the sauna, she had a session with Grete, an amazon Swede who cooed and oohed and ahhed with a Scandinavian sibilance over her for twenty minutes. Her hands knew where the evil lurked in each muscle and how to find the limit of any joint, just shy of her client's scream for mercy. This left Rosy relaxed enough to almost sleep through a facial, manicure, and shampoo prior to a complimentary glass of cheap Chablis served from an expensive decanter by René, the artiste and proprietor.

She noted that he chose the peak of psychological vulnerability, when her hair hung wet and slicked upon her head, to make his pitch. She listened to the routine about the latest style he intended to inflict on her, then placed her usual order. "Take a little off, René, and I warn you, if I don't recognize myself when you're finished, I'm going to throw up on your Persian cat."

As the chastened René got huffily but carefully to work, a trace of a smile slipped through the façade that delivered the line. She was thinking that Charlie would have loved the scene.

But then, she'd been thinking about Charlie most of the morning. The night before, when she'd seen Lucy on fire, the water all around them, she'd had to make a choice. Lucy would be burned, or she would drive her into the water. Bam. She'd done it. She was drowning. Then he was there, pulling her up, an island she could climb. After that, she knew. He was what he seemed.

She wasn't so naive as to forget that water held no fear for him, so saving her was no big deal. Somehow her own reaction to Lucy's danger had freed her feelings for Charlie. If she could do something good, maybe he could, too. If she could dive into fire and not get burned, maybe she could chance letting her feelings go.

Then, when she felt that molten lady lava stirring, she didn't fight it, let it flood all over Charlie and licked him dry. Waking in the darkness of the morning, she'd felt no need for a safety net. He wouldn't drop her. Maybe she didn't need another scam . . . the thought gave her a feeling like a new mink coat. She hadn't been so happy since her wedding night. Of the marriage that had gone so dreadfully wrong.

And what had gone before that marriage. Her romantic college career, she thought bitterly. . . .

Her concept of what men were all about began with her mother's counsel. She told Rosy not to rely on them; they were undependable. And in her view interchangeable. She advised her never to judge a marriage until it was over and she saw the settlement. Her favorite quote she attributed to Zsa Zsa Gabor.

When asked whether a woman should return the ring after a broken engagement, she allegedly said, "Von must alvays return za ring, dahling . . . but, of course, keep za stone." Or words to that effect; the phrasing changed according to how many martinis her mother had had.

Her mother practiced her preachings through four marriages, becoming more secure financially as she progressed. Rosy had been a liability in her life-style, especially as she grew old enough to present chronological contradiction to whatever age her mother was using at the time. She had been bundled off to a long series of camps, boarding schools, school-sponsored tours of Europe.

In a youth hostel in Venice, she failed to find enlightenment in the act of losing her virginity, likewise in a fumbling encounter with a boy from a neighboring prep school. Her friends assured her it got better.

When she arrived at college, somewhat unaccustomed to her newly long legs and a figure run positively amok with femininity, she was bowled over by an invitation to a fraternity party by a boy who looked as though he'd jumped life-size from the front of a Wheaties box. The new friends she'd made were wild with envy when she left the dorm with him.

She wasn't really taken in when, after pouring several glasses of mysterious punch into her, he took her upstairs to his room, turned out all the lights, cajoled her out of her clothes with some timeworn lines about how everybody at college did it. She wanted to be taken in. She was all for it. She'd waited too long already in girls' schools and girls' camps and chaperoned buses. Let's see about this thing called grown-up lovemaking.

He showed her with all his heart. He went to the bathroom, came back, and showed her again. The second time, he seemed larger inside of her, but he held her hands so she couldn't explore him. He went to the bathroom again, came back wearing a new cologne, showed her again.

Then, lying there alone in the dark, she confronted a horrifying thought, which she did her best to explain away. She

79

preferred to discount her thought as an aberration of the strange punch, of which she'd drunk too much, or as a manifestation of her inexperience with the mechanics of masculinity. Her body trembled from the intensity of the effort to make the idea go away.

But when she heard bare feet returning to the room, she rolled off the bed, flipped on the light, and found herself facing a naked stranger. He covered himself with his hands and ran out the door to the bathroom. She heard a chorus of laughter coming from the room that shared the bath.

The boy from the Wheaties box came sauntering in in his silk briefs, a charming smile on his face. He held his hands open and said, "Hey, don't be mad, okay? It's just a joke."

The boys' version of the story immediately spread and gave her pariah status during sorority rush. The joke kept coming back to haunt her in various forms for the next four years as the details got fuzzy in the retelling, but the fact became common knowledge that she'd pulled the train for the quarterback and the rest of the starting backfield in her freshman year. Every now and then, she'd be walking across the campus toward the library or somewhere, and she'd hear a falsetto voice from a dorm window calling, "Oh, Mona! Ooooh, Mooona!" Her nickname. Although she never heard an explanation, she knew it began as Moaner. It made her ill. It never went away.

The experience left her with a loathing of leering masculinity. The marriage it drove her into did worse . . . it showed her that love could be just as destructive.

Lying beside Charlie in the dark, suspended between new hope and evil memories, the unexpected gnarlings of psyche produced by the marriage bloomed anew. It had led her to an ironic belief in God: unless some seditious spatula was stirring the filling, once in a while things would go right. Something was always putting blisters on dancing feet and expiration dates on the drug called love.

What could go wrong this time? She didn't know, but she knew something could, in some new and horrible surprise attack. This time, she'd at least be prepared . . . she'd have a grubstake. She wouldn't let go of the trapeze without a net beneath her.

When she emerged from All of Me, although she looked much the same as she had on entering, she felt as though she were wearing a costume. Her carriage reflected the change, through smaller steps, a more erect bearing, and a pace that was studiously unhurried. She prowled the city, stopped in each lunch place Frank Singleton had listed for Jason Richards, but he was in none of them. She called his office, was told he'd left for the day.

"Is he in court?"

"No. He's out on personal business."

Smiling, she hung up the phone. She thought about going back to the marina to get her car, looked at her watch, and realized she still had time to catch the Bettors' Special from South Station. If she found Jason Richards at Rockland Park, it would be useful to need a ride.

Her path took her along the edge of Boston Common, one of those inner-city havens where the richest and the poorest mingled without really touching. Bums and brokers, heiresses and whores; each strolling the greenbelt trying to cop a little peace in the midst of a personal tournament of urban swat and swat back. She heard a voice with some familiar note in it, turned to see the big blond girl stoop to kiss an old woman on the cheek, say in wonderful Baastonese, "See ya lata, Ma. We'll catch a flick; that wicked Clint Eastwood at the Caaney, okay?" It was Gerte without her Svedish accent.

Rosy laughed out loud and felt the fear that drove her from Charlie Gamble's berth that morning subside. It was giving way to another feeling that she recognized and welcomed. Power. She felt it in her step and in her acceptance of the ways in which the city worked. Jason Richards would be a piece of cake.

After stanching the flow of seawater into the bilge with a wooden plug kept on hand against the possibility of a failed seacock, Charlie determined that the bullet hole was only inches below the waterline, and that moving everything with weight toward the stern would raise the bow enough for him to repair the fiberglass.

Before he began the work, he yielded to the prickly feeling on his neck and told Lew the truth about the hit-and-run and the gunshot. They kicked it around and decided Rust must have gone completely nutso. Charlie asked him if he had a handgun he could borrow.

"You mean you're gonna hang around and wait for him to try again?"

"Rosy was gone when all this happened; I don't know where she is, but she left a note saying she'd be back tonight or call in the morning. Besides, that plug is a joke . . . before I go anywhere, I have to fiberglass that hole."

Lew shook his head. "Keep some extra. If that guy's still around, you may need it to patch your ass."

Charlie took the .32-caliber Savage automatic Lew handed him, slid the top back to cock it, fingered the safety into place, and said, "Just flick that and shoot, right?"

Lew raised an eyebrow. "Yeah. Then duck: 'cause you probably missed."

Thirty minutes later Charlie was lying on his back in his dinghy, bouncing around beneath *Squareknot*'s bow. The coveralls he was wearing concealed the pistol jammed into the waistband of his cutoffs. It would have been nerve-racking under ideal conditions to work with the rapidly congealing mess . . . he was using triple catalyst so he could do several layers quickly. Every time a wake jostled him against the boat and the metal of the gun clinked against the hull, he got a gory image of the thing going off, carrying his privates on a booster ride to the bottom of the harbor. Putting it down, however, seemed even more foolish.

The fact that Lew appeared beside him on the dock undetected confirmed that view. Lew traveled with all the stealth of a water buffalo with church bells for balls. He had an oddly shaped package in his hand which Charlie realized was his shotgun in a garbage bag. "You might as well load the guy's gun for him as lie out here in the open like this, Gamble."

"Possibly, but since you're standing in the line of fire, you needn't act superior about it. In my case, this hole could sink me and my darling *Squareknot* in about five minutes, so it's just a case of selective but reasonable cowardice. You, on the other hand, appear to be bucking for the foolish hero award."

Lew shuffled around a bit, squinting his eyes at the spaces between parked cars and the knots of tourists moving on the far bulkhead. Then Charlie's reference to sinking distracted him, got him talking about a friend of his who'd smacked into a railroad tie that was floating just under the surface.

"Goddamn, I don't know why he didn't sink!"

Lew always had an ear for a good sinking story. He had one of those instant lifeboat packages that could be activated in five seconds by yanking a ripcord. The resulting inflated raft was stocked with canned food, water, and such necessities of survival as fishing gear, a pocketknife, signal flares, and toilet paper. It was designed to keep two people alive at sea for weeks if boredom didn't kill them.

"That's right, Lew. He was just lucky."

"You know Smeltz? The guy with the yellow Bertram over on the far dock? He had a Rybovitch, best damn sportfisherman money can buy; paid four hundred thousand for it, used. One day, not a cloud in the sky, ocean like glass, he's steaming thirty knots, pretty as ya please, suckin' on a col' brewsky, and wham! Damn thing sank out from un'er 'im in less'n a minute. When they pulled 'er up, she had a telephone pole sticking out of the damn bow like it was a giant Popsicle."

"No shit?"

" 'T's 'em damn hunks a lumber floatin' just un'er the surface ya can't see that getcha."

"Ya never know, Lew."

The Turf Club at Rockland Park was a steeply tiered, private area of the clubhouse where people rented permanent boxes by the season. On a slow Tuesday, they didn't pay much attention to nonmembers wandering in. Mostly it was a tax write-off for small businessmen who wanted a stylish way to entertain customers . . . a subtle way to slip some money under the table to a buyer: "Hey, this ticket's a winner, Claude. Didn't you buy this one?"

Rosy strolled among the boxes until she saw the plastic sign bearing the name of Jason Richards's law firm. Jason was in attendance, by himself. He was poring over a computer printout, a pencil in his hand. In person, he was more chunky than fat; had the thick shoulders and arms of a former athlete gone to rich food and luxury. His suit was expensive, but worn without attention to neatness or fit; his graying hair was unabashedly slicked back from a receding hairline.

Noting the empty box beside his, Rosy tipped the usher to seat her next to Jason. He glanced at her, looked away without interest. She got tired of waiting for him to make a move, leaned over, and said to him, "I can't seem to hit a winner today. How about a tip on the next race?"

"Don't bet." His tone was not friendly.

She watched him ignore his own advice and place a bet after

much consultation and riffling of the computer sheets. When the race ended, he took two tickets out of his pocket, pitched one onto the floor and shifted the other one to a different pocket, made a note on the paper. Rosy persisted.

"I won't hurt your odds. I'm only betting two bucks a race."

"I'll tell you what," he said. "You give me the two bucks and tell me who you want it on. If you win, I'll pay ya double what the track pays."

"Pretty sure I don't know what I'm doing, huh? Is it that obvious?"

He shrugged. "The horses are all losers. The sheets don't help. Every bet's a crap shoot. Seven horses. You have one chance in seven of hitting it."

"I notice you're betting."

He looked exasperated, shrugged as though giving in to something, held up the computer sheet. "I had a theory there had to be a way to beat these bastards . . . hired a little old lady in Boston and put a computer terminal in her apartment; gave her a subscription to every racing form in the country. She keeps records on every horse that gets his name in print.

"I figured a computer would make it like the card counters in blackjack: just enough help to turn the odds in my favor. I designed the program myself. Weighted probabilities on any race based on lineage, racing record by track condition, and recorded times, with a factor thrown in for the jockey that's up on a given day based on his record in the last two years, last one year, and last month. The goal is to find one race a day I can pick with better than fifty-fifty odds."

"Pretty impressive," Rosy said.

"Yeah, impressive is what it is," he said.

"How's it work so far?"

" 'Bout as well as betting lucky colors," he said, "but I think, today, if your color happened to be pink, you'd be doing slightly better than my program."

Rosy laughed. "Maybe the little old lady is throwing in coded data on you; making a fortune while you scratch your head."

His head swiveled toward her, and she got the impression he

was taking his first real look at her. "Now, that's cynical. If you can't trust a little old lady, who can you trust?"

"There are theories on that one, too," she said, smiling slowly at him as she did. "But I'm not sure how you'd get them on a computer. Probably do just as well to trust left-handed, blue-eyed mulattoes with two brothers named Mary; assume anybody else is gonna screw you if you give 'em a chance."

"Does that mean nobody's trustworthy?"

"Now, that's cynical," she said. "It just means you can't predict who's honest, and the odds will be a little in your favor if you assume the worst."

"I guess that's what makes a horse race," he said. "Can I buy you a drink . . . ?"

"Rosy," she said, answering the tone question. "Sure, I'll take a slippery nipple, erect," she said, smiling into his eyes, letting him decide if the choice of drink was a message or an indication of general low character. "And while you're up, put two dollars on Ouija's Darling, to win, for me."

"You betting a hunch?"

"No, a tip. She's carrying pink."

The bartender knew what a slippery nipple was: layered Baileys Irish Cream on top of sambuca, with an added squirt of grenadine that settled through the translucent syrup to form a red nodule on the round bottom of the miniglass, leaving no doubt that this final touch was what made it "erect."

Jason puzzled over the beautiful girl with the cynical rap. He thought she might actually have solved the riddle of why his rational betting system hadn't yet paid dividends. It wasn't a big deal to him. He'd done it on a whim. He could afford the wages he paid the old lady who plugged all the numbers for him.

Short, fat, aware of himself, aware of most follies, he had little else on which to spend the outrageous sums that his expertise on arcane matters of corporate finance earned for him. His computer hobby was more fun than another whim, the Ferrari he'd bought, then never drove because it embarrassed him, sort of like walking around with his fly open or something. His computer gave him a way to relax; the horse racing idea was a mere offshoot of that. It was a way to forget the hard-nosed attitude he needed to survive in downtown Boston's litigious milieu; mathematics had for him a comforting predictability that human behavior frequently lacked. Maybe that was why it took the girl to alert him to how simple it would be for the old broad to tinker with the software; plant a depth charge that would screw it up, give him garbage, and keep the good data for herself.

The girl, Rosy, wasn't your usual back-barn slut looking for a tipster. No, she was only playing at that, like he played at the computer system. But she had a seriousness about her, under the game. He could feel it bubbling. His law practice had taught him one lesson over and over: unusual behavior is rarely accidental, and never altruistic, so don't agree to anything you don't understand. On the other hand, sometimes one had to give a little to get a little of something else, and she was definitely something else.

By late afternoon, Charlie had finished the fiberglass, and Lew had gone home after convincing him, without much difficulty, that one thing he couldn't do was spend the night on board. The murderer had already shown himself to be flexible in his style of mayhem, having used a green Mercury and a gun powerful enough to leave a hole fit to spit Ping-Pong balls through, and next he might pour gasoline down one of the dorades and follow it with a lit cigarette. Charlie agreed to lock *Squareknot* and join him aboard *Lew-Sea* for "bobbycued poke chops" but sent him ahead while he checked something out.

Rosy had left one of her bags behind. He thought it might contain something to tell him where she was. If he could find her, there was no reason to hang around waiting for Rust's assassin to try again. They couldn't track him on an ocean, and he had no misgivings about flight in the face of derangement.

He took the bag out of the settee locker where he'd stowed it reflexively, then hesitated, feeling that going through her stuff might be a creepy kind of violation. He imagined her showing up, catching him at it. His discomfiture deepened riffling through small stacks of lace and silk triangles in pastel colors. What he sought was an address book, maybe an envelope addressed to her, some document that would suggest her whereabouts. But he found only clothing.

Disappointed, he tried to restore the contents to their original neatness, thinking despite himself that he was glad to find things folded with care. Keeping things well ordered is beyond optional on a blue-water sailboat, where a snarled locker might cause the moment's delay that is the difference between a stanched emergency and a sunken ship. (Lew referred to these nautical sermonettes as "Charlie's Saltines.")

Putting the bag back in the locker, he realized he'd missed a pouch on the outside of the bag. In that he found the keys to the Ferrari. He'd been intrigued by the fact that she'd left the car behind. Did it mean she was within walking distance or that she was expecting a ride with someone else? Another man? He fought that idea off with the fact that he too found getting around Boston easier without the hassle of fighting traffic and finding a place to park.

He also found a small jewelry box covered in black velvet. It contained a few pairs of earrings and a lavish necklace of diamonds on settings that looked like small flower stems. He held it up and whistled. Knowing not a thing about gems, but something about Rosy's style, he assumed the diamonds to be genuine. He read the inscription on the underside of the lid of the box: "Michael Barkum, Fine Jewelry and Gems, Since 1950, Washington Street, Boston."

Still no address book. He took the keys and walked off the dock, went to Rosy's car, and unlocked it. With some haste, assuming there was an alarm, he put the key in the ignition and started it to kill the alarm, then turned it off. For a small car, it held one hell of a lot of clothing, but nothing that would tell him where she was. Even the registration was gone, probably in her purse.

The only thing he found that inspired curiosity was a manila file folder. It contained sales prospect sheets. He'd used similar forms himself in the computer business, an organized way to remember minutiae about the people one called on. Apparently, they were the work of someone named Singleton, the name in the space for "Salesman's Name." Each sheet had a man's picture clipped to it, and each man stood by a Ferrari, a different car in each picture. In the background of one, he saw a street sign that read "Cambridge Classics." He'd passed the dealership, knew where it was.

He put the file back and tried out various explanations as he walked back to *Lew-Sea*. Was Singleton a friend? Maybe the car had been recently purchased, used, the file left there by accident by the salesman.

He put the keys back in her bag, then used the phone to see if Cambridge Classics might still be open, but they were closed for the day. Charlie guessed anyone who could afford a Ferrari didn't have to shop after work.

He took the wireless phone with him in case Rosy called. He almost left a note, but then he realized the murderer might read it; decided Rosy would know where to look for him. He scanned the shore and the water, the bridges, alert to any eyes looking his way. He'd frequently found the scene peaceful, the proximity to urban snarl somehow emphasizing the separateness of the waterfront. Now it seemed to crawl with humanity, encroaching and close, furtive and dangerous. After a moment, he jumped from his port quarter to *Lew-Sea*, hoped he hadn't been observed.

They ate pork chops without lights in the deepening gloom that follows sunset so they could see out but weren't illuminated like a store window. Charlie admired Lucy's ability to listen to her husband's stories as though she were hearing them for the first time. In a way she was, as Lew was not the sort to confine himself too strictly to facts when telling sea stories, an art worthy of its own reality, so they tended to acquire more color with each rendition. Distracted, the only way Charlie could tell when one ended was when Lucy squealed and said, "Ain't that somethin', honey?"

After dinner, seated so they could watch the approach on the dock, Lew declined when Charlie said, "Wanna get stupid?" and offered him some of the marijuana he was smoking. Funny thing. When Charlie got stoned, it always made Lew paranoid; got him going about his Scylla and Charybdis, "them floaters just under the surface," and pirates. He got out his latest clipping about some defenseless cruiser getting terrorized, read Charlie the heavily underlined passage from *Waterway Guide* that told of the million tons per year of floating debris from derelict docks breaking up in New York Harbor.

Charlie realized he'd gone too far in the effort to calm his nerves when he was jostled awake by Lucy covering him with a blanket on the salon berth. "That's okay, honey. Lew says to let you sleep. He'll sit up awhile, and nobody knows you're here."

Before Charlie slept again, he realized that Lucy probably had no idea what his first name was, because Lew was the social butterfly, always collaring people and bringing them back to the boat for her to feed, and he always used last names.

10

At one A.M., Jason Richards was in his Jaguar XJ-12, doing close to eighty miles an hour on Route 128 north. Jason wasn't thinking of the road. He still hadn't figured out what the brunette was after, but he had a good idea what she was willing to trade. He was eager to be home.

Her name was Rosy, supposedly, but Jason had only her word on that and a promise to show him the body parts that led to the nickname. He suspected she'd seen him pass a short stack of C-notes through the bettors' window. That was why she'd gotten herself seated next to his box. With that body and clothes, she could have been a star jockey's kept woman. With that face, she could have done cosmetic ads. With the balls to pretend to be attracted to Jason's looks, she should have been sold in pressurized cans.

Jason had never been much of a success with women. He'd given it enough thought in his teens and twenties to last a lifetime. By age fifty, divorced from the woman who married him for his money without understanding the fine print in the prenuptial agreement, he was comfortable enough to be philosophical about his physical shortcomings and forget any misgivings he might have had about gorgeous whores. For them, he had what it took.

Rosy had the gall to tell him she'd been watching him because she found him very mysterious looking. He smiled at that but thought to himself that mysterious must be another name for short, fat, and rich. He had no delusions about his appearance and was content to have money rather than looks. He'd made do too long to worry about it.

Which was what he was thinking when he looked over at her, started drifting off to the shoulder of the highway, looked back up just in time to miss an old Impala clunker that was sitting on the side of the road.

"Jesus!" he said, embarrassed, thinking maybe the broad had him more hot and bothered than he wanted to admit.

"You're not falling asleep, are you, Jason? I could drive if you want."

Ouch, that one hurt. She thinks I'm in my dotage. We'll see when I get that dress off of her. He smiled at her. "That's okay. Wasn't concentrating. We'll be home in about two minutes."

As they curved onto the exit, Jason had to crowd the right shoulder of the road to avoid the flashing warning lights indicating they were coming to some obstacle. He slowed to thirty as the curve tightened, then saw a cop standing in the way, signaling them with his flashlight to stop.

"We got a cop here. Must have been a bad accident."

"Oh, I hope nobody was hurt!" she said.

The cop was walking up to the window as Jason rolled it down. "What's the trouble, Officer?" In Jason's neighborhood, cops were always friendly. He wasn't concerned about the alcohol on his breath.

The cop shined his light into their faces. As he did so, he reached in and turned the car off.

"What the hell are you do—" Jason's voice stopped when he saw the gun. There was a giggle as the cop put the gun against Jason's neck. His other hand still held the light on them.

"Folks, this ain't your night. Don't nobody wiggle a finger and I won't wiggle mine, but the idea is, I'm gonna steal this car and everything in it that ain't breathin'."

"Damn," Rosy said. Jason thought he heard more exasperation in her tone than fear. Her party spoiled.

"Okay, pal, stay calm, we aren't moving. You can have the car." Jason watched the flashlight for jittery motions, but it seemed steady. That struck him as good news. If they went step by step, there was no reason it should be anything worse than a robbery.

"Open your door and get out slowly, both of you." He stepped back from the car and slightly to the rear. They got out. The flashlight under his arm, the man threw a plastic garbage bag onto the hood. "Now empty your pockets into that. Take all your jewelry and watches off, too, and be quick, now." They started doing as they were told. "Wait a minute!" Coughlin shouted. He giggled. "You wouldn't happen to have a gun on you now, would you, fat man?"

"No, no guns," Jason said. He was surprised that his voice was steady. Just get through the steps, he thought to himself, and this character will move on.

"Okay, then empty the pockets, but remember I'm a half ounce of pressure away from pulling this trigger. I'm gonna pat ya down when ya finish, and I better not find anything in yer pockets when I do."

Rosy was taking things out of her purse one at a time, when Coughlin grabbed it, upending it onto the hood. "This ain't a scavenger hunt, girlie, just put it all in and quit farting around there!"

When they were finished, the cop shined the light on the ground behind them. "Pick up that tape, fatso, and tape her hands behind her back."

Jason could feel relief flooding over him as he taped Rosy up. There was no reason for bonds if he was going to shoot them, so they were going to be okay. He could already see himself laughing and telling his partners over drinks how he got mugged in the middle of a goddamned exit ramp from 128, two miles from some of the most expensive real estate on the north shore.

93

An electronic voice came from the cop's hip. "Jesus, Coughlin, a state cop just passed, headed your way." For what seemed a long moment, they all froze.

Coughlin grabbed the bag and threw it into the Jag. "Get in the car! You're driving, fatso!" He ran around to the far side, dragging Rosy by the arm. A knife appeared in his hand with which he slit the tape on her wrists. He pushed her into the front passenger seat, reached in to unlock the rear door, got in. "Drive!" They started around the rest of the exit. When they got to the stop sign, the radio crackled again.

"Relax, he passed the exit."

Jason heard. But he knew something terrible had just happened, a highwayman's stupid mistake that could cost him his life: the speaker on the radio had named the phony cop . . . Coughlin. He sat at the stop sign, hoping that if they made one stupid mistake, they'd make two. The gunman was fishing in the garbage bag.

"You live around here, fatso?"

"Yes." He saw the guy had his wallet, was looking for identification.

"How far?"

"Two miles."

He spoke into the radio. "Okay, Bead-brain, we're waiting at the stop sign at the end of the exit. Come on, and pick up the flashers on the way!" He'd found the ID and was reading it for confirmation. "What's your address?" he asked Jason.

"Three ninety-two Broken Oak Drive."

"Anybody else home?"

"No." This made the guy giggle.

"Perfecto, fatso, perfecto! You're having a late-night party, and I'll bet we're invited."

Jason didn't respond. The gun rammed into the back of his neck. "How about it, fatso, ain't we invited?"

"You're invited."

"That's better." He giggled and twisted around as headlights came up behind them. "Okay, let's roll. Drive slowly. Nothing to attract attention." Jason kept hoping he'd see the village police. What would he do? Jerk the wheel, crash right into them? Something good might come of it. Maybe they'd see the car behind him, realize it didn't belong. They passed the small shopping center. "Hey, turn in here and stop!"

Bead drove up next to them. Coughlin rolled the window down and spoke. "Park it, and let's all go in this one . . . no sense attracting attention with that tank you're driving."

Bead got in the back with Coughlin and started to speak. "What the fuck, I thought you said we'z leavin' them in the—" Coughlin backhanded him in the gut, knocked the wind out of him.

"Shut up. You've done enough talking for one night."

Jason lost all hope.

Bead didn't feel much better.

Rosy was trying to remember why she'd thought she needed one more scam. At that moment, she'd have willingly sold the necklace for a dime on the dollar and told Charlie to weigh anchor and point her south. She couldn't get her thoughts organized to figure out where they were going or what was going to happen. She just kept thinking that the guy with the gun and the giggle struck her as being, on a scale of one to a hundred, about ninety-nine on the spooky-weirdo meter.

11

Maybe it was the less sea-kindly motion of *Lew-Sea* compared with the ballasted stability of *Squareknot* that awakened Charlie from a deep sleep. Or maybe it was the emergency wake-up function that everybody has, to a varying extent—the suprasensory stuff that rouses a mother when her baby coughs three rooms away, after she's slept through the U.S. Marine Band's rendition of "The Star-Spangled Banner" from the television five feet from the bed. For whatever reason, Charlie Gamble's eyes flipped open with an almost metallic click. He lay sweaty, sea damp, and shirtless in a pair of blue jeans on the salon bunk of *Lew-Sea*. He sensed that he'd heard something out of sync with the common beat.

Through the open porthole he heard the muted cacophony of halyards tapping in the breeze against their masts, the slap-slop of the eternally moving water on hollow hulls, and the coming-going doppler drone of eighteen-wheelers crossing the Mystic River Bridge.

He sat up to look through the starboard porthole toward *Squareknot*. Crouched in the cockpit, apparently absorbed in picking the companionway lock, was a shadowed figure whose head swiveled in watch for possible interruptions.

Charlie's first reaction was relief at not being on board, the sleeping target of a stealthy maniac with a handful of lethal steel. The thought caused a shiver, and he watched for a few seconds before it dawned on him that the killer might not just find him missing and leave.

He might be there to plant some device that would explode when he opened a door or a drawer. Or he might know enough about boats to realize that once inside, he could slide open a hatch, relock the companionway door, and lie below in wait for Charlie's return. In his mind's eye, he saw himself opening the hatch to a roar of point-blank gunfire.

He thought of using Lew's phone to call the cops, but it was too easy to imagine a chain of events that ended with Rust describing his blackmail scheme in a courtroom. There seemed to be no way out of it . . . he couldn't keep his secure observer's post another minute. Once the guy got inside, there was no avenue of flank attack.

He retrieved the pistol from where he'd stashed it under his pillow. Both boats were stern to the dock. With the utmost care, mindful of the intruder fifteen feet away, praying that Lew had a phobia about squeaking hinges, he slowly opened *Lew-Sea's* main hatch. He counted on the lapping of the water and the distant sound of traffic to muffle any chance rustlings. With the step/freeze stealth of a setter on solo point, he crawled to the stern. He could hear the scratchy probing in the lock. He rolled soundlessly to the far side, waited for a loud truck on the bridge to provide noise cover, then slipped over the transom onto *Lew-Sea's* stern quarter. In a crouch, the gun at ready, he listened. There it was . . . the probing continued. He hadn't been detected, yet.

He had a moment of indecision. His initial thought had been to get to the dock, then approach the other vessel, and the intruder, from the rear. Now it occurred to him, crouched on *Lea-Sea's* stern swimming platform, that his weight would cause the rusted metal couplings of the dock sections to scream like jungle birds.

Then he heard a bright click that meant now or never. The

lock had popped open. He imagined both hands occupied in removing the lock and opening the door, so the pistol wouldn't be ready. His rise and two barefooted steps across the stern gave him time to gauge the enemy's distance, and he landed with his right foot in the center of the killer's back. His flying weight drove the guy's chin into the hatch, and his body crumpled down the now open companionway. He reached inside and flipped a light on.

Over the gun pointed ahead of him, he saw the depth of his miscalculation: the killer's gun had been in his hand. Only silence had saved him. He scrambled below, removed the pistol from the inert hand, and stepped on the spine of the slowly reviving prone body. He placed the gun at the base of the skull and said, "Don't move," but the man was too groggy to obey. He sort of writhed around a bit, shook his head, rolled over, blinked, and focused.

"Son of a goddamn bitch," he said. "Where the hell did you come from?"

"Out of the sky, shithead, where do you think? It must be embarrassing for you to learn that you've been trying to murder Superman."

The hit man was neither amused nor scared. "Who said anything about murder? I was breaking and entering, and that's all ya got on me, so cut the shit and let's get down to the station and get this over with. I'll be on the street before daylight."

Charlie realized he couldn't impress the guy with threats, that any hesitation would weaken his position, so he started right in by driving the edge of his foot into the guy's face as he tried to raise himself erect. His head bounced on the cabin sole and rebounded upward in a spray of broken-nose blood.

Charlie closed the door behind him while the intruder snuffled and moaned and sobbed, put his head back with his finger under his nose. Rogers came walking out of the forward cabin, stopped, and shook his paw when he stepped in the blood.

"Now, let's start again. First of all, this is neither a police station nor a court of law, nor do I have any intention of taking you to either one. The only judge you might be seeing is the one they told you about in Sunday school. Unless you show me an attitude of complete cooperation, you're going to be seeing Him in the next couple of minutes. *Capishe?*" So close to Boston's Italian North End, Charlie figured the simple Italian, familiar to any kid from the streets of Boston, might be more frightening in its insinuation than an FBI badge.

"Okay," he said. Charlie noticed that he held his eyes on Rogers, who'd sat down to frank observation of the visitor. Their faces were inches apart.

"Who hired you to kill me?"

"I don't know."

Charlie stepped forward ready to launch another kick. The guy scrabbled backward, warding off the expected blow with his arm and sputtering, "Listen to me, listen to me!"

"One more bullshit lie and you're lobster food, punk."

"I never even seen him. . . . I got a phone call, and somebody told me if I wanted to score big and easy, to look for an envelope taped to the bottom of a particular park bench in Quincy Market."

He snuffled, and Charlie handed him a paper towel. He blew his nose noisily into it. "Ya broke my fucking nose, ya bastard."

"You're not really expecting sympathy after three attempts to kill me, are you?"

"You can't prove that."

"I don't have to prove it. You were telling me about an envelope in Quincy Market . . ." Charlie said, a movement of his leg making the alternative clear.

"Okay, okay. I find it, and it has half a five-thousand-dollar bill in it."

"A five-thousand-dollar bill? They don't even make those anymore."

"That's what they said at the bank I took it to. But it's still good if I had both halves. The note says to be standing by a group of phones at Logan Airport the next day at five P.M. if I want the other half. I go, one of the phones rings, and this guy tells me he seen my picture in the paper when I got acquitted for murder. He wants to hire me. . . . He wants you and the broad dead."

"What broad?"

"The one you was with on here yesterday. . . . I seen you here; thought you'd both be here when I came this morning when the marina was less crowded."

Rosy?! Jesus, Charlie thought, Rust must be completely deranged, killing not just his blackmailer but a total stranger as well, a poor girl who happens to be keeping him company.

"There was another envelope taped to the bottom of the phone. It had pictures of you guys and directions to the marina, the name of the boat."

"You must be some cut-rate killer; two for five thousand."

"Fuck you. There was another half in the second envelope; with another serial number. I'd a gotten ten, and the banker said it'd be worth more to a collector."

The guy was no shrewd negotiator. He seemed to think Charlie would have more respect for him because of the higher figure. Charlie held out his hand, palm up, fingers saying gimme, gimme.

"I ain't got 'em on me."

"Sure. You gave them to a friend to keep, right?"

"Right."

Charlie vaulted from the table where he'd perched looking down at the guy and landed on his gut. He doubled up, and Charlie relieved him of the bulge on his hip.

The driver's license said William O'Neill, a name that seemed familiar, and the picture was a good likeness. Under the secret flap in the money compartment were two halves of different five-thousand-dollar bills. Also there were three wrinkled photos. One showed Rosy and Charlie in *Squareknot*'s cockpit. The other two were straight-on shots, one of himself, one of Rosy. Rosy stood beside her car. He'd been caught easing a spring line on *Squareknot*. All could have been taken from a great distance with a telephoto lens. The overhead angle suggested the walkway of the bridge.

Charlie held the gun on O'Neill, still doubled wretchedly

over his gut, blood running out of his nose, tears making streaks through the red. He couldn't have been more than twenty-two or twenty-three years old. Charlie suppressed a wave of pity by remembering the pain of his encounter with the Mercury.

With his free hand, Charlie picked up the one-piece phone, flipped the On button with his thumb, and punched 411. The operator said there was only one O'Neill on that street, but it wasn't William. He took the number anyway, dialed, and asked the woman who answered in a voice textured by sleep, tar, and nicotine for William.

"Hold on." The phone clanked onto a hard surface. He waited about thirty seconds. The voice that returned was angry. "Billy ain't here, and who do you think you are, calling here this time a night? I work, ya know, and I need my sleep. Who is this?"

"Is this his mother?"

"Yeah, who's this?"

"Never mind. I'll call him later." He hung up. So it was feasible. Rust could have seen the wild-eyed sociopath in the papers and just called him up. Damn. Half-assed way to find a contract murderer. The method of payment was pretty ingenious for Rust—he being a man whom nobody had ever known to come up with a creative idea of his own—half of a bill, so neither of them can spend the half he has . . . makes names unnecessary, and the buyer has nothing to gain from not paying up, so the hit man can be confident of payment when the job's done.

"If you succeeded, how were you to contact the buyer to get the other half of the bill?"

"He said he'd watch the papers and call me with instructions. I said if I got you out on the boat, they might not find the bodies, so he told me to draw two circles in chalk on the back of the bench in the market if I needed to contact him and he'd call me within twenty-four hours."

Charlie put the driver's license, the pictures, and the halves of currency into his jeans pocket. He emptied the bullets from O'Neill's gun, then tossed it to him. Taking it back from him, he inspected the bloody blotches on the gun and smiled at O'Neill. "That was just to be sure there are good prints on it," he said.

"Now, here are the facts of life, O'Neill. I'm not taking you to the cops because I happen to have friends who are much more efficient and much less particular about the legalities of their methods. I'm not gonna kill you because I might find you useful someday. One minute after I kick your ass outa here, I'm gonna be on the phone to my friends. They have expensive reasons for wanting me alive. I'm gonna give this gun with your prints on it to them. I'm gonna tell them about our little discussion. If I suddenly become dead or missing, either they will find you and kill you very slowly, or they will shoot a wino with your gun, leave it by the body, and let the cops find you. Once you're in prison, you're easy meat for my friends. Are you following me, O'Neill?"

"Are you telling me you're Mafia?"

"Shit, O'Neill, does my name sound Italian to you?"

"I don't know your fucking name."

"Well, don't sweat it. Just trust me. My friends are well connected, and they will know that if I turn up dead or missing, one William O'Neill is the first sucker down, got it?"

O'Neill looked at him through baleful eyes. "Yeah, I got it."

"One more thing."

"What's that?"

"Don't take any phone calls for a couple of weeks. I want your employer to think you're still on the case, so he won't take other measures. I may decide to check by calling you myself. If I get you, my friends do their thing, *capishe*?"

"Yeah."

Charlie sent O'Neill on his halting way, still limping from the anchor-smashed toes, groggy and bloody from the evening's exertions. Then he began talking into his cupped hand, loud enough for O'Neill to hear: "Guido, *paisano*, how the hell are they hanging, you old garlic fart?"

He heard Lew calling from *Lew-Sea*: "Hey, Gamble, thought you were gonna lay low over here."

"Changed my mind, Lew."

"Well, then keep it down over there. We're trying to sleep, ya know?"

"Sorry, Lew. Good night, Lucy."

"Good night, honey."

Jesus Christ. Nobody knows my name.

Charlie wasn't so cool he could indulge in such violent negotiations and then flop back into the bunk for the rest of his night's sleep. He watched O'Neill drive out of the brilliantly lit parking lot, right past Rosy's Ferrari still parked there. He craned his head around and sniffed the air. There was a freshening breeze, and he concluded that a little night sail would help him calm down.

He unplugged the shore-power cord and telephone jack, started the Volvo diesel, dropped the mooring lines, and slipped into the channel sparkling with Boston's night lights. He had the main and a one-ten jib up in ten minutes, and in twelve was ghosting down harbor, propped into the heeling cockpit. The clear thinking came on hard in slo-mo visions of bouncing heads and freeze-frames of tears mixed with blood. He softened it with a nonskid tumbler of ice and rum in one hand and a lumpy reefer in the other.

It seemed odd that Rust hadn't used his name. O'Neill was just a tool, and a poor, randomly selected tool at that. Nonetheless, he'd nearly succeeded, and Charlie couldn't kid himself that getting rid of O'Neill would necessarily get rid of Rust, although he hoped he had him neutralized for a while.

The source of his familiarity with William O'Neill's name had returned. His mother called him Billy, but Charlie had been thinking of other things, hadn't made the connection until after he'd gone. Billy O'Neill.

A year before, the papers had been full of details about O'Neill's trial. He'd killed his landlady with a tire iron when she told him she was evicting him for playing loud music all the time, keeping her awake. He'd stuffed her body in her own car after it got dark, taken her out of town, and buried her in a forrest near Topsfield.

While he was doing that, one of her kids had come to visit, known something was wrong because the car was gone and the old lady was scared to death of driving at night. When he'd found the blood by her tenant's apartment door, he'd called the police.

The cops who'd spotted the car and pulled Billy over weren't Boston's seared veterans; they were rural cops who'd sensed something really big when they'd found blood and a shovel in the trunk. They'd figured it would be hard to prove without a body, so they'd bent a few police procedures in their eagerness to be heroes.

The A.C.L.U. had been outraged by O'Neill's damaged condition on arrival at the jail. Much attention had focused on the two cops and the methods by which they'd convinced Billy O'Neill to lead them to the buried remains before taking him to the station for booking. They'd claimed Billy had come to them in tears, his remorse driving him to confession. Billy had claimed they'd tortured him and threatened to kill him. His confession was vitiated by the overzealous interrogation without benefit of counsel through which it had been obtained.

The two policemen had resigned amid much media hoopla that alternately canonized and condemned them for their roles in the affair. Billy had walked, with grisly portfolio and about fifty pounds of free page-one advertising for his future career. Nobody doubted he was the murderer, but the law machine, such as it was, spit him back onto the street.

Charlie remembered the headline, POLICE BRUTALITY!, and Lew saying, "Of course they were brutal, ya bunch of assholes! Somebody has to be! Ya wanna send Gandhi to negotiate with Qaddafi?"

The night breeze felt clean, cool, and strong. *Squareknot* responded to its power with a headlong rush past the blinking light of a buoy. Boats don't use headlights like a car, only small colored lights so other mariners can see them. One trusts navigation skills to avoid fixed obstacles, watches for the running lights of other vessels, steers the boat by compass into the safety of clear water marked by darkness.

Charlie thought about feeling safer in that race to darkness than in the glare of lights that others trusted to ward off demons. He realized the demons had adapted to the light; they'd grown bold. It all began with people huddled around a campfire that scared the beast. But when the beast squats at the fire, only the darkness is safe.

Charlie realized his shock was turning to fury that a murderer could be found in the evening paper and sent to his boat to kill him in his sleep. Okay, Rust knew he couldn't call the cops. Did he feel secure in his house in Wellesley, behind locked doors? How prepared would he be for a madman flying through his window in a shower of broken glass?

12

The headlamps of Jason Richards's Jaguar XJ-12 burned a tunnel of light up a paved driveway through mature forest, then carved two switchbacks as the grade steepened. Wilbur Coughlin bounced up and down on the backseat.

"Hoo, hoo, hoooo! Look at this! With all these trees, your neighbors prob'ly don't even know wha'chew look like, fatso!"

They emerged from the trees onto a level expanse of lawn, went through a brick-and-concrete *porte cochère* into a small courtyard. The brick house in the Queen Anne style reeked of old New England and sedate money. "Park by the door . . . no! You got a garage?"

"Yes."

"Use it."

The drive led them around to the left. There was a high wall circumscribing the house and immediate grounds. They came up short at a closed garage door.

"You got a 'lectric-eye door?"

"Yes."

"Where's the doohickey runs it?"

"In the glove compartment."

"You get it, girlie."

Rosy pushed the button, and the compartment dropped open. She quickly reached in and got the device, pressed it, and the door started to rise. Her heart was pumping hard enough to raise it on the hydraulics of her blood pressure. In the glove box was a small pearl-handled automatic. She sat slightly forward in an effort to block the view into the compartment with her body. If Coughlin saw her reach for it, she knew he would blow her head off from behind before she could spin halfway around. She knew guns had safeties but had no idea where one would be, and even if she had, she could never shoot fast enough to get the two of them. She saw Jason's eyes cut toward her frantically, saying something, but she didn't know what.

He started the car rolling into the two-car garage, and Coughlin reacted to the other car they found parked inside. "Hoo, hooo, Bead, look at that! It's a goddamned Ferrari!"

She saw Jason put his hand down, palm up, between them. His mouth was contorted as though he were about to scream. Focusing her eyes to the left toward the car, she slid her right hand slowly into the box and felt the barrel of the gun. She pulled it out and clutched it against her belly. With Coughlin behind them, the one-foot-open space between the bucket seats seemed like a floodlit cavern in the dim glow of the automatic light that had come on as the garage door opened. Coughlin jumped out of the right rear door and ran around the front toward the Ferrari. She slipped the gun into Jason's hand, realizing as she did so that Jason had just missed the chance to step on the gas and pinion Coughlin against the back of the garage. The left rear door opened, and Bead screamed as he dove to the pavement, "He's got a gun, Coughlin!"

Jason was pointing the gun through the windshield when Coughlin spun and saw him squeezing the trigger with all his might, an eerie high-pitched wail coming through his clenched teeth.

"The safety!" she shouted, too late. The windshield blew in from the close-range force of Coughlin's forty-five automatic.

She felt flecks of glass all over her upper body, and her hands went to her face and felt stuff sticking out of it. She looked to-ward Jason's screams. His right shoulder was gone, and blood was everywhere. She looked for the gun but didn't see it.

Then the driver's door flew open, and Coughlin jerked the screaming Jason out onto the ground with one hand. He slid behind the wheel and rammed his gun into her side. His eyes and mouth were wide open. He seemed to be choking. Then she realized he was laughing soundlessly as he caught his breath and squealed with sick adrenaline.

Finally she saw Jason's gun, now slippery red on the floor, and Coughlin saw it, too. He picked it up and showed it to her. "See? See? I got 'em both now, girl!" He examined the gun quickly, slid the top back and forth with a guffaw, fired through the space where the windshield had been. Its sound was an anemic pop, pop, after the roar of the forty-five. "See? Ya gotta cock 'em or they don't work good!" Still grinding the barrel of the forty-five painfully into her ribs, he screamed, "Bead!" and held the smaller gun behind him out the door. Bead took it, then Wilbur grabbed her hair and dragged her out onto the garage floor. "Watch 'em!" He disappeared through the door that led into the house.

Bead was ashen. Rosy sensed the possibility of an alliance with him based on fear of the randomly violent energy pouring from Coughlin. "He's crazy, you know that. You could be dead soon, too."

Jason was failing fast, now moaning where he lay in a widen-ing pool of blood.

"Shut up," Bead said, and stepped back so they were both in front of him.

"You screwed up, Bead, and he'll kill you for it, sooner or later."

"Shut up, I said!"

"You used his name on the radio. We heard it. That's what he meant when he said you've done enough talking for one night." She could see it register on his face. Like Jason, seeing his own death. "If you shoot him, I'll forget I heard your name, too. You can drive that Ferrari out of here, and I'll owe you my life. You weren't even there when he robbed us. We'll say he was alone, that we shot him."

Then Coughlin was back in the room, scooping Jason up like a leaky garbage bag. He half dragged him, stumbling and semiconscious, into the house. He talked excitedly as he went: "There's nobody else here, Bead. Only one closet has clothes . . . the fat man lives alone, and this place is loaded! Close this garage door and keep her here. I gotta do somethin' quick." He closed the door leading to the house behind him as he left.

As soon as they were gone, Rosy started again, her voice an urgent whisper: "You know what he's going to do; he's going to finish killing Jason, and you'll have a murder charge on your head unless you do what I told you and . . ."

His voice came out in a husky whisper. "You stupid cunt, whaddaya think my chances'd be of killing him outright with a goddamned twenty-two pistol? The guy's an ox. I could shoot him five times and he'd still blow my head off with that cannon he's carrying." Holding the gun awkwardly in front of him, he sidled toward the wall, pressed the button that closed the garage door.

Rosy's heart leaped. She'd been right. He knew he was in danger. He just didn't know how to get out of it. She had to find a plan that would give him enough confidence to run. "Well, he's gonna do it anyway unless we do something," she said, feeling the panic choking her, knowing she had to get through to the small man whose eyes were dilated by his own terror. "Let's get in the car and get the hell out of here before he comes back."

"He'd hear it and be here before we could back out. We'd be dead in the driveway."

She had him thinking and knew it could be her last chance. "I can drive. You sit in the passenger seat and fire away at the door as we back out. He'll duck back. Nobody would walk into a barrage of bullets! He won't get himself shot just to stop us."

He was shaking his head back and forth. "This guy don't

know fear, lady. He thinks he's Superman. I seen 'im tear into a small crowd of niggers when we was in the joint, no weapon but his fists and feet. Most guys'd tell ya that's suicide. He did well enough that none of 'em ever got up the nerve to shiv 'im. They just started calling him Crazo, and he thought it was a compliment.

"He'll come blasting out of that door expecting the bullets to bounce off his fucking chest. Forget it. I'll take my chances being his partner, 'cause I damn sure don't want him for an enemy." Both of them caught their breath at a shrill childlike scream that came long and eerie from some distant corner of the house. She saw Bead struggling to swallow.

"You have no chance—"

Bead's voice cut her off, nothing if not earnest. "Lady, if he hears you talking like that, he might shoot me f'r list'nin'. Now shut up, or I'm gonna shut you up."

She stared at him, calculating that there was no way she could overpower the man, small and frail though he was. She leaned back against the car, her eyes rolled upward as her mind wallowed in a vain attempt to fathom a plan of escape.

Then she saw the light bulb. It was screwed into the device that raised the garage door. It was a security feature of the door opener. She'd seen the feature elsewhere. It went on as the door opened; would go off some measured amount of time after the door closed.

No sooner had the thought formed than the garage was plunged into darkness. She could hear Bead's feet scuffling in the dark. He was talking.

"Don't move. Stay where you are. . . ." He was bumping into things as he searched the wall for a light switch.

A door . . . there was a regular walk-through door beside the car entrance to the garage. In the darkness, she was disoriented. She dropped, crawling on her hands and knees as silently as she could toward where she thought it was. Her hands were wet and sticky on the concrete, and she realized she'd gone through the puddle of Jason's blood . . . the wrong direction. She reversed herself, then drove her left shoulder painfully into the side of a car. It gave her a point of reference, and she followed it by feel to its rear bumper.

Bead was cursing and making a racket as he floundered over the accumulated accretions of the garage; something made of glass shattered.

Rosy lunged by memory toward where she thought the door should be. Immediately she found the doorknob, but it wouldn't turn. She felt its shape and realized it had a twist button in the center. She twisted it, it popped out, the knob turned, and still the door wouldn't open. She ran her hands along the edge of the door. At head level there was a slide bolt. She threw it back just as the room was bathed in light. Bead yelled, "Freeze!" his voice only feet behind her. The garage door was sliding open. He'd found the button, and the security light was on again. For three seconds she was poised on the brink of running into the darkness, her only hope; yes, she would run and Bead would miss her. . . .

No. His hand was on her shoulder, pulling her back. He saw the light switch now, above the button for the door. He flipped it, and a bank of fluorescents came on. He hit the button, and the garage door closed. They stared at each other, both of them breathing hard.

"The light, Bead. Unscrew the light bulb."

"Shut up," he said, his voice sullen.

"Wait in the darkness. Empty the gun into him when he comes out. If he can't see you, he can't shoot you."

He gaped at her, his cheeks fluttering with each labored breath. "You shut up. You think I'm stupid or something?"

Finally, she slumped against the bumper of the Jaguar. My God, she thought, I'm going to die. She remembered the stinging pain on her face. Slowly, carefully, she picked bits of glass from her skin.

Then Coughlin returned . . . alone. His demeanor had changed. He shuffled in with the gun hanging loosely from his fingers, swaggered between the cars, smiling. He looked at her and giggled.

"Girl, you're a mess. Take her inside and let her clean herself up, but don't take your eyes off her for a second. Even if she has to pee-pee." Bead took her by the arm and started her inside.

"Bead!" They stopped and turned in his direction." You must be good luck. If you hadn't used my name on the radio, we'd a left 'em in the ditch like we planned . . . old-fashioned highway robbery. We'd a taken off with the car and cash and shit and never even knowed we was leaving all this behind." He laughed at the enormity of it. "And if you hadn't shouted when that guy had the gun, he might of figgered it out and given me a headache." He ambled toward Bead as he spoke, capping a huge paw on his shoulder. "So I owe you one. . . . Hell, we'll clear fifty, sixty grand on this job easy, 'tween the cars and all the shit he's got inside, even at fence prices. Bead-brain, you ain't too swift, but I think I like having you f'r a partner!"

Bead smiled nervously. He sort of shrugged, and Rosy knew that all the pressure she'd put on him had just evaporated to nothing. He's so stupid, she thought, that he really believes this maniac is going to keep him for a good-luck charm, give him half of fifty thousand for the privilege.

They entered through the kitchen, which would have made Betty Crocker envious: fancy pots and utensils hanging from a circular wrought-iron rack over a large central island; big commercial stainless-steel stove; wall-mounted ovens; Mexican-tile floor with a high-gloss sealer and stand-easy rubber mats on the floor by the work spaces; two big side-by-side refrigerator/freezers. She took note of a thick free-standing butcher block that had a slot filled with workmanlike knives. She couldn't help also noticing a small round sink with a disposal and a high curving spout in the center of the block. How handy, she thought, and wondered if she was losing her mind.

The interior of the old house had been gutted and redone by an architect who liked open spaces. It had bright colors juxtaposed with white, white walls and lots of glass and chrome.

In the bathroom, her insides flip-flopped at the sight of her face, a red fingerpainting. Her fingers trembled as she bathed it in cold water, patting gently, Bead standing there staring at her, breathing through his mouth.

When she had patted it dry, leaving red spots of blood on the towel, she saw the damage was merely small scratches. She caught herself being relieved that she wouldn't be permanently scarred, instantly realized how pointless that was, since she probably had only minutes or hours to live. The cool water had calmed her down. What was happening wasn't happening to her. It was a situation on a show she was watching.

How could she have gotten out of the berth that morning, leaving Charlie in the dark, thinking how it would only take her a week or so to get some money to fall back on . . . money, she now realized, she didn't even need. She'd intentionally made the note to him vague, to give herself time to work the scam.

How would he react to her failure to return? It dawned on her that he'd just think she'd taken off . . . a rich girl on some kind of fugue that was over. He wouldn't wait for an explanation; he'd trust his instincts. Sooner or later, he'd leave her bag in her car and sail off. She knew Charlie well enough to be certain that before he left he would put the bag in her car and leave the keys with Lew. He wouldn't leave a note or a forwarding address.

They found Coughlin sitting in a chrome chair with oversized beige Ultrasuede cushions billowing out of the frame. The low lighting came from cans aimed at the walls above head level, drawing attention to the two-story height of the room. At first, she thought the thing at his feet was a rug. Then she realized it was Jason. A dark stain on the white carpet encircled the top of his body. She caught her breath, and Coughlin giggled at her reaction.

"Don't worry 'bout him, girl, his troubles are over. Yours are just getting started." He watched her as though he were expecting her head to roll off onto the floor and he didn't want to miss the bounce.

Rosy was searching her brain for a way out. Her only bargaining chip was sex. They were gonna take that if they wanted it, and Coughlin was probably hoping she'd fight like a tiger with copperheads for legs. She told herself that these were not master criminals. They were random-action run-amoks, with no plan and no discipline. Already Bead had used the name that changed the game; Coughlin had run in front of the car, giving Jason a chance he'd not been ready to use. At any moment, the next chance could come. She had to stay ready. Jason had only gotten one.

"Shouldn't we be getting this stuff in the car and getting the hell outa here, Coughlin?" Bead said. His tone was tentative. He thought Coughlin was calm, maybe too calm, but one didn't push too hard so soon after a performance like the one he'd just witnessed.

"Oh, let's us jus' crash for the night; take care of business in the morning."

"Hell, we don't know who might be coming by here."

"We don't?"

"We don't know who might come to check when this guy don't show up at work tomorrow."

"We don't?"

"No . . . we don't . . . do we?"

Coughlin reached out with a lazy arm and hit a button on the stereo. There was a bizarre contrapuntal duet of laughter and screaming. It was nauseating. The look on Coughlin's face was beatific as the voices came through clearly from the large wall-mounted speakers:

"Say it again! This time don't whine."

Then Jason's voice, struggling for control: "This is Jason Richards. I have a family emergency which is taking me out of town for at least a week. Cancel my appointments and see that my court dates are covered or postponed. I'll be in touch by telephone in a few days."

Then Coughlin's voice again. "Now remember, fatso. I'm gonna try to keep you alive. But if a cleaning lady or anybody else shows up that you haven't told me about, the first bullet is going to go through your kneecaps, then your elbows, then I split the difference. So start talking! Tell me every person that just might show up here in the next few days."

"Okay, okay, don't hurt me again. . . . There's a cleaning service. They come twice a week, Mondays and Thursdays. . . . Their number is in the little book on the kitchen desk."

"The name, what's the name?"

"North Shore Cleaning . . . ah . . . North Shore House Cleaning."

"Who else?"

"Yard service . . . Calvin Jones; in the book!"

"Who else?"

"That's all."

"Anybody who does is dead, Jason."

"There's nobody."

"Relatives?"

"They're out of state."

"Friends?"

"They wouldn't come without calling first."

"Who else?"

The scream that followed was like a small child burned on a stovetop. It took him a while to settle down. Coughlin smirked as they listened to a few minutes of Jason fighting to regain his control, no sounds from Crazo on the tape.

"Nobody, I swear it."

Jason's frantic breathing could be heard over the tinkling laughter and the word "good." Then there was a single thud, and the tape was quiet.

Coughlin reached out and poked the button that stopped the tape. Then he held a little microphone up in the air for them to see. "He liked to dictate for his secretary here at home. It was sitting here on the arm of the chair." He smiled. "It gave me an idea."

Bead and Rosy stood nervously while he rewound the tape, found the beginning of the part he wanted. He picked up a business card, displaying it to them with a flourish. He pointed his gun at Rosy. "Boom!" he said. "You wanna die right now, make a little noise while I'm makin' this call." He dialed, then dropped the receiver into a modem that sat beside the phone. They could hear the ringing on the other end. Then a taped voice:

"You've reached the offices of Wickam, Richards, Margolis, and Graham. Our offices are closed from five in the afternoon until eight-thirty in the morning. If you need immediate legal assistance, hang up and call 555-6342. An operator will answer to put you in contact with an attorney. If your business can wait until tomorrow, please leave your name, phone number, and a brief message at the sound of the tone. We'll return your call during regular business hours. Thank you."

Coughlin pressed the button to start the tape just before the tone, so the click wouldn't be recorded. Jason's voice told them he was leaving town. He sounded a lot like a man upset by a family emergency . . . maybe his mother on her deathbed, when he knew she hadn't signed the will.

Bead was grinning as Coughlin hung up the phone. "Wilbur, I gotta hand it to ya . . . nice piece a work there."

"We got us a fortress here, Bead. It's even got a fucking wall around it. And from the looks of it, a few acres of trees outside of that. We'll call the cleaning service and the yard monkeys, tell 'em not to bother this week. Nobody coming, and nobody expecting old Jason here for at least a few days." He turned his eyes on Rosy. "I'm sure you're aces on your back, girlie. You know how to cook?"

"No."

His face registered surprise and then amusement at the rebellious tone in her voice. "Well, you gonna learn, girl. You gonna learn."

His newly calm mood was more frightening than his frenzy. She'd seen those changes before. She knew why he'd been quiet while Jason screamed. That was the road to this guy's nut. At least, that was one of them. She hoped there were others. He looked strong as hell, the cop suit stretched tight around his shoulders and thighs. His eyes had an urgent look, as though the world he saw was stuck on fast forward. She was sure he'd be horny again before too long.

Charlie was the first early-morning customer at the rent-a-car place across from Government Center. His intentions were violent and illegal, and he didn't want his trip to Rust's house recorded on a taxi driver's log. He'd been to the house before, and he had no difficulty locating it. On a drive-by, he noticed a "For Sale" sign in front.

He parked around a corner and walked back, darted into the trees when he was sure no cars were coming. There were no lights visible as he approached the house, and he thought his plan of crashing in on Rust and his wife in bed still looked pretty good. He didn't know exactly what he'd say but figured the point was to scare the guy so much he'd back off.

He guessed where the bedroom would be. Up close to the windows, he could see enough to tell he was going to have to find another idea: there was no furniture. Rust was gone.

Stunned, he decided that didn't necessarily mean Rust was innocent. If he were really into this thing, why wouldn't he go to ground, hide somewhere? Lost in thought, he forgot his stealth, walked down the driveway to the street. Before he realized he was not alone, a voice called, "May I help you?"

A man with slick gray hair looked his way from the adjoining driveway. He was in a white Cadillac with the window rolled down. Charlie approached the car.

"Why, yes, I hope so. . . . I used to work for Wendy Rust at Continental Computer. I was in the area and was going to drop in on him, but now I see he's moved. Can you tell me where he's gone?"

"Oh, I thought you were somebody looking to buy the house. My wife's the real estate agent."

"That would make you Mr. Burwell?" Charlie said, remembering the sign, "Marjorie Burwell, Agent."

"Yes, Spence Burwell," he said, getting out of the car, and giving him a fine, big smile, a handshake that would inspire confidence.

Definitely banking, Charlie thought, stuck in branch management, blew his chances for the trust department or real responsibility. Turning on the charm for a stranger, wasting it. "Charlie G—" He barely caught himself, without knowing why, really. "Glover. Charlie Glover. If your wife's representing them on the house, you must know where they've gone."

Playing coy, he said, "Yes, but I'm not sure Wendy would want me to tell you. He didn't have much good to say about the company last time I saw him."

Figuring everybody liked gossip, he took a shot. "Well, frankly, I can understand that. It's hard to be magnanimous when one is fired from a job."

"Fired?" Spence smiled. "You mean Wendy was fired?"

"Perhaps I'm speaking out of turn. . . ."

"Don't worry about it. I doubt I'll ever see him again. I thought he was an asshole for the ten years he lived next to me, and I don't like him any better now he's moved to Arizona.

"I told my wife he was probably fired. Hell, he used to tell me how great that company was all the time, how I should get out of banking and get into a real industry. Then, no warning, he up and tells me he got sick of the grind, that the company had gone to the dogs and he'd quit.

"Next thing you know there's a moving van out front and his wife said they were taking the chance to get out of the snow, moving to Scottsdale. Ha, haaa! Wait'll I tell my wife I was right. Why'd they fire him?"

What the hell, Charlie decided. "He was embezzling."

That one rocked old Spence pretty vigorously. "Whooa! No kidding?"

"No kidding. Got caught with his pants right down there around his ankles." Charlie realized he couldn't laugh with Spence too much or it would seem strange that he was trying to visit. "Felt kind of sorry for him, really . . . he wasn't all bad. Scottsdale, huh?"

Marjorie, of course, had the phone number and traded him for a few more hastily fabricated tidbits of gossip. Fifteen minutes later Charlie was in a phone booth calling Arizona.

Mrs. Rust answered the phone. Then he heard Wendy's voice say hello.

"Hello, Wendy." He waited for a reaction. If he recognized his voice immediately, it might be an indicator.

"Who's this?" He sounded half-asleep.

"It's Charlie Gamble."

"Gamble. What the hell are you calling me for?" Genuinely surprised, waking up. "Did you call up to gloat? Well, I got news for ya, smart guy: I'm glad to be outa that place, you hear me? If I'd a known how good retirement would be, I'd a quit years ago." Not convincing, but a reasonable lie.

"I did call to gloat, actually, but not about that. O'Neill turned the tables on you, Rust. You made a mistake, and he was just smart enough to backtrack it, find out who you were . . . then I caught him. I've already spoken to the police; just calling to rub it in before they get there."

There was barely a beat of silence. "What? What in blazes are you talking about, Gamble? Have you gone off your nut or something? Who the hell is Neal?"

Charlie, listening intently, with the advantage of surprise, didn't hear a false note. Rust had misheard the name and called him Neal. As quickly as he'd jumped to the conclusion that Rust was his nemesis, he knew that he'd been wrong. The way things were set up with O'Neill, he needed to be in town, unless he had an accomplice, and that was inconsistent with going to all the trouble to mask his identity from O'Neill.

He realized that Rust was giving him a well-rounded cursing on the other end of the line. "Never mind," he said, and hung up.

He stood in the phone booth for a couple of minutes, racking his brain for enemies he might have overlooked. There was nobody else who had a reason for wanting him dead. Nobody stood to make any money on his death, and he hadn't been fooling with anybody's wife . . . unless it was Rosy.

Driving back into Boston, he reassembled the pieces with Rust out of the picture. Rosy had been with him when the first attempt had been made to kill him with a speeding Mercury. Although she wasn't aboard when O'Neill shot at him on the boat, O'Neill may not have known that. When O'Neill hadn't known his name, he'd thought it odd, but now it made sense . . . if the murder attempts were leakage from her past, rather than his.

The thought that he was the target of somebody he didn't even know gave him a groundless feeling, like being told he would die from some unnamed disease of the blood. Making it worse was the thought that Rosy's failure to return the night before might be the result of violent intervention rather than her casual independence. Could it be that she was . . . dead? Captive?

Desperate for a thread that might lead to her whereabouts, he remembered the file folder in the car, from Cambridge Classics, a salesman named Singleton. He realized that the Ferrari dealership was closer than home, and he began the mental navigation that would take him there.

14

Slipping from the loose grip of an unquiet sleep, Rosy wriggled instinctively backward against a source of warmth. She was checked by cutting metal on her raw left wrist. Suddenly aware, her eyes opened and she stared at the handcuffs that tethered her left hand to the head of the brass bed. Her body stiffened at the mental recognition of the source of warmth. Slowly, feeling the insults and indignities she'd suffered the night before, she twisted herself away from Coughlin's back.

He slept naked in the fetal position, facing away from her. She could see goosebumps on his skin, two round scars that she somehow knew were made by bullets that went wide of the spine to the right. He scrabbled toward her with a backward lurch. Afraid her absence would wake him, she suppressed the urge to recoil from his touch. He settled against her, his back nestling into her body held up on the left elbow.

In the morning light streaming into Jason's bedroom, she could see clearly the masculine furniture, burled walnut bureaus, highly polished with brass appointments, matching bedside tables that flanked the scene of her previous night's torture.

Before he'd shackled her, Coughlin had puffed on a cigarette, stalking her in a slow stroll around the master suite. She had backed away, trying to tell him, "Hey, this doesn't have to get anybody hurt, does it?" He'd grabbed her, briefly using the cigarette tip; then he'd let her go and kept stalking, brick by brick building a pyramid of terror.

He'd told her if she did a great striptease, he wouldn't hurt her. He'd laughed at her trembling attempts at undulations and the tears that had rolled from her eyes, said she wasn't half as good as Juanita Jalapeño, and hurt her some more.

She'd screamed and cried, not resisting the verbal release, conscious of trying to do what he wanted to see her do, to satisfy his urge to see her horror. He'd held his finger to his lips and silenced her; he'd shaken his head, then kept walking toward her until he'd backed her into the white-tiled bathroom.

"You're fakin' it, girl. I ain't even got started good yet. I hate it when girls fake it. You try to be quiet now. You'll know when it's really time to scream."

He'd kept her in there for what seemed hours. He'd worked on her in the tub. "Oh, you're disgusting," he'd say, and turn the cold shower on her. "Wash yourself."

Now she saw his clothes where he'd dropped them on the floor by the bed. She wondered if the key to the handcuffs was in the pocket of the pants . . . no matter: out of reach. Then she saw the forty-five sitting on the bedside table beyond him. His leg straightened suddenly, and she thought he was awake, but he pulled it back up and was still again. She calculated the distance to the gun. She thought she could reach it, but she would have to stretch herself cruciform across him to do that. She stared at the oiled black metal of the gun's parts and noted the small slide switch where the right thumb would rest. That must be the safety, she thought. It would slide forward, then she could shoot.

She wondered where Bead was. Would he come crashing into the room at the sound of a shot? . . . Had Coughlin sent him away? She remembered hoping the night before that he would come in to end her ordeal. Had he no mercy, either? But he hadn't come. She had heard no evidence that he was in the house then or now. Would he call through the closed door?

Could she make her voice low enough to imitate Coughlin? The falsetto giggle. She knew she would never forget the giggle. She could do it and say, "Come in here, Bead," in a squeal. He would come. She would kill him, too, for doing nothing while the maniac abused her.

She got up on her knees, then her toes, steadying herself on the sagging bed with her free right hand. She stepped over him, straddling him, and leaned against the handcuffs, stretching for the gun without touching him. Almost . . . almost . . . an inch away . . . touching it . . . Coughlin stirring. . . . She settled herself on the far side of the bed, her shackled arm stretching against his head, her body masking her right hand's braille search for the gun, her eyes watching Coughlin wake up and look into her face. She had the gun, felt the safety switch slide at pressure from her thumb, pulled it beneath her body as Coughlin's eyes widened, seeing her looking at him. She pressed the barrel up under his chin and pulled the trigger.

The click of the empty gun was the loudest noise she had ever heard. Coughlin's mouth erupted with a shiny brass bubble, then another one. Bullets. Brass cartridges bubbling slowly through his lips. Three, four, now the trace of a grin appearing; five, six.

"I thought you'd never wake up, girl. I practically had to sit on you." He laughed in a staccato spasm, rolled off the far side of the bed. He leaned toward her, snatched the gun from her hand. "Little bit of murder in everybody, isn't there, girl?"

She couldn't scream or cry anymore. A crushing weight seemed to push her against the bed. Her limbs were without strength. She waited for what he would do to her, knowing at last that she had been wrong all the times she'd told herself the night before that she could get out alive, she could endure the pain, and she could beat this animal at its own game. She'd been wrong. His relentless madness led him through cunning maneuvers that she couldn't anticipate.

He left her. She heard the shower running. Her body was a loosely connected constellation of brilliant pains. She tried to will her mind to become unconscious, her heart to stop beating, her fear and torment to end itself in the blackness behind her tightly closed eyes.

She'd disappear into that void, never to be exposed again to his eyes. She knew that she could do that. She could leap into the black pool. She stood at its brink, a swimmer poised between too hot and too cold, anticipation and dread. She looked behind her and saw her own body clutching itself into a ball, chained to the bed. She could hear the shower running, and she tried to will her body to rouse itself and follow her, to escape, to jump off, to free-fall out of the universe of nerve endings and eyes. But it shriveled more tightly into itself, cowering, hugging the shackle like a lifeline.

She faced the dark pool again and could feel a soothing breeze on her face. She leaned into the breeze, but she didn't fall. She floated, drifted back onto the ledge, faced herself cringing on the bed, still shackled to the brass rung, still hearing the horrific shower and knowing it would stop, and he would come into the room again. And it did. She opened her eyes at the silence.

Coughlin walked out with a towel around his hips. How odd that he would practice that conventional modesty after his prancing exhibitionism of the night before. He disappeared out the door leading to the upstairs hallway. She could hear him talking to Bead.

"Of course she's alive. . . . She knows other people like Richards . . . single men with big bucks . . . she told me she could tell us where to go and when they are gone and how to get in. . . . Hey, she wants to stay alive, and that's what she's got to trade. . . ."

Her mind drifted away from their conversation, and more of the previous night came back to her. What a mistake she'd made! She thought he was going to kill her. In little bits, he was doing it, letting the life from her. It shrieked as it escaped. Each shriek seemed to send a jolt of power into him that he spent on her, a cycle that would end only when she was empty.

124

She wanted to stay alive. She offered the only things she could think of that they might want . . . her car, worth thirty or forty thousand dollars, parked at the marina, the keys in her bag on board *Squareknot*; the necklace, the one from Dr. Regar, they'd think it was real.

He laughed and said they could get these things anywhere. She told him she could tell them where, when, and how to burglarize other places . . . that she was too valuable to kill. She thought it would make him stop. But it worked the other way. He reveled in her submission, was brought to new levels of sexual frenzy by her promises of riches. When finally she was ready to die, she told him she'd lied. There were no car, no jewels, no reasons to keep her alive.

Now she could hear him laughing again and telling Bead that the little smell pot was turning out to be a gold mine. Now she realized that he would kill Charlie, too, and any of the men she'd victimized, if they happened to be home when she took them to their homes. She would be kept alive and forced to provide the information he knew she had; she'd give them the facts they needed to burglarize those homes she had already robbed in her own way; and he would keep her alive as she'd begged him to do. . . .

Coughlin breezed back into the room with a small canvas bag from which he dressed himself in tan corduroy jeans, a blue muscle shirt, sleeveless, with bright silver threads running through it in a jumbled pattern, and running shoes.

Then, smiling, he came close to the bed. "Now, girl, let's get back to that conversation we was having last night. You was telling me about another Ferrari parked at a marina in Charlestown . . . and a necklace on a boat . . . a diamond necklace, right?"

With neither hope nor enthusiasm, she said automatically, "I was lying. I thought if you believed I had some expensive things, you'd keep me alive. There's no car; no necklace."

His face curled in mock disappointment. "Aw, was girlie afraid? Was girlie making up stories for Wilbur?"

"Yes. I'm sorry," she said, feeling inane, not knowing what to say to this thing that sat now beside her, hovering over her naked body on the bed. She had a sense that she was talking to an avalanche, begging it to hang in air above her.

"Well, you must have a car of some kind, then . . . somewhere. Everybody has a car . . . but I didn't see no keys in your purse, and last night you said the keys to your Ferrari was in your bag on that boat. . . ."

His hand was on her rump, rubbing slow circles, almost pinching but not quite.

"I don't own a car . . . I can't drive. . . ."

"Oh, now there is no car anywhere, huh?"

"No."

"How can I believe that when you just told me you're a liar? I mean I gotta figure you're lying again, right?"

"No."

"Yes. I gotta figure you don't wanna live up to those promises you made last night. . . . After I did what you asked; I kept you alive, and now you want to welsh on our deal."

He shook his head back and forth. When he spoke again his voice was a husky whisper that betrayed the fantasies playing now in the nasty netherworld of his mind. "Girl, here's what you and me gonna do today. We gonna go get your car and your necklace. And we ain't gonna mess around no more in this bedroom, 'cause if we do, we gonna forget about that car and stay here aaaaalllll day, just you and me, and play our little hearts out while Bead loads up all the stuff around this house that sells good and carries it to a business associate of ours. . . . Sooner or later you gonna change your story again, and start saying you got a car and a necklace and friends with houses full of loot, but I ain't gonna believe you then, see. I'm gonna know you're lying to old Wilbur again."

His breath blew on her, and she felt that she was shrinking into herself but couldn't disappear. Then his hand shot out with the speed of a piston and grabbed her hair and held her face close to his as he screamed, "Now which way do you want it, girl?"

She tried to answer but felt herself squeezed like an orange. She couldn't stop the long, long exhaling sob that drained the air from her lungs, the blood from her heart, the brain from her head. It sucked every fleeing final trace of hope from her, even to the flat collapsed bladder of her soul.

15

The look Charlie absorbed from the salesman who approached him at Cambridge Classics was the price he paid for the pleasure of having given all his business suits to the Salvation Army Thrift Store. The vertical sweep took in Charlie's blue jeans and work shirt, put the condescension in the opening line that accompanied the gesture toward the Ferrari he was admiring. "Sixty-eight thousand, before tax and dealer prep. How much are you short?"

"The money I've got," Charlie said. "What I need is a salesman with manners to write it up."

The guy wasn't used to having his rudeness returned. It baffled Charlie why salesmen who sold expensive stuff took on a demeanor that suggested they could afford to buy it themselves. He was opening his mouth for the third time without finding a reply when Charlie said, "Mr. Singleton was recommended by a friend of mine. Fetch him for me, please."

"I assure you, sir, I meant no—"

"Are you Singleton?"

"No, I'm—"

"An asshole, now go get Singleton. Tell him a friend of Rosy Marlette's would like to buy a car."

While the guy was getting Singleton, Charlie realized his nerves were a bit ragged. He caught himself contemplating how much fun it would be to write a check on his Merrill Lynch account for the rolling phallus, just to spite the jerk who wouldn't get the commission. A handsome man in a gray suit appeared, buttoning his jacket. They shook hands and introduced themselves, then Frank Singleton said, "You're a friend of Rosemary's?"

Rosemary, Charlie thought. So much for the friend theory.

"Yes. She mentioned your name. . . ."

"I hope kindly," he said.

Charlie could feel his curiosity, wondering whether a guy dressed as he was might really have the money for a Ferrari. He noticed a gold V-shaped pin on Singleton's lapel. He'd seen them before. It meant he'd had a vasectomy, was advertising himself as a safe screw. Shit. "I'll bet you do. She's a looker, isn't she?"

Charlie had invited the smirk, so he couldn't really fault the guy for it. "Actually," he continued, "I'm looking for her, hoped you might be able to point me in the right direction."

"What makes you think I'd know where she is?"

Charlie shrugged. "Nothing, really . . . just taking a shot in the dark. I only met her recently, and lost track of her . . . don't know where to start looking. She bought her car from you?"

There was some hesitation, then the beginnings of amusement before he answered, "Yes."

"Then you must have an address, phone, stuff like that on the sales agreement."

Singleton was enjoying himself now, seeing that he was in the driver's seat. "If I did, what makes you think I'd share it with you? We're not in the habit of giving out information on our customers."

"Oh? That's a no-no, huh?"

"As you can imagine, Mr. Gamble, our clients come from the top of the financial heap. They wouldn't appreciate our sharing details about them . . . although I doubt that your interest in Rosemary Marlette has anything to do with money."

"You're right. I'm interested in her circle of friends . . . like Jason Richards, who's into horse racing and gourmet cooking." At first Singleton only looked surprised to hear the name of one of his customers. By the time Charlie rattled off the other names he'd read in the file, along with smatterings of detail about their lives, he'd figured out where the information came from and his discomfiture was showing. "What were you telling me about your customers' desire for privacy?"

"How did you get this file?"

Charlie smiled. "I asked you first. What's Rosy's address and phone number? Or would you prefer I take the file to your boss and ask him?"

He didn't like the idea, and it showed. "Rosy's address won't do you any good."

"Why's that?"

"It's obvious what you're after, and you won't get it."

"What makes you so sure? Maybe she just didn't like your line."

That brought a sneer. "Two reasons—one I'm sure of, and the other is an educated guess. To begin with, she's married. I didn't sell the car to her; I sold it to her husband."

In an effort to cover his surprise, Charlie said quickly, "What's the second reason?"

"That's the funny part. She always claimed she was faithful to her husband; kind of strange, because he struck me as a wimp. I couldn't figure it until the last time I saw her.

"See, she told me she wanted the info on my customers to sell them insurance. . . . But I noticed she only wanted the prospects who were single."

"So what?" Charlie said, not liking the way Singleton was looking at him.

"She's looking for a new husband, Mr. Gamble, and she wants one with money." He chuckled and fingered Charlie's shirt. "I don't see her going for you, hotshot."

Charlie was trying to process what he'd just learned, wasn't in the mood for playing with Singleton anymore. "One more try: you gonna give me what I'm asking for, or do I ask your boss?"

Singleton led the way into his office. He went through a file and came out with a contact sheet like the ones Rosy had, only this one was on a Dr. Douglas Marlette, a philosophy professor at Boston University. "Knock yourself out, but don't say I didn't warm you, Gamble."

Charlie looked up from the page, tapped the V pin on Singleton's lapel, said, "Read the article about those in the last issue of the *New England Journal of Medicine?*"

"What article?"

Charlie let just a little amusement show, not enough to be obvious, said, "Read it. You'll find it interesting." He turned to leave.

"What's it say?"

Charlie stared at him. "They've only been doing those on a big scale for a few years, ya know. Never had that many cases to see what the long-range effects might be."

"So?"

He smiled. "So most guys do fine." Gesturing with the sheet of paper, he added, "Thanks for the information."

Charlie left him to wonder about the other guys. He guessed Singleton would spend a couple of days telling himself Charlie was stroking him, but not knowing for sure. Then it would take him another day or so to find a copy of the journal in question and read it; find out that he'd been had, that the strange sensation he'd been feeling in his balls for three days was only his imagination.

Not wanting to chance Singleton having pulled something on him, he found a phone booth and called Dr. Marlette's home just to see if Rosy might answer. But the number had been disconnected. He almost called Boston University but changed his mind. He could see a professorial sort collecting coins; if he was independently wealthy, maybe he'd hang on to discontinued currency like five-thousand-dollar bills. If Douglas Marlette was an angry cuckold who'd hired O'Neill, he'd rather catch the reaction face to face.

He hadn't forgotten his misdirection on Rust. Maybe Douglas was Rosy's brother. He could see Rosy using any old line to keep a slimeball with delusions of boudoir in his place. But he wouldn't have bet the boat on it. Stray cats have never been models of monogamy, and the streak of luck he was riding didn't seem that good.

He wasn't coming up with any good theories on why she'd want dossiers on unmarried Ferrari buyers, either, and that definitely piqued his curiosity. Maybe this cat wasn't stray at all. Maybe she was just plain wild.

16

Coughlin drove Jason's Ferrari with the care of a little old lady. The idling *shuttalug, shuttalug* of the exotic high-performance engine added to Rosy's frustration as they bumped down Tremont Street in Boston's South End. It was an obstacle course of potholes, four lanes wide, sidewalks teeming with various colors of one nonetheless homogeneous group of people: poor folks.

She saw a Latin-looking woman running down the street, her hands holding her swaying print skirt down in front. She caught up with a diapered boy's headlong, chubby-legged sprint, snagged him out of the crosswalk at a run, and returned to the curb, laughing, swinging the child to an ample hip. She reclaimed her place, leaning on a lamppost, flirting with a razor-thin black man who smiled and tickled the baby as he spoke to him.

Coughlin made a show of ignoring Rosy, looking around, right hand dangling limp over the wheel. He was daring her to make an attempt at escape. He'd shown her the gun, replaced it in the holster under his arm; shown her the stiletto, put it under his right leg. "Hey, you think you can jump out of the car, or holler at a cop, you go ahead, girl. But be quick about it, 'cause it's quick draw you're playin', and I'm the champ at quick draw. Quick draw's my thing, ya know what I mean, so you might just wanna sit there quiet while we do this thing and you'll live longer, see, not that I'd kill you right off. . . ." And so on.

When he got going, he had the breath control of an opera singer, the way it came out of him in an endless stream. She'd seen him taking pills. The result reminded her of the old slogan, "Speed kills."

She remembered her attempts to kick him and hit him the night before. Wherever she'd aimed, his hand would be there first, grabbing her, laughing at her frustration, letting go and taunting her to try again, until finally she'd realized she couldn't hit this man. He was just too fast.

He turned down a narrow, one-way side street lined with as-yet-unreclaimed brownstones, dull-eyed faces resting on propped palms on stoops of purplish stone. They made a few turns and came out on a wide street lined with dingy storefront businesses beneath an elevated highway. He pulled to the curb in front of a pawnshop, leaned forward to peer inside the open door, turned the engine off.

When nobody emerged from the doorway, he blew the horn. A stick-thin man of perfect blue-veined paleness, tattoos like bruises on his arms, stepped out the doorway, glanced at them, looked back and forth on the street before strolling back inside as though he hadn't seen anything of interest. Coughlin seemed satisfied, jabbed her leg twice for emphasis as he said, "Sit tight." He got out of the car.

She couldn't believe he would just leave her sitting there. He'd taken the keys. He walked around and sat on the hood. In a moment he shifted his weight, and she could see the minute scratches from the rivets of his jeans in the paint job that probably cost three thousand dollars. It made her angry.

The horn, she thought; attract a crowd. Could she hold the buttons down while he tried to open the door with the key?

A stocky man in his fifties came out of the pawnshop door. He and Coughlin shook in the hands-up style of the sixties. His salt-and-pepper hair was combed across the top of his head the way men do when they're trying to cover the whole thing with what's left over the ears.

They walked around the car, Coughlin talking to him quietly and following him. The man looked squarely at Rosy and elbowed Coughlin, who grinned wolfishly, like maybe the guy wondered if the broad came with the car. Coughlin popped the hood, gave her an amused look as he reached in to release the lock.

What would he do if she jumped out and just started running . . . what would the people on the sidewalk do? She saw him slipping the stiletto quietly between her ribs, dumping her on the car seat, and driving off, nothing lost but the sale. Out here where things seemed normal, there was too much renewed hope not to try. She had to wait for the right moment.

Wouldn't he have to go inside to get paid? Would they be so bold as to exchange money right there on the street? Wouldn't there be a cop she could leap on somewhere, if they were going to leave the car? Her eyes flashed around for police, but there were none in sight. A jumble of desperate thoughts caromed around her brain as the two meen seemed to be getting down to the head-shaking, "you're nuts, take it elsewhere, I damn sure will," dollars and dimes of dickering. As she watched for a chance to bolt, her legs felt heavy and slow, and Coughlin's body seemed spring-loaded under his tight clothes.

Then the man went back in the store, and Coughlin, the son of a bitch, winked at her through the windshield. He paced about, tucked in his shirt beneath the green Celtics windbreaker he used to conceal the gun. He killed a couple of minutes and strolled over to the doorway. Go inside, go inside, she wanted to scream, but the pale wraith, an envelope in hand, met him at the door. A quick shuffle of concealed hands, then Coughlin was walking toward the car, tucking the envelope into his belt.

She had to try; she locked the doors quickly, threw her weight against the horn, and heard deathly silence. "God, it doesn't work unless the ignition is on!" Coughlin looked through the glass at her, a quizzical expression on his face. He shrugged, smiled, said something to the wraith, who tossed him the keys. He dangled them at her and smiled. She opened the door.

"Come on, girl, don't get cute," he said, placing a hand on her elbow. They went off down the street and got into the back of a cab parked a block away. "Charlestown Marina," Coughlin growled.

The black driver was big enough to rival Coughlin; he grinned in the mirror at him and said, "Man, leaving those wheels on that block, I know you can afford the ride," letting him know he'd seen the transaction, thought it was admirable. "Whoowie, yeah, this sport can afford the ride!"

It took the wind out of Rosy; the guy had luck to go with his gall. It was midafternoon, not many people around when the taxi dropped them in front of the marina. Crazo played big dog, gave the cabbie a fifty from the fat white envelope, said, "Find yourself a redhead and lay back a while, Jack."

He smiled and ran his hand over the red Ferrari in the parking lot as they walked past it. On the dock, Rosy knew she'd waited too long. Now she had to pretend to be Coughlin's girlfriend or get Charlie killed . . . no way he could save her from this, and any attempt on her part to solicit his help would be just as good as murder.

So she'd try to blow in for the bag, just tell Charlie their thing was over and get away before he could see that Coughlin was nuts. In her mental rehearsal it took only seconds, and they walked away with Charlie standing openmouthed in the cockpit. He wasn't the type of man who'd beg her to stay, that much she felt sure of . . . but she was equally sure that, if he figured out the situation, he'd try to intervene, expecting maybe a fistfight, and die where he stood.

Then they were by *Squareknot*. The padlock hung there in plain view. Rosy felt relief, said, "He isn't here. It's locked. We can't get in."

Coughlin looked at the lock, then at her, and laughed as though she'd said something ridiculous. He looked around casually, picked up a large screwdriver from a jumble of tools on the deck of a nearby boat, jumped into *Squareknot*'s cockpit, and removed the hasp with one wood-splintering motion, faster than Charlie could unlock it with the key. "Come on, come on, get your stuff."

She went below. She looked around and didn't see the bag, Coughlin staying right beside her every step of the way, spilling the contents of cupboards when he thought she was going too slowly. In three minutes, she'd opened all the doors she knew of, bow to stern, no bag. Coughlin became increasingly agitated. She heard the startling metallic action of the stiletto in his hand. "I don't see it," she said, frantic.

He grabbed her hair again. She felt the tip of the blade on the bottom of her chin. "You tell me, girl, is this the right boat, or are we just lookin' around to attract a cop here? Is this some kind of game you're playin'?"

Her voice sounded far away to her, like someone else's from the other side of a wall, flat and clenched as she tried to talk without opening her mouth against the blade. "It was here, on this seat. I don't know where it is."

Coughlin looked at her for a moment. Then his eyes began to comb the boat, not walking, just looking, turning. He flipped up the back cushions and found the cupboards there, pulled them open: food. Again his eyes danced around, focused on the long settee and lifted up to expose the locker beneath it; there was the bag.

He yanked it out, thrust it at her. "Keys!" he said. She handed them to him with shaking fingers that made them jingle. "Necklace!" he barked. She dug that out, too. He snatched the box and dumped the contents into a meaty palm, starting to giggle now. "Holy shit! You weren't lying, were you, girl! Look at that ice!" He jammed her valuables into the pocket of his windbreaker, handed the bag to her, grabbed her arm. "Come on, let's go."

He half dragged her up the companionway, only to stop in the cockpit when his chest came up against the side-by-sides of Lew Faucet's shotgun.

"No, shit-for-brains, I don't think you're going anywhere. Fact is, my wife's calling the cops right this minute, so you might as well relax." He pushed with the barrel, and Coughlin involuntarily sat on the starboard cockpit seat. Lew's eyes shifted to take in Rosy and registered first curiosity, then surprise and shock. "Rosy!" He looked indecisively toward Coughlin. Before she could warn him, he pointed the shotgun skyward, obviously thinking he'd made a mistake in assuming they were burglars.

"No, look out!" she was saying as he was asking, "What the hell happened to your face—"

Lew never even pulled the trigger. In one seamless motion, Coughlin slammed the stiletto into his chest with his right hand and bludgeoned him with a wrecking-ball left a millisecond later. Lew dropped to the deck like a big ham knocked off the shelf. Coughlin got his arm around Rosy and was off the boat, walking away slowly, softly, calmly, quietly.

They could hear the gradual crescendo of a siren on rapid approach as Coughlin pushed her in the passenger side of the Ferrari and got behind the wheel. He put the key in the ignition, and the engine started turning. It turned and turned, the battery still strong. Rosy saw the mistake Coughlin was making.

He's screwing up, she thought. I knew he would, sooner or later, and I'm going to live. She could see past Coughlin to the squad car racing down the block toward them. Her rage seemed to rise with the sound of the siren. Free at last, that rage welled up from her gut like a surfacing humpback whale, rage at this wide-eyed giggling thing that had tortured her, that had killed Jason and now Lew. Coughlin bared his teeth as the engine kept turning without catching. The black-and-white cruiser careened into the lot and screeched to a halt ten feet from where they sat. Coughlin took his hand off the key before the doors of the cop car opened.

One cop got out right next to Coughlin's door. Coughlin looked at Rosy with such virulent hatred that it moved her back against the glass. She thought he might kill her right then with the stiletto, but the drawn gun in the cop's hand loosened her crow of triumph. "You minidicked pervert, you used the Chapman lock on the other Ferrari, but you panicked; you forgot on this one, didn't you? The car didn't start because you forgot to release the Chapman lock!" She watched his frantic gaze drop to the circular keyhole, grab the key chain where the key to the antitheft device hung in front of him.

She swung at him, connected this time, and it felt good. Left and right, over and over, she hit him as fast as she could, an animal inside her wanting to maim him before the cops took him away. Coughlin ignored her blows, fumbling with the keys.

Then she looked up and couldn't believe her eyes. "Hey, over here, over here!" she shouted as the goddamned cops were running toward the dock. They couldn't hear because the windows were closed—the smoked-glass windows behind which, in shadow and silence, two people were unnoticed by men intent on finding a boat named *Squareknot* where a burglary was in progress. Rosy reached for the door handle, but Coughlin knocked her unconscious, broke her nose with one whirling swipe from the heel of his hand.

17

The building directory showing the room numbers of professors' offices didn't list Douglas Marlette. Charlie asked the secretary in the department head's office, was told there was nobody by that name on staff. He asked if there had been in the past. She growled, dabbed liquid paper on the page she was typing, and said, "Whadda I look like, the department historian?"

"I just thought you might know."

"I've only been here two weeks, and that's too long. These professors are all nuts." She stopped and looked at him. "Are you a professor?"

"No."

"Good. I need the job, I just don't happen to like it."

"This Dr. Marlette . . . I was told he taught here. . . . Who might be able to tell me where he's gone?"

After a jumble of instructions that made nothing clear, except that she had trouble keeping left and right in their places, she sighed and got up. She led him through a series of corridors, telling him on the way that she was too busy to do his research, but she'd introduce him to Dr. Bowler, who'd been there for years and had been known to importune the bust of Socrates for an hour and a half of conversation. Without explanation, she donned what Charlie had by now seen was a gas mask, rapped twice with authority on the door, opened it, and led him into a very smoky office. Red-eyed in the gray mist sat a very skinny man with stringy black hair and a cigarette dangling from his lip. He looked up, and the ashes fell into the book he was reading.

"Dr. Bowler, this is Charlie Gamble, and he's interested in what you might know about an alleged professor here named Douglas Marlette." She turned to Charlie, and he thought he saw an evil glint in the eye that squinted through the glass hole in the leather mask. "I don't lend out the mask. Stay at your own risk." She closed the door behind her as she left.

Bowler half stood, extended his hand, and Charlie shook it. "Are you a student here? A professor?"

"No, I'm a mechanic, actually. I'm just trying to find someone, and the path has led to Dr. Marlette. Do you know where he is these days?"

Dr. Bowler rubbed his eyes and squinted through the smoke. "Are you a relative . . . friend of his?"

"No. I've never met him."

"Well . . . I guess it won't be too much of a shock, then. . . . Douglas Marlette has been dead for more than two years."

"Oh," Charlie said, hoping the relief didn't show. "Did you know him well?"

"Yes, we came here about the same time, in the early seventies; we got tenure the same year. I'd say I knew him as well as anyone did."

"Then you knew his wife?"

"Rosy? Of course."

"Do you know where she is now?"

"I haven't seen her since the funeral. She was in very bad shape, as you can imagine . . . well, not knowing the circumstances, you probably can't."

"What circumstances?"

Dr. Bowler stared at him. "I don't know you, Mr. Gamble. Maybe I should ask why you want to know."

Bowler's raspy voice wasn't without empathy. Charlie hoped

141

he'd respond without suspicion to a simple request for help. "I met Rosy a week ago. She stayed with me on my sailboat for several days, then left me a note saying she'd be back in a day or two and disappeared. She left her car and a suitcase, so I know she'll be back, but I have pressing reasons to leave the dock where she'll be looking for me. . . . Trouble is, I have no idea how to get in touch with her."

"You're . . . lovers, then?"

"I guess you'd say so."

"You guess?"

"Technically we are. I couldn't say for sure how she feels. She hasn't told me a lot about her past . . . as you can tell by the fact I didn't know her husband was dead. I suppose I'm waiting to see what happens."

Dr. Bowler lit a cigarette from the butt of the old one, looked out the window, came to a decision. "Douglas and Rosy's marriage was a strange union with an even stranger ending."

"How so?"

"Douglas was an intellectual monk. He was not an attractive man physically. I suspect that he faced that fact years ago, opted not to compete for women rather than subject himself to rejection. His life was his work.

"He was a great lecturer, absolutely the best I ever heard. He'd learned from the professionals, of course. He'd been a prodigy tent preacher in Oklahoma and West Texas, was carted from meeting to meeting, where he'd whip the faithful into a frenzy with his mother's teachings; he had an uncanny command of biblical detail for one so young, and a natural bent for the dramatic. That kind of thing gets less cute and less convincing when the babe's mouth gets hair and pimples sprouting round it . . .

"During his hiatus for puberty and young manhood, he majored in religion at SMU, went from there to Yale Divinity School, where he contracted the most profound case of atheism imaginable. Switching to the philosophy department, he went on for a doctorate specializing in the truly depressing stuff of Nietzsche, Heidegger, and Sartre."

Bowler was standing now, gesturing broadly with the burning cigarette, pacing around the room, talking sometimes to the wall, sometimes to a spot a couple of feet over Charlie's head. His tone was gathering dramatic steam. "By the time Rosy got here, he was a bona-fide guru of the godless—a campus celebrity; his classes were all oversubscribed. He was funny looking, but he had the voice of a herald and could hold the attention of a roomful of college kids, so completely co-opt their raging postadolescent hormones that had he passed a plate after one of his lectures, every last one of them would have contributed his or her weekly beer and reefer money. Whatever else happened during the hour, he left them staring into the unknowable void of helpless impotence and ignorance. Lord, the man could make you cry!"

"Rosy was his student? Later married him?"

"It isn't unusual, really; marriage, maybe, but not the emotion. The older man who knows the answer, has it all worked out in advance; easier than working it out on one's own. The strange part was that Rosy was so beautiful . . . the ones who go for the old profs are usually as homely and lonely as we are."

Bowler gave Charlie time to make some comment to the effect that he wasn't homely, smiled and shrugged when he didn't. "I don't know what made Rosy tick, but her attraction to Douglas wasn't a fluke. I saw her react to the flirtations of grad students far more charming than Douglas, ostensibly more suited to her. She could be positively arctic in her rebuffs."

"It's easy to picture," Charlie said.

"You can also imagine Douglas's surprise upon realizing that a woman of Rosy's beauty was in love with him. All those years of being too reticent to ask a woman out . . . suddenly he finds himself the candle to this gorgeous moth who thinks he's a philosophical savior of Western civilization."

"A savior?"

"Douglas had two passions: one was his pedagogical role in the classroom; the other was a book on which he'd been working for years . . . he meant it to be the ethics that Sartre never

143

produced. The manuscript was piled in stacks around his office. She read parts of it, I imagine, knew it was brilliant because she couldn't understand a single sentence. . . . Of course, who could understand any of that gibberish about the for-itself, in-itself?

"I'd guess that's what captured her imagination. I can see her sitting in her dorm room contemplating the enormity of it: his responsibility to provide sound and reasoned rules for living to a world made bereft of guideposts by God's famous demise. Now there was something to live for! She wished she were part of it.

"The ascetic and the fervent virgin—in spirit, anyway—being ever a volatile combination, she fluttered around him until the tinder caught, married him a few weeks after graduation in a rush of idealistic bliss at how important her life had become. She saw herself, I'm sure, as intellectual sounding board and emotional support for the great man's formerly solitary struggle to save a world lost in despair.

"What Rosy couldn't have foreseen was how much she would change the man's perspective. The history of religion shows that a civilization's idea of God is directly related to the world around it—harsh climate, harsh God; benevolent climate, nice God. Well, Marlette, the poor bugger, suddenly found his book to be a depressing pile of lifeless rationalization, starkly irrele-vant in a life that had become richer than Technicolor.

"Freed from his parchment-drab garret into a July Fourth of the flesh, the urgency of his recondite reconnaissance subsided. His inspired lectures lost their zip. His writing degenerated into cloying sonnets to his wife, which he called 'Rosettes.'

"The head of the department was appalled, asked me to try to talk some sense into the man. Of course he wouldn't listen.

"Even Rosy, ingenue that she was, could see that his fascina-tion for her was turning him into a drooling imbecile. She tried to push him back to his task. He was beside himself with re-morse, wanting only to please her. But once off his path, he had no idea how to return.

"He would confide in me. Having himself lost faith in his

work, he couldn't accept that it was the key to Rosy's love for him; he thought that he needed to make himself over into something he could never be. He tried to regain her approval by stretching himself in new and, some would say, frivolous directions. One day he appeared with a new stereo system and cultivated in his scholarly, exhaustive way a precious passion for jazz. Another day, he spent the money he'd been saving for a sabbatical on a used Ferrari, and gave her the keys. He'd lost all perspective and wanted only to see her smile, at any cost. A man whose life had been dedicated to the pursuit of absolutes, he sank to absolute buffoonery.

"I think Rosy, wanting none of this, happy with what she'd thought she had but unable to fix what she'd broken, blamed herself. Still in love with her ideal, hoping her absence would drive him back to his work, she deserted him. The note she left behind—the poor fellow showed it to me—explained that her need for him, while huge in the dimensions of one soul, was infinitely smaller than the world's need of his work.

"By now fatally paranoid, he decided that she'd left him for a younger man; Milton would love it. 'The mind is its own place, and in itself can make a Heav'n of Hell, a Hell of Heav'n.' Just think of it; she, driven by God knows what strange experiences of her own, marries what she wants, an ascetic; and in the act of doing so, she transforms him into an unlikely voluptuary! Diabolical!

"He mooned about for a few days before burning the manuscript in her honor and taking his final leap of faithlessness from the top of this very building."

"Jesus," Charlie said.

"For Rosy, it must have been like realizing she was some kind of demonic princess: her kisses conferred madness; her rejection, death."

"Dreadful."

"Yes. Are you an ascetic, Mr. Gamble?"

"I'm a Nopey."

Bowler, a professional solver of verbal puzzles, smiled. "The antithesis of a Yuppie?" Charlie nodded. "Yes, that would

fit . . . it would appeal to Rosy . . . maybe overcome whatever it was that caused her usual antipathy for attractive young
men."

"Maybe it helps that I'm neither all that young, nor all that
attractive."

Still smiling, Bowler said, "Perhaps. When you find her, be
careful. If she thinks you're too much in love, she'll probably
be afraid that she'll ruin you, or worse."

Bowler couldn't give him any direction on other threads of
Rosy's past that might be connected to her present. He said
he'd gotten the impression that she was estranged from her
family when he knew her. Charlie thanked him for his insights
and left.

He decided to check the boat, to see if she might have returned. He turned the rental car back in on his way, and in
walking toward the bridge he passed his favorite marine chan-
dlery. Thinking that one way or the other it might be wise to
be prepared for a hasty departure, he went inside, purchased
a large canvas bag, filled it with various spare parts and items
he knew he needed.

Crossing the bridge, he saw her car was gone. If that felt like
a cold shower, the sight of the police cars, the ambulance, and
the crowd around his boat were a tidal wave that left him
barely standing.

He broke into a wobbly run, fighting back tears, his limbs
strangely stiff and uncooperative. The first thought to crys-
tallize was that if Rosy was dead, he'd carry to his grave the
knowledge that if he had called in the police from the beginning, he might have saved her. In preservation of his sanity,
he made an instantaneous transfer of blame from himself to
O'Neill. *He* had done this.

Then he was aware of a new emotion encroaching like thick
rolling concrete into his soul. It hardened in place to forestall
the collapse he'd felt imminent seconds before. It became a
reason for being: to personally ensure that if things were as
he imagined, O'Neill would not again slip through the courts
unscathed. He would never get there alive. His last thought

before he pushed his way through the throng was, *O'Neill's ass is mine.*

Once past the bystanders, what he saw first was a laden stretcher being carefully transferred from *Squareknot* to the dock by two men in white uniforms. Two policemen were helping. There was a plastic mask strapped to her face. . . . *She's alive—wait . . . that's not Rosy. . . .*

Confused, he scanned the scene, saw no other fallen bodies, no Rosy, only gaping faces stunned to silence; and then Lucy. She looked like walking wounded, strangers at her elbows. Her dam broke when she saw Charlie.

"Aaaaahhhhwwww, my God, honey, they've stabbed my Loooooooo!!"

The crowd all turned toward Lucy. Most of them, as a result, missed seeing Charlie pitch forward onto his face, out cold as a cod, a victim of overload, both horror and relief.

"You fainted, that's what happened."

Even groggy, Charlie could hear the disdain in the tone of voice from the fiftyish man who stood next to the salon bunk where he lay amid considerable disarray. He could see that the contents of *Squareknot's* lockers had been scattered about.

"Nothing to be ashamed of . . . a natural human response to severe shock, and men are as human as women." Charlie didn't miss the inflective editorial that, however human it was, the speaker and John Wayne would have been above it. He was a large man, hair more gray than black, once very powerful, now bulky, with thick limbs and torso battling the constraint of his blue suit.

"I'm told you're the owner of this boat . . . Charlie Gamble?"

"That's right. Is Lew going to be all right?"

"I don't know. He suffered what appears to be a deep stab wound in his chest and was apparently hit on the head. He's lost a lot of blood but he's in good hands."

Charlie took a couple of deep breaths to steady himself. "What happened here?"

"We're trying to determine that, Mr. Gamble." He flipped

open a leather wallet that had a badge on one side, an ID on the other: Detective Lieutenant William Jagger. "Apparently, Mr. Faucet saw someone breaking into your boat. He told his wife to call the police, then came out with his shotgun to apprehend the perpetrator." He shook his head. "He should have waited for the police. . . .

"When Mrs. Faucet got off the phone, she looked out the window of her boat and didn't see anybody. . . . She thought maybe they were downstairs on your boat and lay low until she saw two policemen running around the dock." He looked up from his notes to explain. "They didn't know which boat it was, so they were a couple of minutes searching for the emergency for which they'd been summoned." Charlie noted Jagger's careful phrasing and attributed it to years of writing reports and trying to keep defense lawyers who made five times his salary from making him look like a monkey. "When she came out to signal them, she saw her husband crumpled in the cockpit of your boat. . . ."

"Did you catch the person who did it?"

His tone got tougher, either with anger that "the perpetrator" had gotten away or aggressive defensiveness that the cops had been too late. "Not yet. Mr. Faucet was too weak to be questioned. We're hoping he'll be able to help us, for his sake, of course, but also ours.

"Apparently, the perpetrator or perpetrators walked off the dock and escaped. Of course, it could have been someone from another boat, but two people who were here reported having seen a man and a woman walk off the dock and get into a red sports car, possibly a Ferrari. One of the witnesses noted something strange."

"What was that?"

"He said he'd seen the woman on the dock before . . . didn't know her, but he'd seen her around."

Charlie could feel his pulse quicken. "What's strange about that?"

"That isn't the strange part. She was classy looking—the witness's term—looked like a woman you'd expect to see on a

148

yacht. But her face showed signs of a severe beating . . . badly bruised and puffy; and she walked like she might have been hurt or drunk. He said that was what made him watch them and see them get into the car. But he forgot about them when he saw the police arrive . . . didn't make a connection . . . didn't see them drive off. Nobody who saw them actually saw them on this boat, so it could be unrelated. We're still canvassing the dock, looking for people who may have seen something."

He referred to a notebook. "About five ten, curly brunette hair cut fairly short, high cheekbones, blue eyes, strikingly good-looking, like a model. . . . Ring any bells, Mr. Gamble?"

Loud alarms, but he hadn't forgotten the way the cops were hamstrung by due process. If he'd called them earlier, he might have saved Lew, but to tell all now would only be a failure of nerve: his assessment was that Billy O'Neill had stabbed Lew and abducted Rosy, and he could do things to loosen O'Neill's tongue that the law enjoined them from doing. "Wish it did," he said quickly, hoping it wasn't a trap, hoping Jagger hadn't already connected that description with a lady who'd been keeping company with him of late. "Any description of the man?"

"Only that he was large . . . seems the lady was more interesting to look at," he said with an edge in his voice.

Billy O'Neill was large. "You've issued a bulletin for the car?"

Charlie interpreted the raised eyebrow as irritation at crime-show fans who second-guessed his police work. "Yes, but it won't do any good."

"Why's that?"

"It was thirty minutes after the incident before we talked to the witness who mentioned the car. If the couple was involved, then the car probably belongs to some boater who's out cruising, and we'll get a report when the owner gets back that it was stolen. . . . We'll find it abandoned somewhere."

"How do you know it didn't belong to them?"

He enjoyed dragging the answer out slowly. "People who

drive Ferraris don't have to break into boats to earn a living, Mr. Gamble, and people who break into boats and stab people generally don't drive the getaway car home and park it on the curb. Without a license number or immediate chase . . ." He shrugged.

Charlie saw the problem. It gave momentum to his prior instinctive thought: giving them O'Neill's name and the background without proof or better witnesses would also get them nowhere. O'Neill would know the minefield of interrogation as well as Jagger. He wouldn't be sitting with Rosy at his home waiting for the cops to come. On the other hand, he'd talked once before when the interrogation was brutal. Inwardly, Charlie swore he would again.

"Can you give us anything to work on here? Is there anything special an intruder might have been after on your boat, or somebody you might suspect of having a motive other than simple burglary?"

"Not off the top of my head." He concentrated on keeping his voice level. Maybe too level. He'd already seen that the settee cushion was off, and her bag was gone.

"We'll have to ask you to look around a bit, see if you can tell us if anything is missing." Jagger was looking at him intently.

"Of course," Charlie said. How should he be acting? Had Jagger intentionally feigned the early belief that it was a simple burglary to get him off guard, then subtly made a change of course? What was Jagger looking at?

"We'll need to know where you were and what you were doing today while this incident was taking place, Mr. Gamble."

For the first time, he thought of the canvas bag of purchases he'd made, and he looked around for it. Jagger stepped over to the head, reached in, and pulled out the soaking-wet bag.

"This what you're looking for? It fell in the drink when you fainted. We retrieved it. I think we got it before anything fell out." He held it away from him, so the dripping water wouldn't wet his shoes. He looked inside, then up at Charlie. "I'm no sailor, Mr. Gamble. Fact is I'm getting a little seasick just talking to you here, but you seem to be stocking up on some things. Planning a trip of some kind?"

The rendition of ironic innocence, to Charlie's mind, was beneath Peter Falk, but the influence was undeniable. Jesus, he thought. That's all I need. A detective who thinks he's Columbo.

18

Rosy's throat was parched from breathing through her mouth when she came to. She felt sticky, saw the blood down the front of her clothing . . . Jason's clothing; hers had been torn to shreds the night before. A combination of pain and numbness told her there was something terribly wrong with her face.

Coughlin was hunched over the wheel as though he intended to take a bite out of it, but he was disciplined about escape. He drove the entire way to Jason's house without exceeding sixty miles per hour. He giggled when he saw a cop going the opposite direction pay no attention to them.

He had to park her Ferrari outside the garage, because the Jaguar was still there; beside it stood a blue delivery van bearing the graphics of Myra's Flower Shop. Its door was open, and it was apparent that Bead had been loading things into it. Slackjawed, he stood looking at them, a small television in his arms.

Coughlin laughed at him. "Wha'chew gapin' at, Bead-brain?"

Bead's response was to duck his head, do a little side step. It reminded Rosy of a courting pigeon.

"We ran into a little heat, and girlie here tried to signal 'em, didn't you, girlie?" He gripped her arm painfully, and she snorted involuntarily, blowing more blood through her swollen nostrils.

"Oh, messy, messy, messy!" Looking to see if she'd gotten it on his trousers, he shoved her away from him toward the entrance to the house. "This is her car. A little older, but that ain't so bad with Ferraris. Still bring a nice piece of change, but it's prob'ly a mite warm after our near miss this afternoon. We'll need to be more careful getting it to market than we was with the last one.

"I see you got the van. You get what I said for the first load?"

Bead brightened. "Five hundred more than you said."

"Good boy! I knew you had potential!" He pushed Rosy ahead of him into the house. Many of the smaller furnishings had disappeared. It had the look of moving out. He went to the refrigerator and got a beer, washed more pills down with the first swallow.

Rosy stood wondering what would come next. She got a paper towel to dry the blood she could feel on her upper lip. When she touched her nose, alarms went off.

Bead passed through like a servant with aspirations toward invisibility. Coughlin flopped down in the chair with the stain in front of it. He seemed to have forgotten her. She realized the body was gone. Whom did one call for body removal?

She eyed the knife handles protruding from their slots on the butcher block. She went to the sink and used a moistened paper towel to swab some of the blood from her face, gingerly, softly, slowly . . . for what was the rush? Would this be her last luxury? A cool paper-towel bath in a stainless-steel sink? She leaned on her elbows and held the compress to her eyes. She listened for his footfalls but heard none. After a while, she dried her face on a dishtowel that hung by the sink. It had oranges, apples, and bananas printed on it. She looked at the blood on the towel and wondered why he wasn't saying or doing anything.

She knew he could see her from where he sat, thanks to the architect's egalitarian open plan, a plan for a gourmet cook who wants his guests to drink their cocktails and watch the show as he prepares their meal. Or maybe just a lonely man who cooks to have company. She stole a glance and saw that he was looking at her. She looked at the refrigerators, the wide, stainless-steel and cast-iron gas stove, a professional stove, from a restaurant supply.

She tried to imagine Jason padding about the kitchen; to reconcile that with the man she'd met at the racetrack. He'd shown little interest in her until she'd made it obvious that she wanted him to. She wasn't used to that. With him, she'd had the feeling that hustling him would be very difficult, as he didn't seem to harbor illusions about himself. Even his computerized betting scheme . . . he'd laughed when he'd admitted it worked—how had he put it?—about as well as betting lucky colors. He seemed to have more of a what-the-hell attitude than most of the men she'd worked on. His final hour had been his worst. It shouldn't have been that way.

Coughlin watched her vacantly. She saw her suitcase sitting on the floor. Coughlin must have carried it in. She noticed that she was dressed in clothing from Jason's closet: cinched-up trousers and shirt. Earlier that day she'd despaired at the realization that Coughlin was right: "Women wear anything these days, girlie. On you it'll look like the latest from Gay Paree."

Suddenly she couldn't stand waiting anymore, picked up the suitcase, heard herself say, "I'm going to take a shower." She walked out of the room and up the stairs. She thought he'd pounce on her, but he didn't. He just let her go.

She went into her bedroom. She caught herself thinking of it as her room, her sanctuary, a place where he couldn't see her, if only for a moment's relief. Surprised that she'd actually gotten there alone, she looked around, wondered what to do.

A telephone. Only to satisfy herself that it was dead, she picked it up and felt her pulse leap into her temples when she heard a dial tone.

She put it down gently. She trembled as she tried to fathom such a simple idea. Call the cops. Maybe he was so intent on feeling the speed come on that he just didn't give a damn. She went into the bathroom and started the shower. She crept back to peer out the door, over the balcony. Coughlin still sat in the

154

chair with his back toward her. She picked up the phone, dialed 911, and heard a ring. Before anyone answered, the left side of her head exploded.

Shaken awake, she saw Coughlin looking down at her. How could anything so large be so swift and so silent? It couldn't have taken him five seconds to make it up the stairs and along the balcony, and still she'd heard not a trace of movement behind her in the room.

He dragged her, stumbling, into the bathroom and told her to shower. He watched as she undressed and watched through the glass door as she washed herself. What did he think, she'd kill herself if left alone? Would she? How many more would die before the ordeal ended? Would she be one of them?

He spoke to her loudly above the noise of the water. "Now tonight we gonna start on your other friends' houses. You gonna show us, and I don't want you snuffling blood all over me while we're doin' it. So you blow your nose good in there and put some cotton in it when you get done."

She heard an echo in his voice, someone else speaking—a mother? father? lover? Who'd said that to him, who'd been so callous about *his* blood?

Then he was gone, and for the first time she felt the massaging warmth of the water on her body. She flinched when it hit the burns. She'd had so many bruises, so much pain.

What was next? Coughlin planned for her to lead them to other men, who would let her in the door only to be tortured and killed. It brought her own use of them into sharp relief; she pitied them now for the way she'd victimized them, leaving them open to Coughlin's greater evil.

Then he was back with her suitcase. "Your bag, madam," he said, and closed the door on her. She let the water run a long time over her wounds. She found some salve for burns in the medicine chest and rubbed it into the livid spots from Coughlin's cigarettes. She dressed herself slowly, looking at her bruised face, the crooked, swollen nose.

When she was dressed in a clean white blouse and a pair of

155

yellow slacks, she stood before the mirror, and holding a towel under her chin, she screamed from what her vanity made her do.

Coughlin burst into the room and stopped, looked quizzically at her. "What the hell was that all about, girl?"

Rosy moved the towel long enough to appraise what she'd done. Yes; it was better. She looked at him defiantly. "I was moving my damn nose back into place, you son of a bitch!" she screamed, tears mingling with the fresh flow of blood, feeling embarrassed and childish at the sound of her voice saying "node" instead of "nose."

Coughlin was waiting on the bed when Rosy emerged from the bathroom. He smiled. "There ya go. All clean. Don'cha feel better now?"

"Yes," she said.

He patted the bed. "Sit down here, girl."

He was smoking a cigarette. He made a little show of it, blowing smoke rings. She sat near the foot of the bed. He got up and moved closer to her, smiled at her, took a big movie drag on the cigarette.

"Now . . . let's talk business. I want to know who you's talkin' 'bout last night, when you said you could take us to other houses like this one."

She stared back at him, visions of Lew hitting the deck looming before her. How could she lead Coughlin to more victims?

"Now don't you get any idea about bein' tricky, girlie. 'Cause we're talkin' last chance here, got it?" He spoke softly, shook his finger at her. "I shoulda killed you for what you done today, tryin' to call them cops, beatin' on me when I's tryin' t' concentrate. But I didn't. I didn't 'cause I figured you to lead us somewhere else worth goin'."

She felt relief in there somewhere. For what? For Charlie. Charlie had not been home—that was something. It was her first chance to appreciate that. Events were moving so quickly that she couldn't react before something else was happening. What day was it? Desperately she tried to walk herself back

156

through days to one she recognized so she could give it a name. She had gone to the races—what day's races?

Coughlin was calmly enumerating the things he hadn't yet done to her but would find fun. Various ways of breaking bones, removing eyelids and fingernails and other vulnerable tissue.

What day's races? Tuesday's races. How many days ago? Four? Three? A year? Lord God, yesterday, so long ago. Today was Wednesday. That means something. . . . Who's not home Wednesday? His voice is talking faster; he wants me to answer him. Someone isn't home Wednesdays. Then she remembered.

"Okay. I'll take you. I know a house we can get into. His name is Anthony Panoff. There's an alarm, but I know where there's a hidden key, unless he moved it after I left him."

Coughlin smiled at this. "Moved it after you left? Why would a man do that? He prob'ly wakes up at noises in the night and hopes it's you sneakin' back in. And tonight he'll get his wish." He giggled. "He'll die happy."

"Goddamn you," she said. "You don't have to kill him. If we go early enough, he won't be there. He never gets home until close to midnight on Wednesday night."

She hated it that Coughlin was probably right. Anthony Panoff probably did miss her, wish that she'd come back to him. He didn't seem the type to hold a grudge.

He used to stare at her, give her the feeling he just enjoyed looking at her. She used to tell herself it was dehumanizing, the way he stared at her. In the moment of telling Coughlin about him, though, she thought maybe Anthony Panoff had looked at her as he would at a painting he dearly loved. Dehumanizing? Maybe. But she couldn't find the rancor she'd thought she owed him in return.

It required all of Charlie's concentration to deal with Detective Jagger while his mind kept straying to more pressing matters. He knew Lew might be at that very moment conscious, telling the cops that Rosy had been there when he was stabbed. Lew, or possibly a new witness who knew Rosy, could cut short the time he had to act on his own.

He told Jagger he'd spent the day price-shopping various marine stores before buying his supplies where he had. It was a safe story. The reason he shopped there was that the store had a huge selection and worked on a smaller margin than its competitors. An investigator would find that he'd bought at the least expensive source.

Before Jagger's car was out of the parking lot, Charlie was on his way to the hospital, where he was told that Lew was still in surgery. He found Lucy in the surgical waiting room, a friend from the marina with her. She and Charlie hugged each other. Her composure was back—tense, but solid. Word had been sent out by the surgeon that although Lew had lost a lot of blood, they had him stabilized and were doing repair work. They were guardedly optimistic, and she would hear more in an hour or so.

Lucy subtly pulled him away from her friend. Leaning close

to his ear, she said, "Lew was still conscious when I got to him. Said Rosy was with the guy who stabbed him; she tried to warn him, but the guy was quick as a mongoose.

"He said I should talk to you before I told the cops; that you might want to keep them out of it. What's going on?"

"I don't know myself, but I have a couple of lines on how to find out. That's why I need the time you and Lew can give me."

He felt her hold on his arm tighten. "He said something else, honey. He said he barely recognized her. She's been through the mill. You better find her fast. He said if you do, don't take chances. Shoot the guy before he gets in arm's reach."

"I appreciate you sticking your neck out this way," Charlie said.

Lucy's face was a study in uncertainties. But she patted his arm, said, "Rosy could have watched me burn."

It was fully dark by the time Charlie picked up another rental car, found the building where O'Neill lived with his mother: on a run-down street off West Broadway in South Boston. In Boston, the streets were laid out by wandering cows, their tracks later paved. Half the signs are always missing, according to popular wisdom, because the locals know where they are, and the cows can't read. Finding an address is no mean feat in the best neighborhoods, of which this was not an example.

Here the brownstones still bore the grime of generations, no fancy sand-blasted rejuvenation or polished-brass numbers like the Boston reborn in the Back Bay. The buildings were jammed shoulder to shoulder with granite stairs leading to front doors that once needed paint and now needed to be replaced. The potholes in the asphalt were less deep than in some parts of the city, only because here they were partially filled with refuse that spilled from the curb and which nobody bothered to move.

The uncrowded and poorly lit street suited Charlie's purpose well. He couldn't be sure of finding O'Neill there, but he didn't have any better plan. He'd called on the phone and been told

Billy was out. Maybe he was inside, obedient to the injunction against answering phones, but Charlie was willing to hang his chances on the nocturnal leanings of those who live by nefarious means. He clung to the thought that O'Neill would have no reason to take Rosy with him if he intended to murder her.

He lined up his mirrors to give him a good view in both directions, then slumped behind the wheel and succumbed to the wandering mind of one who waits.

Counting his options if O'Neill didn't show, he didn't get beyond one . . . that being the other valuable in Rosy's bag, the necklace. It looked valuable enough that a merchant might remember it. If the car led to her husband, maybe the necklace would lead somewhere different. Trouble was, her bag was gone, and he was struggling to remember the name of the jeweler.

He worried over Lew. A man who grew bored on ships designed and equipped for colossal destruction, then realized how slender life's supports were only when he assumed command of the tiny boat of his retirement. The death he feared was from drowning or rabble pirates, so he fortified himself with lifeboat and shotgun and seldom left the dock. Then, in his finest hour, in the act of repelling the long-expected pirate, he gets taken by surprise, paranoid precautions to no avail.

"There he is," he said softly to himself when he saw a dark figure approaching from behind, a block away, on his side of the street. The figure walked with the pronounced limp of a man who'd recently suffered the shattering effect on his metatarsals of a mushroom anchor driven by the adrenaline of fear.

He calculated that O'Neill would cross the street before he reached the car. He got out and began walking straight toward the figure. He counted on the darkness to shield his features and walked casually erect.

When they were abreast, he hooked an arm and swung himself behind O'Neill, pressing the gun into his back decisively, and told him to keep walking. They goose-stepped the half block back to the car. Charlie patted him down and came up with a short but stout iron crowbar that would open doors or heads with equal dispatch. He pushed O'Neill into the passenger side and shoved him across behind the wheel, getting in behind him.

"Start the car and drive."

Now O'Neill recognized the voice. "Hey, man, wattaya hasslin' me for?"

"Drive." He shoved the gun into O'Neill's ribs.

For ten minutes, O'Neill drove and at the same time swore he'd done as he was told. He thought his employer had called, but he'd told his mother to say he wasn't in. Charlie asked no questions. He didn't want to ask until O'Neill was one hundred percent sure that to lie was to die. He wavered inside when O'Neill asked the question "Why would I keep after it when you took the two pieces of those five-thousand-dollar bills? What would I have to gain?" But he answered himself silently with the conclusion that O'Neill could have held the hope of getting them back, not to mention his doubt that O'Neill operated on what anyone would call a rational game plan to begin with. What was rational about what he had done to his landlady?

They got to the boatyard, and Charlie slipped a noose he'd made over O'Neill's neck and led him out of the car. He held his hand at the small of his back with the unobtrusive noose tight as they walked to *Squareknot*. Below, he put his marline-spike seamanship to work, trussed him securely to the salon table, and gagged him with a dishrag and chafe tape.

Before long, they were motoring into a two-foot chop as they passed the macabre, irregular gong of the sea buoy into the glimmer and gloom of moonlit ocean. The wind was blowing, but Charlie used the diesel for convenience, and they pounded in rolling surges into an easterly breeze.

He abandoned the wheel for a moment to check on O'Neill. Through a porthole, he watched him struggling in a vain attempt to wiggle free. Rogers sat sphinxlike on the gimbeled stove, watching him. Squirm, you bastard, he mouthed silently, confident that the knots would hold, and returned to the wheel. When he was far enough out that boat traffic had thinned sufficiently, he shifted into neutral. He brought O'Neill on deck, removed the gag, and let him scream his questions about what the fuck was going on and what was he gonna do to him. He listened for what he wanted to hear and counted on the drama of not speaking to add to the natural chill of the night.

When O'Neill didn't volunteer Rosy's whereabouts, he became more and more sure that she was dead. He rove a line through a reefing block on the boom, attached one end to O'Neill's still-bound hands and the other end to a two-speed Genoa winch. He rigged a line from the bow cleat to pull the boom out to port over the water.

"Where is she?"

"Where is who, you crazy—"

Charlie shoved him over the stern. After checking to be sure the line was clear of the prop, he shifted into forward and towed him for about ten seconds, watching his futile thrashings in the moonlight astern. He adjusted his course away from the only set of running lights in view. Over the deep rumble of the diesel, over the wind's whooshing and whistling on water and rigging, he heard one distant, garbled shriek.

Then he shifted back into neutral, winched O'Neill back aboard.

He sputtered and choked and cried. When he finally recovered enough to speak, Charlie put his face up close to his, said, "O'Neill, Rosy is gone. You took her. I understand that business is business. You got one way to live . . . that's tell me where she is. I'll take you to the police, and you'll have a chance to try to beat the system again. Maybe your confession to me will be just as invalid as the one you got away with last time. But you keep playing dumb, you go back in the water and drown right now. Where is she, freak?"

Charlie could see O'Neill's eyes widen, his mouth open and close; the guy was too terrified to speak. That was fine. He could wait. When something got out, it would be the truth. Charlie's mood was rising on the hope that he might finally learn where Rosy was. At last O'Neill spoke in short, gasping

162

spurts. "Don't kill me, man. I done what you said. I ain't been near yer boat. I ain't seen the girl."

Charlie's rage burst out through his arms and hands; he picked Billy O'Neill up without the aid of the winch and executed a writhing, shrieking, medicine-ball chest pass that sent Billy back into the water. He threw the lever to engage the diesel and went to hull speed. He put the helm over and headed back in. Turning from upwind to downwind put a feeling of calm on the boat, cut the wind noise in half. The moonlight was forward now, decorated by the blinking red and green dots of the channel buoys. He looked behind him toward where Billy was being trolled like shark bait; there was not enough light to see, and he heard no screams.

In the stillness, a conclusion grabbed him as though it crouched with eyeteeth dripping on the chrome ship's wheel: I didn't kill him for the evil in him; I killed him because I've been swinging at shadows since this mess got started, and I'm damn sick of hitting air; because Rosy may be dead because of me, and it's easier to blame him than it is to accept that truth.

Was O'Neill dead yet? He shifted into neutral and cranked the winch until O'Neill hung like a melted wax man over the deck. He dropped him down and pressed hard on his chest. Water shot out, and he repeated it to the same effect. He turned him over and slammed his back several times, turned him over again and breathed three times into his lungs, and slammed him on the chest and screamed, "Breathe, you son of a bitch!"

He did. He breathed. He vomited and breathed. Charlie dragged him below and ran hot water from the shower over him to warm him up. He dried him and put some of his own clothes on him, while Billy O'Neill remained half-conscious and befuddled.

He slapped his face to try to get some awareness going, asked him, "O'Neill! O'Neill! You said the contractor didn't know my name. Did he call the lady by name?"

It took a minute, but he finally said, "Rosemary something."

For Charlie it was confirmation that the murder attempts came from her past, not his. He thought that might ease his guilt. It didn't help.

He left O'Neill on the bunk and drove the boat back to the slip. He wrapped him in a blanket, led him to the car, and drove him home. Before he let him out of the car, he said, "New rules, O'Neill. I might think of a use for you. If I want you, I'll call and tell your mother it's Rosemary. Answer the phone if a man's voice identifies himself as Rosemary. Other than that, the deal's the same. Got it?"

O'Neill seemed sleepy, groggy, demented, but he nodded. Charlie helped him to his door and left.

As he drove off, stalked by exhaustion, he had a moment of near panic realizing what he'd done. The son of a bitch is a killer, and now he'll know I'm not. O'Neill will put himself in my place, see that he'd have killed me, that I let him go. Will he come back, looking for the pieces of money?

He couldn't think. His consciousness had become a spiraling, looping vortex of frustration, thoughts tumbling like dice in a rolling barrel. One name emerged: Michael Barkum . . . Washington Street. Yes, that was it. Maybe he'd learn something new.

20

Coughlin handcuffed Rosy to the refrigerator at the home of Anthony Panoff, one of her earliest scam victims. As Coughlin had predicted, he hadn't moved the keys.

He was a mostly retired CPA, senior partner of a major firm. He was a widower whose children had moved to other cities. One mark of his success was a Ferrari; another was a seaside cottage at Hyannis on Cape Cod to which he repaired every Tuesday and Wednesday. He preferred the less crowded mid-week to the weekends on the Cape, considered it a benefit of semiretirement that he could avoid the masses at his favorite restaurants. He returned on Wednesday, late enough to avoid Boston's heavy traffic. That fact would save him, assuming the robbery didn't take too long.

It also might save her, she thought, treasuring a secret, listening to a commotion in the front of the house over discovery of a floor safe under an Oriental rug. A phone call was made. She couldn't hear the exchange. The sounds of objects being carried out mingled with Coughlin's escalating glee.

She slipped her fingers into the front of her blouse, pulled out the little card she'd snatched from the kitchen counter while Coughlin was talking to Bead at Jason's house. It was the business card Coughlin had taken from Jason's wallet. It had the business address, but Rosy figured it might bring help if she could manage to leave it at the scene of the robbery.

Should she drop it on the floor, push it partly under the refrigerator? She could open the fridge, flip it onto the shelf. She saw a stack of unopened mail on the counter close by . . . left by the maid for Panoff's return. He'd be sure to go through it . . . but maybe not, on a day he discovered a robbery. Trouble was, anywhere else she could reach, Coughlin might see it, or investigators might not.

She slipped her left foot out of its shoe, managed to transfer the card from fingers to toes. She raised her foot up onto the counter, twisted it so the card fell facedown. Then she pushed it carefully beneath the stack. One little corner protruded a bit, but she was satisfied.

Finally, sweaty, flushed from the activity, the two of them came back into the kitchen, and Coughlin made a big joke of his ability to effortlessly open the refrigerator by picking her up and moving her with the door. He raised her by putting his hand between her legs, doing a one-armed curl. They treated themselves to John's Molson Golden. He crotch-curled her several times in feigned indecision over whether to have a snack as well, opening and closing the door, each time changing his mind. Bead laughed obediently and beamed at his unpredictable leader. Rosy gritted her teeth, the message hidden giving her some spirit back.

"Here, have some beer, girlie, we're celebratin'." Since her hands were cuffed to the door, he tilted it to her lips, as if bottle-feeding a calf, laughed as part of it ran down her cheeks. She guzzled some of it from sheer inability to resist anymore. "Look at that, look at that, like a blind pup on a warm tit!

"You ain't so glamorous no more, girlie, but you sure know your rich folks, don't you? Why, hell, if I'd a knowed I could get in these places with pussy, I'd a had me a sex change years ago, ain't that right, Bead?"

"That's right, Wilbur, I would a, too!"

"That's how you done it, ain't it, girlie?'

He held her hair now and grinned at her. "Ain't that it? You

166

poontanged your way to fame and fortune, didn't you?" He tightened his grip and shook her to get his answer.

"Yes, that's what I did," she said, feeling her face protest at the effort. This seemed to please him.

"Well, tonight your old boyfriend is the fuckee and we're the fuckers," he said, and let her go. He ambled about the kitchen looking at stuff in cupboards as though it were an afterthought, not taking anything, just looking. He paused by the stack of mail, and she thought, No, he's gonna look for checks, but he turned away.

What's going on here, anyway? she wondered. Burglars'-union rules: beer break every forty minutes? They sat and discussed the value of various items of their plunder like two women at the prior viewing of an antique show. She began to worry that Anthony Panoff might get home before they finished. She couldn't see a clock in the room.

Bead was partial to the sterling flatware and "teapot stuff." Coughlin strutted a surprising familiarity with the value of Royal Doulton and Limoges. He explained to Bead that he'd learned it from a book lent to him by a con up at Attica, laughed at how he didn't waste his time reading smut and pounding his pud the way most a them goons up there did; he was into self-improvement—taught himself about antiques and shit like that; figgered it'd come in handy.

Rosy heard a car outside the house and saw the swing of headlights across the yard. Her heart leaped in joy and dread that she might be saved—or see another man die.

" 'At's him all right," Bead said.

"Well, it's about time he got here. I hope he cracks safes faster than he drives," Coughlin quibbled, but his heart wasn't in it. His life was going too well. He was on a roll.

"Hell, Wilbur, we only called him forty minutes ago, and he had to come all the way up here from Boston. I told you he'd come, didn't I?"

"Yeah, well, you tell him like I said that he only gets half what's in the safe, no share on the rest?"

"I told him, I told him. He un'erstands. You'll see. Ol'

Bernie's a pro, he don't expect to make no profit on nothing he don't work for."

They left the kitchen, went to welcome their safe-cracking consultant. Rosy was crying again, the warmth of the beer releasing emotions long since paralyzed by fear and defeat. She could hear the distant clamor of feet ascending the stairs and vainly jerked at the handcuffs, thinking maybe the handle of the refrigerator would break. In a frenzy, she yanked the door back and forth until the rattle of bottles on its shelves made her stop in fear of attracting Coughlin.

Waiting, she remembered that Panoff had wrapped the diamonds clumsily in shiny gold paper and fashioned a bow from ribbon that clashed. . . . She remembered that he'd been quite prim and businesslike about it, no fussy baggage of inane endearments. And she knew then that he'd seen it for exactly what it was . . . a deal. She remembered that he'd watched her undress later, indulging himself with a rare glass of brandy. With his tie still knotted, white shirt with starched French cuffs still impeccably correct, he'd sat for a long time in the chair near the bed. He'd looked at her body, but his expression at the time had made her think that he was remembering something from long ago.

The next morning she'd asked herself if she'd been bought. She'd left shortly after he went to his office. She hadn't seen him since.

Then they were all clamoring into the kitchen for the well-lighted, claw-footed oak table. Bernie yelped when he saw her, covered his face, "Cripes, why didn't you tell me there was somebody in here?"

Coughlin laughed. "Who, girlie? Hell, she won't tell."

Bead got to the point. "She's seen us do murder, Bernie."

Exchange of glances. Bernie seemed to shrug; was it indifference or a shiver?

They unfolded a sheet on the table and began to separate the contents. Coughlin was reading names of companies and cackling about Panoff getting bearer bonds, probably for looking the other way when he found piles of stinko in some company's financial statements.

Bernie stopped him. "Wait a minute. These things are hard to put a value on . . . stock certificates, jewelry . . . how the hell we gonna divide it?"

Coughlin didn't hesitate. "We fence it first, then split the money."

"Huh-uh. I was clear on the phone. We split before we leave here. I take my share and fence it myself. I got no yen to go to jail because of somebody else's carelessness." He looked at Rosy as he said it.

Coughlin's hand was instantly leveling a gun across the table and leaning after it. "Well then, maybe you'd rather take nothing, you're so careful. That way there ain't no way you'll get caught with it."

Bernie smiled. "I ain't that careful, but I am careful enough I got your balls one foot in front of my barrel here."

From where Rosy sat, she could see he told the truth. His hand under the table focused a gun on Coughlin's groin. She could see the barrel trembling. Would Coughlin trust a clean kill and blow him apart? Rosy was sure he would. She remembered the speed that had killed Lew. "He think's he's invulnerable," Bead had said. She suddenly realized that this could be her salvation. If Bernie was faster than Lew, and he had the advantage that Coughlin couldn't reach his gun, under the table, to deflect it . . . Bead would be the only obstacle to her escape.

"Wait a minute, you guys. Stay cool." Bead's voice quavered, but they were listening to him, watching each other. "We can do it another way . . . so everybody's happy . . . way we divided cake when we's kids. . . ."

Coughlin stole a glance at him as though he thought Bead had lost his mind. "What the hell are you talking about, Bead-brain?"

"One divides, the other chooses . . . that keeps everybody fair. You know a little about stocks and such, Wilbur, and

Bernie, you've boosted every kind a rock anybody ever thought of. Coughlin divides the stock into two piles; Bernie chooses one. Bernie divides the jewelry; Coughlin chooses one. That way ya both gotta try to make it an even split, or you might be screwing yourself."

They continued to stare each other down as they thought it over. "Don't that make more sense than bleeding to death? One cuts, the other chooses? Even-Steven?" Bead said.

Coughlin started giggling first. Then Bernie joined in with a gravelly bubbling from his gut. Coughlin surprised Rosy by putting his gun down first. Then it struck her that he thought killing was cool, so he probably didn't think Bernie was cool enough to shoot him when it looked to be avoidable.

Before long, Bernie was eyeballing the jewels—no doubt jewels once worn by the deceased Mrs. Panoff. He used a glass like Michael's, separated them into piles. Coughlin was mumbling and moving his lips as he tried to divine the relative value of stocks he'd probably never heard of, but he was willing to divide rather than risk having his balls blown off.

Bead was watching it all, beaming in proprietary pride at the management acumen that had enabled him to keep the beasts from tearing each other apart. He still thought that he and Coughlin were partners.

Now Rosy was beginning to wonder if maybe he didn't understand Coughlin better than she did, and whether there might be some way to deal with the creature. What was changing her mind was the way he'd allowed a compromise with Bernie.

Before long they were back in the van, Rosy between the two of them, Bead driving. He said, "I ain't never had a better haul than this."

"Like I told ya: ya wanna steal somethin', ya gotta go where they got somethin'. This ain't nothin' compared to what Lolly Gaines an' me hauled outa Overland Park, Kansas, couple years ago."

"Yeah, howdja do it?"

"Lolly had worked humpin' furniture for Mayflower. He

knew the ropes. We spent a few bucks to hire an answering service, make some cards and forms.

"We rode around lookin' for rich-lookin' houses with 'For Sale' signs. We knocked on the doors, tol' 'em we's movers. Some lady took us up on it . . . thought she's really gonna stick it to us, 'cause our quote was prob'ly half what Allied give 'er.

"We show up in a Ryder truck he's rented with false ID, got two niggers we hired off the street to do the work emptyin' her whole fucking house into the trailer. The lady give us a big ol' pitcher a ice tea. Me and Lolly sat there drinking tea and list'nin' to the radio while the niggers loaded up. Couple hours later, we drove the whole damn truck into a warehouse in St. Louis and walked out with thirty grand in a grocery bag."

They talked around her in excited appraisal of the take from Anthony Panoff's house: stereo equipment, Oriental rugs, cashmere overcoats, televisions, silver, china, clocks, and assorted furnishings and bric-a-brac. When they got to the jewels and stocks, suddenly realizing there would never come a time that she could broach the topic without attracting attention to herself, she lurched into it without taking time to think.

"Wilbur, there's something I've been wondering about."

"Oh-hoooo, girlie wants to chat now? No more cat's got her tongue? Whatchew wond'rin' about?"

"All that stuff that Bernie took . . . half the jewels, half the stocks. You let him go with it. I kept expecting you to shoot him and keep it. Why didn't you?"

Rosy could feel the tension from Bead. He wanted to know the answer, too, but was afraid to ask. So was she, but she didn't have anything to lose.

Coughlin didn't answer her. She could see a tight look on his face in the glow from the dashboard lights. She'd already guessed at the answer, but she had to chance goading him to answer it himself.

"You were chicken, weren't you? He had a gun, and you weren't so brave that you'd chance his getting you—"

He elbowed her in the chest, knocking the wind out of her.

"I'm chicken, huh? Well, I'll tell you somethin', girlie, I killed guys with guns! Shit, liquor stores, Seven-Elevens, and I let 'em go for 'em, too; didn't shoot 'em down empty-handed. I could see it in their faces, they had 'em, and I waited till they reached for 'em every time. None of 'em got close, see, and neither would that asshole Bernie. I coulda put lead between his ears, and he'd never have pulled the trigger."

She forced her lungs to fill up slowly, small gasps, building to a full breath. "Then, why didn't you?" She braced herself for another blow.

" 'Cause I don't kill guys I'm doing business with, see; I know about guys like that. Sooner or later it comes back, and they get theirs. They get theirs between the ribs when it gets around. Ya gotta keep it straight. There's them, and there's us. They got it, and we're takin' it. And I ain't one a these assholes shoots the guys on their side."

There it was. Even Coughlin had rules. She waited for him to settle down before she said in the toughest voice she could muster, "Hey, Bead-brain, how about a cigarette?"

Bead elbowed her ineffectually, swerving the car. "You watch your mouth, bitch!"

"You watch the damn road, will ya?" she said.

"Yeah," Coughlin said, "watch the fucking road. You gonna break all our loot before we get to payday here."

"And gimme a cigarette," Rosy persisted. "It's the least you can do after you guys muscled in on my territory."

"Your territory?" Coughlin was curious. And amused. Bead didn't know exactly what he was. "Give her a cigarette, Bead."

"What?!"

"You heard me, Bead, now give her a goddamned cigarette!"

He did. She reached forward awkwardly with the cuffed hands and punched the cigarette lighter.

"What's this about your territory, girlie?"

"Well, I've been working these old guys for two years now. You think I'm not doing exactly what you're doing?"

"Oh, yeah? Tell me about it."

She lit the cigarette and dragged deeply, the nicotine making her light-headed, loose. It gave her confidence. "I'm not into guns. That's your thing. But I've been taking their stuff just like you. . . . You use a gun and muscle; I have to con 'em. They got it; we don't. I got tired of being the sucker with nothing."

Coughlin predictably jumped on that one. "So you did some sucking for something, huh?"

Bead joined in. "Yeah, I bet she did, Wilbur, you're right about that."

"What're you laughing at, asshole? Coughlin told you to toot his root, I bet you'd dive on the big tool with more gusto than I would!"

The van weaved precariously as Bead struggled to get beyond the hands she got up before he could hit her.

Between his howls of laughter, Coughlin yelled, "Bead, you break any of that china back there, it's comin' outa your share! Drive the car straight, or you're gonna be walkin'."

I'm doing it, I'm laughing; something I didn't think I'd ever do again, and I'm looking back at a wild-eyed bastard who's laughing, too. He's laughing with me at Bead; we're laughing together. We have a common interest: dumping on Bead-brain.

She was there, she knew she was. She was ready for step two: she put the cigarette, now slightly crooked from the tussle, but still smoking, into her mouth and extended her wrists in front of Coughlin. "Come on, Wilbur. Are these things really necessary? What am I gonna do, beat you up if you take 'em off so I can smoke a cigarette without cutting myself?"

"It ain't smart, Coughlin. It ain't smart," Bead piped up.

Coughlin's own suspicions showed on his face. Rosy smiled as she held his gaze. "That's rich, isn't it, Wilbur? Bead-brain talking about what's smart?"

"The bitch is trying to trick you, Wilbur."

"Shut your face, Bead, I don't need your advice!"

"Come on, Wilbur. I'm doing more for you than this runt. Least you can do is let me smoke a damn cigarette without these things on. Or are you afraid, like him?"

She kept on smiling: Here it is, big fella, you deranged maniac, what could silly little me do to big old you, who aren't afraid of anything? Half joke and half dare, betting that Coughlin didn't pass up many dares.

And what man wouldn't have a charitable spot for a woman who has just told his buddy that he's got a big tool? Even maniacs have egos; especially maniacs have egos. She hoped and prayed and smiled and looked back into his squinting eyes until finally he dug in his pocket for the key and opened the cuffs.

Her first thought when her hands were free was to stick the cigarette in his eye. It was almost impossible not to try, but she remembered his speed and smiled and rubbed her wrists gently, caught Coughlin's eye, winked at him—yes, she actually winked at him, the way he had at her through the windshield of the Ferrari. Then she put her hands by her ears and wiggled her fingers and blew a raspberry at Bead. "Take that, shithead."

He gave her a look that dripped malevolence, but he kept his hands on the wheel. Things were going entirely too fast for him to keep up.

Coughlin smiled back at her. Chuckling, he reached out and gently corralled a handful of her hair, not pulling hard, just grasping the handle. The man was crazy about pulling girls' hair. And why not? He was crazy about everything. "I think you liked what I gave you last night, girlie."

Oh, God, where's this going? she thought, and took the plunge. "Not the pain, Wilbur, not the beating and burns. Maybe some people like it, but I don't. . . ." She could see the thin smile freezing on his face and let him wonder whether she'd go on for a moment before adding, "But the other stuff was good, Wilbur. I like strong men, and if I hadn't been in so much pain, I wouldn't have been complaining.

"That's why I was glad to hear you have principles, Wilbur. You don't kill people you work with. We're working together, Wilbur. I did my share tonight, and I have more addresses just like this one. I pay my way. Long as I know you aren't going to kill me, maybe we could find a way to pass the time till you let me go."

Rosy knew she was going too fast, but now that she was going she couldn't stop.

"I couldn't go to the cops. I did these men before you did. After I took their money and ran, they would never believe I wasn't a willing participant in the robbery, so there's no way I'd ever go to the cops. If I did, I'd be the one in jail faster than you. . . ."

He tightened his grip in a little spasm that made her shut up. Something told her not to smile then, not to suppress the fear she felt. He was thinking about sex, and she didn't hide the fact that she knew she was completely in his power and scared out of her wits. That might help now. No sense hiding fear when fear is what people want to see.

He stared at her, and she felt she'd blown it. She'd played the cards too quickly, and he was realizing that it was just a way to get out alive. He'd been only playing along and would put her through another session of pain. The thought made her feel faint, and her hair took more of the weight of her head. Slowly he let her go and looked ahead at the road coming at them in the car's self-made tunnel of light.

She took another drag on the cigarette when she noticed it was still in her hand. Quiet. That's what he'd want now . . . a quiet and submissive woman. It wouldn't do to go any further.

The booty rattled behind them, reminding her of Anthony Panoff and the necklace he'd bought for her from Michael for thirty thousand dollars . . . when he could have given her something from his floor safe. Why didn't he? The question made her uncomfortable.

She looked at it from a new perspective and wondered if she'd been wrong about her whole scam. She'd seen it as refusing to sell. Maybe she had sold. She'd displayed the product and given little bits of free sample to stimulate the market. With the necklace they bought only what she tacitly offered for sale. Then, she'd failed to make delivery after they'd paid in advance.

The cigarette was out. She put it in the ashtray.

With her hands free, she told herself, anything was possible.

Even cuffed, she'd snatched and planted the business card. She had Coughlin thinking. That was bound to get him in trouble, she thought.

What would she look like after the abuse she'd taken? Would her looks be spoiled with a broken nose . . . and other ugly scars? She'd felt so close to some understanding with Charlie. What he took from her didn't diminish her. How would he feel now? Was she ruined for him? Could he still love her?

Was that the wrong word, love? Of course it was. How could he love her? He didn't know her. His passion for her . . . the heat she felt from him . . . did it get beyond something oozing and bubbling from his glands; hormonal tides for which she was the moon? Would he still feel it if he saw her looking the way she did now?

If that's all it was, why did she care? she asked herself. Because she wanted him to feel it. She felt it, too, but she felt more than that, and thought he did, too. Something that was an attitude about the world, and he was her access to it. She could feel better about the rest, because of what she could see in him . . . as though he were a prism through which an ugly world looked not so bad.

What would he think of her if he really knew her? If she saw him again, now that she could see what she'd really done, would she tell him how she'd lived? Could she make him understand? No. Never.

She thought it was about the time that Anthony Panoff would be getting home. How long before he read the card?

If I were free, what would I do tomorrow?

In bed that night, Coughlin still inflicted pain, but the sense of menace was tempered by the fact that she knew he would keep her alive for more burglaries, and he'd left the cuffs off. She thought his heart wasn't in it; reasoned that he wasn't accustomed to regular sex. Like a black widow or a praying mantis, and for the same reason, his mates were one-night stands. The smile she was intermittently able to show him felt like a Halloween mask.

He settled, finally, and seemed to be drifting off to sleep. She was wide awake. She saw herself creeping naked to the front door, throwing it open, running silently into the night . . . no wasted noise or motion that might awaken him . . . as she'd done from Dr. Regar, only this time she'd have no Ferrari.

Then he rolled off the bed, got the cuffs, and attached her ankle to a brass rung.

"You don't need those, Wilbur. I'm starting to like you."

He snorted, "Yeah, well, I wouldn't want you wandering off . . . not long's you got more boyfriends. Don't take it personal. Think of it as business insurance."

She wondered if she should have said "love" instead of "like." Could he be aware that either one was absurd? Does he know he's loathsome? Or does he think inflicting pain gives him charisma? Are there really such people? She didn't know how to play it.

"There's only one more, Wilbur . . . only one more place I can lead you." It wasn't true, but she had to find an end to it. If the police didn't come, it had to end anyway. Whenever, she expected him to torture her for more, but she had resolved that either he was going to kill her at the end, or he wasn't. Where the end came probably wouldn't matter. He surprised her.

"Well, we can't stay here forever, anyway."

She couldn't stop herself from asking, "Then what, Wilbur? Are you going to kill me or let me go?"

Something in her voice seemed to rouse him. He rolled to his elbow and peered at her in the dim light that spilled through the open bathroom doorway.

"Of course I'm gonna kill you, girlie. Soon as you run out of boyfriends or do one more thing to get us caught. You don't think I bought that horseshit about us being partners, do ya?" He giggled and crawled on top of her again.

This time she didn't even whimper as tears rolled down her cheeks. She wiped them away and bared her teeth at him when he raised himself to look down at her as his lower body undulated its invasions. She could only play out the role and hope he'd change his mind.

When she finally slept, she dreamed of doors that shattered as SWAT teams burst through them. Her heart sank lower each time her eyes snapped open, each time she saw that nothing had changed.

Anthony Panoff looked at the scene in disgust: police all over the place with their little crime-stopper kits. He really didn't care about the items stolen—they had faded into the background years ago, and they were insured. It was just going to be an outrageous inconvenience to replace them. The idea hit him that it might be easier to just sell the musty old place, get a small apartment on Beacon Hill, spend more time at the Cape. The thought gave him small relief.

He spotted the stack of mail on the counter, picked it up, and flipped through it halfheartedly. When he saw Jason's card, he figured the maid had found it somewhere, like under the cushion of a chair. He couldn't remember meeting the man, and the last thing he needed was another attorney. He tossed it in the trash.

21

While guzzling morning coffee in an effort to clear the adhesions in his brain, Charlie called the hospital and learned that Lew's condition was listed as stable. He hurried through a shower and walked to Mass General; he found Lucy sitting beside the bed. Lew appeared to be sleeping.

She came into the hall when she saw Charlie. Lew had been in surgery for four hours as they'd struggled to put one of his lungs and surrounding muscle and blood vessels back together; he'd waked up long enough to talk to her and allay her fear of his being brain-impaired from the dangerous amount of blood he'd lost.

Charlie was appalled at how frail he looked, suspended between, and dependent upon, tubes that led into and out of him in humiliating ways. His usual ruddy complexion was sallowed and sagging. His right eye was swollen shut.

Lucy touched him, and he opened the other one, raised his head toward Charlie. "Didja find her?" he asked, his voice rasping but urgent.

"Not yet. But I still have ideas. I might get lucky this morning. Don't try to talk, buddy."

"I blew it. Had the gun on 'im, saw Rosy, and thought I'd

made a mistake. I pointed at the sky. He nailed me before I could blink."

"How could you know she'd be with a killer? You did what you could. If you insist on talking, tell me what he looked like."

"Big as me. Dark brown hair, late thirties. Last thing I saw was his teeth. Yellowed. One of the front ones only half there. He was grinning. He liked it."

Charlie put his hand on his shoulder. "Try to play sleepy with the cops for another day. See if your doctor can keep them away until tomorrow. If I don't get anywhere today, we'll tell them the truth. Easier if you don't have to change your story."

On his way to Michael Barkum's store, Charlie contended with the part of his brain he called the chorus of the mean-spirited. Regarding Rosy, there was an emerging consensus: the lady's bad news, with a guttural *bad*. The chorus offered the seductive argument that since it wasn't his karma creating the storm, he had no obligation to stay and ride it out. The more he learned, the less his intuitions painted Rosy as an innocent bystander.

He remembered, however, that when he had thought the poison was leaking from sunken barrels in his own past, he had just wanted to grab Rosy and leave. Was it fair to assume the worst about Rosy, now that he knew it was her past acting up? The chorus said, Who cares about fair, we're talking lethal weapons here, but he kept walking until he stood in front of Barkum's window.

As he focused on the necklace of daffodil diamonds, his hand moved unbidden to feel under his shirt for the Savage automatic tucked into his waistband. Then it occurred to him that there could be two of them; that nobody would be fool enough to abduct a woman, then hang her jewelry in a window the next day. Still, he couldn't help feeling he was on the right track, and that made the pistol comforting.

Finding the door locked, he pushed the button by the brass plaque. He jumped when a voice by his hand said, "We're not opening today . . . sickness in the family."

Without knowing whether the intercom was one way or two way, Charlie said, "I just want to talk with you."

No response. He pushed the button again. "We're not buying today, either. Please come back tomorrow."

"I want to buy the necklace in the window."

The answer came quickly, and Charlie heard a certain urgency in the voice now. "Who is down there?"

"Charlie Gamble. I'm a friend of Rosy Marlette's."

"Wait there, Mr. Gamble. I'll be right down."

In a moment Charlie saw a small, vigorous man with a tuft of white hair and a squinted right eye coming down the stairs. He had a newspaper in his hand. They introduced themselves, and Michael asked where they could go to talk; he said the bell would drive him nuts if they stayed at his store. Charlie suggested the coffee shop at the Parker House.

When they had their coffee Michael said, "What has happened?"

"I was hoping you could tell me."

"How did you know to come to me? Why did you come?"

"I came because I'm trying to find Rosy. I saw a jewelry box with your logo on it and thought you might be able to tell me where to look. I really didn't expect the reception I got, though. How do you know Rosy . . . and how did you know my name?"

Michael hesitated, thinking, his mouth poised in the shape of an "O," then said, "I'm afraid Rosy and I are . . . partners in crime." Charlie could see the statement caused him some pain. "She mentioned your name to me a few days ago. Now I think she's in an awful fix, and needs help or she may be killed. It's trouble of her own devising, I'm afraid, but I intend to try to help her anyway, despite the fact that it may be dangerous. Knowing that, are you prepared to get involved, or would you prefer to stay out of it?"

"Get involved? There have been three attempts on my life in the last few days, Michael. You're the first person I've run into who may know why. What the hell is going on?"

Michael insisted on hearing Charlie's story first. He listened

181

with puzzlement and horror to the tales of hit and run, the purple-haired gunman, and Lew's undoing. When the story ended, Michael took a moment to struggle over some internal conflict before he said, "You've made nothing clear to me, but Rosy has been playing a dangerous game . . . with my help, I regret to say. It seems to have backfired. It will take some explaining."

Charlie soon realized that meant Michael intended to tell her life story, which he proceeded to do insofar as he knew it, including her mother's marriages, her college career, and her marriage to Douglas Marlette. He was surprised that Charlie already knew that part.

He skipped to two years before, when Rosy came into his shop, asked for an appraisal of a diamond necklace. He gave her a retail figure of thirty thousand. She left, pleased. Days later, she returned wanting to sell it. Naive about the necessary margins of business, she was disappointed by his low offer. Seeing her distress, he tried to be kind.

She left, only to return again and invite him to lunch to discuss a business proposition. Michael bashfully admitted that he accepted without question only because of the pleasure he took in her company. They dined at the Ritz, and he could tell she was a woman of some breeding and intelligence before she broached the topic on her mind. . . .

Rosy said, "Michael, I wanted to get to know you before I got to the point. Now that I have, I think maybe I've picked the wrong man."

"Not knowing your mission, I can't argue, but I humbly submit that I hope you're wrong."

She smiled. "You're very gallant. But you may be wishing your own downfall."

"My downfall, Rosy? That happened before you were born."

"I can't believe that. It's obvious that you're a very upright individual, and my proposition may be beneath you."

"I appreciate your vote of confidence, but what you take for my uprightness may be nothing more than the lot in life of a bent old man. Who would sin with me?"

"Now you're teasing me."

"Come, come. Out with it. What is on your mind?"

She was visibly reluctant, but she began. "I find myself the object of flattering attentions from a man who wants to give me a gift. He's quite a bit older than I, and I assure you, our relationship is one that is strictly platonic. I can't explain it, really . . . unless maybe he sees me as sort of an adopted niece."

"Is that all? That is no mystery to me, my dear. I'm sure it's quite proper" ("What an old fool I was," Michael averred as he told the tale) "and you'll give him great pleasure by accepting his gift. Perhaps I could show him a nice string of pearls?"

"He's wealthy, actually, and his generosity may well outstrip a string of pearls."

"Well, in that case . . . you have a beautiful necklace; perhaps diamond earrings, or a brooch, to set it off?" ("I confess," Michael told Charlie, "my merchant's blood was rising.")

"If I may be candid, what I need is not a fancy present, but money. I could live for months on the amount he'd spend on a frivolity. Now, I just can't bring myself to say this to my, ah . . . uncle; I mean, he isn't really an uncle, and how would it look, a woman taking money from a man?"

"Quite," Michael agreed, somewhat taken aback.

"As you know, Michael, I have that necklace, a bequest from my mother" ("The girls all say that." Michael leered. "She later admitted to me that the necklace was a present from a very rich man she barely knew. It was that gift which gave birth to the idea for a scam") "which you've told me is worth thirty thousand dollars at retail. I have an idea that would enable me to keep the necklace in her memory, but also sell it, if you'd help me."

"And how do you intend to do that?"

"Suppose I were fo give the necklace to you, then send my uncle to your store. . . . Would you sell it to him and pass the money through to me? That way, when he gives me the necklace, I'll have both. It will solve my money problems, and I'll still have Mother's necklace. I'd pay you a commission, of course," she added quickly.

Michael smiled as he recounted the interview to Charlie. "Well, of course, initially I was shocked. But I'll admit I was also amused. The thought of some old reprobate doting on this young beauty, and that she'd concocted such a scheme to turn his affections into cold cash! I'll tell you, Charlie, in the gem business, one learns to roll with the punches. It's a crazy world."

Resigning himself to the fact that Michael was a very deliberate storyteller, Charlie ordered more coffee. Michael accepted with a nod and the words, "Two sugars."

"Also, I realized there was, in fact, nothing illegal about what Rosy was proposing; conniving and dishonest, certainly, but illegal, no. I could take her necklace on a consignment basis and sell it to whomever I pleased. It's done all the time. It was a mark of her naiveté that she'd told me the background at all. I agreed to do it for a ten percent commission."

Charlie chuckled. "Her naiveté? You know damn well the commission would normally be more like fifty percent on such a deal, Michael. To me, it sounds more like guile than naiveté, and it worked."

Michael blushed but made no further attempt to cover the fact that he'd allowed Rosy to manipulate him. "Maybe. In fact, I became so fond of her that, on a whim, after the transaction, I gave her the full amount. I told her that she could think of me as another doting uncle.

"Well, I think that first episode was every bit as innocent as Rosy described it . . . dear God, I hope so, anyway. The old goat was twenty years older than I am if he was a day!" Michael's disapproval was clearly aimed at his peer, who should have known better. "Had it stopped there, it would have remained a charming episode in the dull later years of a jeweler.

"But a few months later, Rosy reappeared. She had another

'uncle.' To my everlasting opprobrium—I should have known when to stop—a cycle was begun. Rosy kept sending the necklace out to catch thirty grand. The uncles got younger—not as young as she, but young enough that they were difficult to cast as aspiring to uncledom, if you see what I mean. I scolded her, of course, but I lacked conviction, because I didn't want her to disappear. I know it sounds foolish, but you must understand that life can grow dull . . . and Rosy was a very appealing exception."

Charlie realized now the reason for Michael's insistence on telling how he and Rosy became involved in their hustle. His contrition was evident: he was in confession; he wanted Charlie to understand.

"How many times did you see her? How many 'uncles' were there?" Charlie asked.

"There were . . . four, in two years' time, but I saw her more than that."

From his years in business, Charlie was not without honed instincts at catching lies. He thought four might be a low figure, that Michael was trying to minimize her transgressions, and maybe his own.

"We'd become friends, I think, because sometimes she'd call even when no business was discussed, and we'd meet for lunch."

Charlie didn't say it, but in sales it's called a rapport call . . . building the perception of friendship with a useless visit, the intent being ongoing control of a valuable ally. He suspected Michael knew that but didn't want to believe it. Whether Rosy did was a question he couldn't answer.

"She'd tell me about her trips around the globe. That's what she did with the money—traveled. Aimlessly, it seemed, but I enjoyed her travelogues. And I drew her out. Even as I tried to dissuade her from her philandering, I began to get the picture of a past that made her behavior comprehensible."

Charlie refilled his cup and offered some to Michael.

"No, thank you . . . aging kidneys."

"This is all very enlightening, Michael, but where is she?"

"I'm afraid there's more to my story, yes. What I've told you so far is really preamble. . . . I didn't want you to think she was an experienced criminal. I think that would be a mistake. I wanted you to understand the events that brought her to her unsavory . . . ah . . . profession, before I told you that when I saw her last week . . . her intent was to work one more scam."

"You mean, that's where she went when she disappeared? To hustle some guy into buying her necklace?!"

"Precisely." Michael watched him for a moment.

"Sweet bleeding Jesus," was all he could manage.

"On Monday, she called on the phone to tell me the mark's name. I scolded her—halfheartedly, I'm afraid—but to my great surprise, she told me she planned to leave with you, but she was gun-shy. I hope you'll agree, based on what I've told you about her past, that she may have been justified in that. She wanted enough money to bail out if you turned out to be . . . a disappointment."

Charlie was still trying to decide whether to be pleased that Rosy had said she was leaving with him or pissed that she didn't trust him, when Michael went on.

"Then I read in this morning's paper a report of the stabbing on your boat. The description of the couple the police were searching for . . . it must have been Rosy, the hostage of a violent criminal. Alarmed, I tried to prove myself wrong by calling the home of Jason Richards . . . the mark." Charlie recognized the name, but he didn't interrupt. "The phone was out of order. I called his office and was told that he is out of town on a family emergency. Under the circumstances, it only increased my fears. Then I saw this in the same paper."

He handed a newspaper to Charlie, directed his attention to an article that detailed a robbery at the residence of one Anthony Panoff, well-known Boston businessman, founder of the largest independent CPA firm in town. The thieves had known where to find hidden keys, with which they'd turned off the alarms and gained access to the house. They had also known Mr. Panoff's schedule well enough to plan the burglary during his habitual midweek trip to Hyannis. Charlie looked up from the clipping.

"Anthony Panoff," Michael said, "was one of the men to whom I sold her necklace."

"So you've decided that three maybes add up to a certainty?"

"Yes. I don't know what's going on, Charlie, but I'm certain that Rosy wasn't a willing accomplice in the crime that took place on your boat, or the robbery of Mr. Panoff. She has taken some shortcuts, but these things are beyond her. I want you to help me find her and get her away from whoever is controlling her."

Charlie watched the white-browed eye that blinked excitedly at him from across the table and thought Michael was ridiculous in the role of rescuer. He wondered if the assessment wouldn't also apply to himself. "Are you sure this isn't beyond us now, Michael? Shouldn't we go to the police?"

His smile showed embarrassment, a cover for stronger emotions. "Charlie, Rosy is . . . special. I've watched her ruining herself and tried my damnedest to make her stop. . . . I told her once that I was through, that I wouldn't be a party to her game anymore. I thought what she was doing would destroy her from within. She said she would only find someone else to help her. I relented, but I was losing hope, really, that I would see her make a turnaround.

"I was wrong. Something is still intact. She's ready to begin again. Her feeling for you was what she needed to pull her out of her dive. She almost made it."

Much as Charlie had hoped Rosy's professions of love were genuine, on the heels of the story he'd just heard, he didn't feel the elation he had thought that news would bring.

"Whatever is happening," Michael continued, "I know it isn't her doing. You know it isn't her doing"—Do I? Charlie wondered—"but that may be hard to prove in court. The legal process, possible time in jail—it could be a setback from which she'd never recover. With your help, I thought maybe we could handle it some other way."

Charlie could see that Michael was suffering. He was

hopelessly in love with Rosy, though he tried to conceal it beneath a veneer of unclelike concern. He probably didn't know it himself. He was certain that she was innocent.

Charlie was in love with her, too, but, well versed in love's notorious myopia, still reeling from the morning's revelations, he wasn't eager to place any bets on her innocence. But then, on his sliding hierarchy of human characteristics, innocence wasn't very highly ranked lately. Sometimes it seemed little more than a booby prize, the withered thing a person got to keep when he couldn't muster the will and the wherewithal to fight fire with fire.

"So what do you suggest we do, Michael?"

His relief was evident, though he didn't smile. "I'd say we have to reconnoiter Jason Richards's house, see what we can learn."

22

Charlie crept around Jason's house looking in the windows. Only with great difficulty had he convinced Michael to wait in the car. Finally, Michael had seen the wisdom in somebody being able to go for help if Rosy's captors got the upper hand. He'd agreed to give Charlie an hour, then give it up and summon the police, hoping there'd still be somebody to save.

Charlie found life in the kitchen, a large, athletic-looking man, seated by a butcher-block island, a gun beside his hand, and Rosy . . . Jesus, Rosy! What's happened to your poor face?

The rage that welled up in him almost pushed him to break the glass and fire at the man. Then he realized there might be others in another room. He might only get her killed.

It took time to move around the rest of the windows without being detected. He couldn't check the upstairs but decided to chance it. He'd moved to the back door, was about to burst in and fire at the man point-blank, when he heard an engine coming up the driveway. He concealed himself in some shrubbery, waited to see what he was up against. As soon as he did, he heard the voice of the man in the kitchen with startling clarity. He was saying something about a doctor. Charlie realized there was a sheet-metal exhaust vent beside his ear.

· · ·

Rosy kept looking at the black handles of the knives that protruded from the butcher block in the kitchen. She remembered reading in a novel that plunging one into a person's body isn't the simple task it's made out to be . . . that it takes a huge amount of force to shove the thing home to a vital organ, that the blade could break on a bone, that the victim seldom keels over dead at the first thrust. And she hadn't forgotten Coughlin's speed. Still, Coughlin was intentionally tempting her by leaving them at hand while he watched her fix him a steak. He was succeeding.

Bead was on a trip to a fence in Boston, selling the spoils of the Anthony Panoff robbery. Coughlin sat on an oaken stool beside the butcher block. His face showed both concentration and amusement as he watched her move around the kitchen.

She fixed a plate for each of them: steak, potato, and canned peas. She put the plates on the cutting table and sat across from him. He smirked at her and began to eat. He chewed with his mouth open.

"Sorta homey, ain't it? Like we's married or somethin'."

"Yes, I guess it is." It took all of her control to carry off a semblance of normalcy; terse commands to puppet-wire nerves that pulled the planes of her face and made her broken nose throb in protest.

He laughed at her response. She didn't know if it was because he was proud of himself for winning her over or because he found her persistent attempt to lull him with her pretense of criminal partnership so transparent. She had nothing to lose.

All night and all morning she'd expected the cops to arrive. Finally she'd admitted to herself that something had gone wrong with the business card.

"Soon as Bead gets back from droppin' off the stuff from last night, we'll take another load from here. Then we're ready for another one, girlie. Where we goin' tonight?"

"A doctor's house." It was the only remaining place where she felt she could predict that nobody would be at home.

"Wooo, doggies, a doctor, huh? They got lots of scratch, and

I got the itch! But you know that, don't you, girlie? You know I got the itch, don't you?"

"Yeah, Wilbur, you got the itch."

He stopped laughing suddenly, ate a mouthful of food. "He likely to be there?"

"Not if we're early. He and some friends of his play poker from nine to midnight every Thursday. We can get in and out with no trouble, just like last night."

They heard a car coming into the garage, and Coughlin walked out the door with his gun in his hand. She could hear him talking to Bead and stood up with the wild thought that she might make the front door and be gone before he remembered he'd left her uncuffed and unwatched. He was giving Bead hell over something that was still in the van that he was supposed to have unloaded. She started across the floor, stopping when she heard them coming her way. In the last instant, her eyes fell on the Sabatier knives. She snatched one of medium length and slipped it into her blouse as they stepped into the kitchen.

"No, you dumb shit," Coughlin was saying, "we ain't gonna take it later with the stuff from tonight's job. Why take a chance on an extra burglary count by carryin' stuff from two jobs at once? We unload everything as fast as possible. That way we don't hold on to no evidence. It's the smart way to do it.

"You believe this guy, girlie? He wants to take the loot from one job along in the van to the next job."

"Dumb, Bead, really dumb!" she said. Coughlin had latched on to her game of the night before, and every time he wanted to rag on Bead now, he included her in the attack. He liked seeing Bead squirm under it. Any chance she'd ever had of making Bead an ally was now long gone.

Bead managed a little burst in his defense. "Hell, Wilbur, ya said don't take less than two hundred for them fancy candlesticks, and he wouldn't go over one fifty."

"Because he figured you for dumb enough to take it. You

watch. We gotta take the rest a this shit in anyway. This time we'll go with you, and I'll get two fifty."

Rosy drew a laugh from Coughlin by telling Bead she could have gotten more than one fifty for the candelabra, and she wasn't even a thief. "At least I wasn't until you guys came along."

A new idea was rising with the knife in her blouse. Maybe if she could drop it by the bed before he saw it. . . . When he was asleep . . . both hands into his throat, where the artery was near the surface. Then she realized she'd said this was the last one tonight. Maybe she wouldn't be alive when Coughlin slept next. Maybe she'd never make it back from the robbery. "By the way, Wilbur, I remembered another place we can hit tomorrow."

He giggled. "Girl, you're too much."

Bead looked at the remains of the steaks on the plates and checked the stove to see if there was one for him. There wasn't.

Coughlin and Bead loaded the few remaining valuables at Jason's house in a matter of minutes. Soon the three of them piled into the van, Rosy sitting in the middle smoking a cigarette.

Charlie made sure they were gone before he stirred from the shrubbery where he'd been hiding. The things he'd heard told him he had some time, so he didn't want to go cowboying in, one against two, end up with all the wrong people dead.

One thing he grudgingly conceded: Michael had been right about the cops. If it had been a cop in his place, Rosy would be a long time explaining: fixing a meal, bantering with a thug, telling him where they were going to rob next, serving food, smiling at him, sitting down to eat beside a rack of knives.

Charlie had no idea how she'd gotten into the fix, but he had no trouble explaining her behavior as biding her time toward a chance to get out of it. But then, he knew her a little—and a judge and jury wouldn't. A stranger watching might even have thought she was the ringleader, the goons working for her. A district attorney would have used her nefarious scamming past to sew her into a sack of accusation more convincing than truth.

Checking his watch, he saw he still had fifteen minutes before Michael would leave without him. He entered through the open garage door and crept into the house. He'd just seen them leave, but the oddness of being in a stranger's home made him stand still for a full minute listening. Where was Jason Richards? Maybe there were others.

The kitchen looked like a fraternity had camped there, dirty dishes piled in the sink, garbage overflowing the pail, empty cans around the counter. There were pieces of furniture missing around the living room, depressions in the carpet where things had been. He saw the stain in front of a chair and decided it had to be blood.

Upstairs he found the master bedroom. The covers were in disarray. There was blood on the sheets. In the bathroom, there were more flecks of blood around the white tile floor. He picked up a crumpled piece of cloth. It was a woman's dress. It appeared to have been pulled apart. He held it to his face and breathed a fragrance that was Rosy.

On the vanity was a pack of Marlboros and a butane lighter. Someone had stamped out three or four cigarettes . . . next to those was another article of clothing, a pair of panties, also torn. Looking at them, he thought at first they had a sloppy pattern of lace. Something made him look more closely. He saw that the holes in the panties had black edges. His fingers began to tremble as the reality behind the clues came into focus, and he leaned into the john and retched for a long, long time.

He washed his face and rinsed out his mouth, his mind struggling to make the pieces fit into place. He stumbled down the stairs. He got out to the garage and remembered something. He ran back in and raced from closet to closet, throwing open the doors. In the downstairs bedroom, he found the rest of Jason Richards, the part that hadn't leaked onto the floor.

He heard a footfall behind him and whirled, the gun outstretched before him.

"Don't shoot, it's me!" Michael shouted.

"Jesus, I told you to wait in the car!" Charlie said, letting himself buckle backward onto the bed, running his hand through his hair.

"I saw a van drive out. Didn't know whether you might have been caught. When you didn't follow, I decided to check." Michael carried a golf club.

"That wouldn't have done much good, Michael," Charlie told him. "These people are rougher than that." He pointed into the closet.

Michael looked, swallowed hard, turned back to Charlie. "Where's Rosy?"

"She's with them . . . two of them, guns in evidence. . . . I couldn't charge them without taking a chance on her being killed in the process." He remembered Rosy saying they were going to a doctor's house. "Were any of Rosy's marks doctors?"

It was a visible effort for him to concentrate, his squinted eye winking, fingers rubbing his brow vigorously. "Yes. One. The last one."

"Where does he live?"

"I don't know . . . I have his address at the office. . . ."

"Do you know his name?"

His breathing was rushed. His mouth open, he stared at Charlie. "I have his name written down at the shop, but I've forgotten it. I can't think of it."

They walked back into the kitchen, both of them deep in thought. Charlie paused by the butcher block. Overlapping the horrific images of Rosy's ordeal was the idea that something on it was different. An exercise . . . what's wrong with this picture?

He looked at his watch. "Come on. Let's go!"

He took Michael's arm and hustled him down the driveway and along the street to the place where they'd pulled Michael's car off the road. As they were driving toward Boston, Michael pressed to know what Charlie had found.

He spoke angrily. "Forget that! Empty your mind of everything but that doctor's name. Rosy's life may depend on your thinking of it before we have to drive all the way to your shop."

194

He drove Michael's car faster than a Dodge Aries is meant to go. What he'd seen upstairs had made things plain: Rosy's captor wasn't just brutal; he was terribly, lethally, capriciously mad, wired so loosely that the smallest fleck of surprise might cause the short circuit that would end her life. The next place they would predictably be was this doctor's house, and he couldn't risk putting the resolution off beyond that time.

He'd solved the puzzle of the butcher-block scene: through the window, he'd seen four knives there, and now there were three. Rosy had stolen one, and that meant she was desperate enough to try to use it. Even with the adrenaline of desperation, she'd never get by the eyes that he'd seen watching her, waiting for her to try.

He played scene after scene in his mind, wondering if he could get by them either. Two men . . . a house he didn't know . . . when would Rosy make a move with the knife she'd lifted? How would he get to them without her being in the way—reach for the sky, ingrates? Fat chance.

Michael was thinking out loud, going through his last conversation with Rosy in an attempt to jog his memory with some association. "The doctor . . . was violent with her. The first time it ever happened. I'd seen his arrogance when he came into my shop. Not a nice man. She'd fled his house in fear the night before she met you. What is his name, the scoundrel?"

Charlie heard what he said, and tumblers clicked into place. The thugs with Rosy didn't explain the attempts on his life. He remembered how Rosy's Ferrari stood out in the parking lot at the marina. He remembered a man watching them from the bridge. As he thought it through, it seemed preposterous, but he was beginning to think the way to stay alive was to strive for the nastiest interpretation of the partial picture one got of reality, connect the dots with meanness, treat it as a working hypothesis.

At Michael's office, they would learn where the next crime would take place. He could only hope that he would get to the unnamed doctor's house first, and that scouting the terrain early would provide some advantage. The margin was slim, but it was all he had.

By the time Michael had run into his store and gotten Regar's name and address, Charlie had thought of a few things he might need. He stopped at the boat to get them before they hurried north.

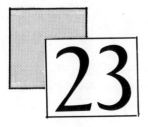

23

"Never get old, Gamble. The muscles slide low on the bones, like falling socks, and the brain becomes a rusty bucket. I used to have a great memory."

"How do you know? Maybe you've just forgotten that you were always forgetful."

Michael sneered at him.

Charlie's preparations had consumed more time than he had wanted, but he didn't expect Rosy and her captors until nine. When he pulled over, concealing the Dodge behind some trees a few hundred yards from Regar's house, it was eight o'clock, and that seemed time enough.

"Remember what happened when you sneaked in behind me. I could have killed you by accident. So stay put!"

"Your chosen illustration does nothing to instill confidence. Maybe you should stay here, and I should go in with the gun."

"Screw you. If the van gets here and leaves before I get back, get to a phone and call the cops." He closed the car door and started up the hill through the woods.

From the trees, he could see a cedar-shingled house with white trim, a big old beachy New England affair. There were pools of light on the surrounding lawn and lights on inside. A lawn sprinkler sprayed water in circles to the left of the door.

He couldn't tell from his vantage point whether it was occupied or not. He decided to head for the shadows beside the house and struck out, only to dart back into the woods when the door swung open.

The man who emerged walked with an aggressive stride. He cut off the sprinkler and went into the garage on the far side of the house. A motor started, and a black Ferrari shot across the lighted cobblestones and disappeared down the hill. Charlie waited until he heard it stop at the street, then go through a couple of gears down the road, apparently in a hurry. Dr. Regar, off to a game of poker.

Circling the house, looking in the windows, he decided nobody was there. An upstairs window, above an old-fashioned front porch, was partially open. He donned the latex gloves he'd brought to be sure he left no prints . . . he kept them on the boat for painting. He climbed onto the porch roof, slit the screen with his rigging knife, and flipped the hooks that held it in place.

As silently as he could, he moved from room to room until he was sure he was alone. The house had the tidy/tornado contrast of a bachelor who has a maid come in twice a week: beds in the guest rooms just a bit too smooth; ashtrays sparkling clean; magazines, current issues only, in a fanned stack on the coffee table . . . that balanced by a sink full of dishes, an unmade master's bed, and a cluttered office where the maid was probably forbidden to go.

He tried to imagine how burglars would move through the house, tried to envision how he would capture two armed men without putting Rosy at even greater risk. In the movies, the bad guys were always grabbing the lady and using her as a shield. What would they do with Rosy while they were rifling the house?

The character of Regar came into focus as Charlie moved through the rooms. The place was full of trophies, some of them silver. The guy was an equestrian and a marksman. There were pictures on the wall of him in jodhpurs, in jackets with patches over the shoulders and rifles across his arms. He didn't smile in photos. He looked humorless as hell.

Three exterior doors triangulated the house: center front, in a hallway that separated the living and dining rooms; left rear, from the kitchen to the attached garage; right rear, from the study into a screen porch that jutted out from that corner of the house.

The study was the room most lived in. An Apple computer sat on a side table next to the desk, which was a huge mahogany affair with a square of glass on which to write; across two walls, built-in shelves with medical books and journals lined up on them went from floor to ceiling.

One shelf was conceded to inane gifts from relatives who were impressed by having a doctor in the family. It was a regular menagerie of plaster-of-Paris doctors with stethoscopes and reflectors over their eyes. Charlie was reminded of how good it had felt to toss all the sailboat junk people had given him when he'd cleared out of his house on the heels of his divorce.

Then he noticed what the thieves would probably have seen first when they walked into the room—framed on the walls, in tight eye-level rows, were felt-mounted coins. Charlie didn't know diddly about rare coins, but he knew an expensive framing job when he saw it. Maybe they weren't worth much, but they had the look of something inherited from a grandfather.

He froze upon noticing a small box on the wall, partially concealed by curtains that could be pulled to conceal the collection; it made him wonder if there were cop cars at that moment on silent approach to the house. It was an alarm system. Examining the thing closely, he saw that it was turned off, the key in the hole. The doctor must have forgotten to activate it in his haste. It seemed strange, but then how many people sit on their seat belts? We get too familiar with ever-present risks. When on, it had a row of concealed beams that would have been interrupted by opening the curtains or an attempt to move the coins . . . apparently on the theory that any thief would be relaxed by the time he got that far into the house . . .

wouldn't notice the paraphernalia until it was too late. The frames were in regular rows; a blank space indicated one frame was missing. He spotted the empty frame, sitting on the floor, leaned up against a bookcase.

He unlocked all of the exterior doors so he'd have easy access and egress when the time came.

Hiding in a closet would be the worst—one guy opens it, the other hears a ruckus and grabs Rosy. It all depended on what they did. He preferred to wait for them outside the house, watch through the windows for an opportunity. They would have to carry things and would probably tie Rosy up somewhere. He opened all the curtains and blinds so he could see what was going on from the yard.

He hoped they'd leave Rosy tied up in the van. That way he could just grab her and split . . . down the driveway, which turned a short distance from the house, taking to the woods only if he heard pursuit. That would avoid the clamor of two people crashing blindly through the undergrowth. Once at the car and rolling, they'd be indistinguishable from other traffic.

He completed the circle back at the study.

He sat down at the desk, took a brown paper bag from the pocket of his jacket. He took Billy O'Neill's revolver halfway out of its plastic bag. He could see the bloody fingerprints on the barrel and the handle. He taped the plastic bag over the butt only, hoping that would preserve O'Neill's prints. Part of his afternoon had been spent leaving a package for O'Neill, getting him on the phone to tell him where it was. Part of the package was torn money. Although the number would have to be played by ear, if he found what he was looking for, he had a few measures planned for O'Neill.

He sat the gun on top of the desk in readiness and began a systematic search of the desk and files. He went through it quickly, as the organization made it possible to scan by category. In ten minutes, he'd not found what he was looking for. He had found a forty-five automatic in one of the drawers. He added it to his pockets, realizing he was getting heavy, with Lew's, O'Neill's, and Regar's hardware. It was comforting, like knowing there were extra dry socks aboard on a cold-weather voyage.

He was about to begin again, more thoroughly, when he saw in plain view the thing for which he searched. He marveled at Dr. Regar's gall.

He lifted one edge of the glass on the desktop and removed the picture of Rosy and the envelope that was beside it. He'd seen the picture before. He took from his pocket the pictures he'd taken from O'Neill's wallet. One of them matched the print Regar had under glass on his desk. In the envelope were the torn halves of two five-thousand-dollar bills and pictures of Charlie and *Squareknot*. Remembering that one drawer had contained packages of prints, he tried the envelope on top and saw that it contained the negatives.

After a moment's thought, he put the pictures and the money in his pocket. He was concentrating on how this would affect his plan when the sound of an engine from the garage made him drop to the floor. He reached up for the gun. The approach to the garage, on the far side of the house, was such that he doubted anyone could have seen him. He slipped quietly out onto the screen porch and, from there, around the house toward the back side of the garage.

He recognized the constricted tenor voice of the large man who had sat eating with Rosy at Jason Richards's house. "It's as empty as the others, the door's wide open. Let's go, Bead; come on, girlie, you know the routine. You don't really think I'm gonna leave you sittin' here unguarded, do ya?" A squeal of pain from Rosy accompanied the sound of steps entering the house.

Routine? Charlie peered into the garage to confirm what he'd heard. They had not left her in the car. O'Neill's gun felt unwieldy in his hand. Regar's was better. He slid the magazine out of the handle, made sure it was loaded, cocked it, worked the safety to be certain it was off.

Rosy stood handcuffed to the refrigerator. Apparently, it was one of Coughlin's rules: Always cuff the hostage to the refrigerator. This time, at least, one hand was free, the other cuffed to the appliance. She was thinking about the nature of courage as she listened to the hoots and hollers of Coughlin and Bead moving around the house. She fingered the knife beneath her blouse, then pulled it out and looked at it. The blade appeared to be quite sharp.

A story came back to her, one told by a girl from Alaska, a girl she'd been friendly with in college. The girl's grandfather had been something of an adventurer. He'd made and lost several small fortunes by the time the girl was twelve.

That winter, the old man was traveling a frozen river between two wilderness settlements on his snowmobile when it conked out. He got out his tools and went to work on the machine. Lying on his back on the ice to get at some part, he'd reached one hand up to try the starter. The machine was in gear, and the thick rubber track jumped forward, dragging his other hand and wrist into the machine. He was trapped. He couldn't reach his tools with the free hand.

The shooting pain of shattered bones dimmed to numbness with the cold. He kept himself calm with the thought that someone would pass on the well-traveled river and stop to help him. As the meager winter light drained from the sky, however, he had to face the fact that the time for travel was over. Nightfall and temperatures of thirty below zero meant that he would freeze into a bizarre statue of the coupling of man and machine. No more pilgrims abroad that day.

He tied his scarf around the trapped arm, using his teeth and free hand to get it very tight. Then he used the only tool he could reach, his pocketknife, to cut the arm off at the elbow. It took about ten minutes to saw through the tough joint. He bound the arm as best he could, managed with his tools to get the severed hand and wrist out of the track, and drove the five miles farther to town, a feat in itself, with one hand, on a bucking snowmobile.

Rosy wondered if her will to live was that great. She put the blade on her wrist, tried to think of it as something that wasn't part of her. Do big cuts only hurt the same as small cuts, or does the pain go up exponentially? She wondered whether she could keep from screaming and bringing Coughlin running into the room. The blade was sharp . . . blood was running in little drops from the gentle pressure. It didn't hurt even as much as the cuffs. She tried to decide whether to flail at it in one grinding swoop or to go slowly and carefully. She moved the wrist, watching its action, trying to figure out where the path of least resistance would be.

Then a noise behind her made her turn in time to see Charlie grab the hand that held the knife.

"What the hell are you doing?" he asked in an urgent whisper.

"Oh, Charlie," she said, nearly fainting. "He's so fast. I couldn't get away. He killed Jason and Lew, Charlie. He'll kill you."

"Lew's still alive, and he hasn't killed me yet." He jerked at the cuff that held the door. "Where's the key?"

"In his pocket. Charlie, run! Get the police. Don't let him catch you here."

Charlie was thinking of the bolt cutters on the boat, which would have gone through the cuffs like tissue paper. Damn!

Through the window he'd seen the knife she held on her wrist. His logical deduction had been that she was about to kill herself. It affected him like a starter's gun. He'd rushed in unprepared.

Now footsteps came from the other side of the house. Bead appeared in the doorway, a stack of framed coins in his arms. Charlie pointed the gun at him. Afraid of alerting the other one, he said nothing. Wide-eyed, Bead stared at him. Charlie listened for the footsteps of the other guy, trying to decide what to do.

Bead said, "Who the hell are you?"

Charlie put his finger to his lips and motioned for him to move out of the doorway. He stepped aside himself, so they were both out of the line of view, and Coughlin would be in the room before he saw them—with his arms full, Charlie hoped. He waited. Five seconds.

From behind him, Rosy whispered, "Charlie, Lew had his gun on the other one, but he moved so fast! Don't make the same mistake. Kill him as soon as he walks in, Charlie! It's the only way. Otherwise, he'll kill us."

Charlie puzzled over the alien idea of shooting a man down on sight. He remembered the burn holes in Rosy's underwear and decided he could.

From behind her, another voice, also whispering. "That's right, girlie."

Charlie's head spun toward the sound, just in time to see Coughlin drape his arm lazily over Rosy's shoulder, the gun in his other hand pointed casually at the ceiling, his eyes focused on Charlie like a dragster watching the starting light.

"Think you can beat me, sucker? Think you might hit the girl if you do?" Crazo let a big grin crawl slowly over his features, followed by the squeal of adrenal giggles. "Look at 'im pointing on that door like a dumb setter on a rabbit hole. Don't he know there's a back door, girlie?"

The next squeal was Rosy's as she drove the knife upward into his neck. The plume of red that shot from around the blade opened his eyes in surprise. A flash of metal over his head came down, driving him to his knees, revealing Michael with a sand wedge in his hands. Afraid to fire at him between Michael and Rosy, Charlie dove toward him, his gun straight out in front. Coughlin managed to get his own gun up, but Charlie fired first and blew him onto his back. His head came up, and Charlie fired again, this time a foot away from his face. As he did so he realized the man was already dead, the movement of the head no more than a rebound.

Charlie's ears were ringing from the contained explosions. At first he couldn't place the muffled racket, like listening through a pillow. Then he saw Michael's gaze over his shoulder, heard his voice falsetto and far away, saw him throw the golf club toward the side of the room where last he'd seen the man holding a stack of frames. Even as Charlie whirled, his mind tagged the noise he'd heard as shattering frames, and he knew there would be a gun in Bead's hand. Bead had to fend off the flying golf club, and before he could level Jason's twenty-two, Charlie caught up with him, firing into his chest. He watched as Bead was jolted backward like an actor getting the hook.

The distant wail, he realized then, was Rosy, right beside his ear. He went through Coughlin's pockets and came up with the necklace that had been in Rosy's bag, then the key to the handcuffs. He freed her wrist. Shoulders heaving with uneven sobs, Rosy leaned into his arms. Michael took the gun from Charlie's hand, and they stood there for a couple of minutes while Rosy caught her breath.

Charlie led Rosy outside, where a brisk New England sea breeze blew. He breathed deeply and told her to do the same. They leaned into each other and moved in slow, aimless circles around the yard. When Rosy was composed enough to listen, Charlie began with what had to be done.

His voice was gentle. "Rosy, I know all about your scam with the necklace, the reason you were with Jason Richards, the fact that you were with that maniac in there when Lew was stabbed. Michael told me a lot of stuff, too . . . so I could help him find you."

Her arm tightened around him, afraid of where the talk would lead. "There's a lot more going on here, too, that you don't know about yet. I can't take the time to explain because we've got to get out of here. Regar will be back about midnight, or so you told Coughlin. That's three hours from now. What we do between now and then may determine whether you spend time in jail or go free. So you've got to help me. Can you do that?"

She didn't answer, and he wondered if she would be able to talk at all for a while. "Can you tell me what happened? Can you answer some questions?" Her face contorted in pain. "Can you hold on and tell me how you fell into the hands of these men; what has happened in the last few days? Then you can rest for a long time. We'll go away, where you can rest a long, long time."

Sounds were still distant from the ringing in his ears. It reminded him of being in an airplane on rapid descent, when the pressure in the ears didn't equalize, and it feels like the whole world's had the volume turned down. He barely heard her say, "Would you take a woman with a broken nose to Tortola?"

Two and a half hours later, Charlie stood alone in Dr. Regar's kitchen and looked around. It wasn't perfect, but it would have to do. The bodies were gone, the blood basically removed, but there were faint stains on the floor and on the walls that he knew would be more visible in daylight, would be easily identified for what they were when a police team went over the house. They'd find lead in the walls, too, lead that had passed through bodies—the bodies of Coughlin and Bead, now hastily crammed into a toolshed outside the house. One way or the other, they wouldn't be there long.

He looked at his watch. Michael and Rosy should be finished at Jason's, gathering her possessions and wiping down every conceivable surface that could carry one of her fingerprints. Charlie had washed the dishes there himself, helped them for a while, after taking Coughlin's van there to get it out of the way, then returned alone in Rosy's Ferrari to do the clean-up at Regar's. Regar was due back in half an hour.

He picked up the phone, dialed the number of the phone booth where he'd told Billy O'Neill to wait for his call. Billy's hello didn't sound friendly.

"I see you found the package," Charlie said, imagining Billy O'Neill standing by the pay phone in the roadside bar ten minutes away. When Charlie had told him that afternoon that he was going to get another crack at the ten thousand, Billy had talked a good tough game of not believing him. But Charlie had told him he was leaving his halves of torn money and directions to a phone booth under a brick in the marina yard. He counted on Billy's curiosity to get him moving. Charlie knew that part of the recidivist personality profile was an inability to postpone gratification of desires in a normal fashion. He didn't think Billy would be able to resist the possibility.

"I found it all right, but I'm tired of you guys jerking me

around. I ain't doing nothing for you till I see the mates to these scraps of money you keep tempting me with."

"Aren't you forgetting something, Billy? Like a very nasty pistol with your prints all over it?"

The silence on the other end of the line told Charlie he was suitably reminded now. "You do what I tell you tonight, and you'll get that back, too. Now wouldn't that be worth a little of your valuable time?"

"Doing what?"

"I'm going to leave that to your creative imagination, Billy. Frankly, I don't care what you do beyond carrying a message for me. See, I know who hired you to kill me. He lives about ten minutes from where you are right now. He's due home in about twenty-eight minutes. What I want you to do is tell him I know who he is, and that he better not fuck with me anymore.

"Why don't you send him a telegram?"

"Because I think you'll get his attention better, since you'll know he's got the mates to your pieces of money at his house. You'll probably persuade him to give them to you, and I don't care if you do. For your trouble, you probably earned them. Fact is, he's got a whole lot more money, and I don't care if you take that, too."

"Where's he keep it?"

"What, you think I'm dumb enough to tell you so you can just swoop in there, rob him, and disappear? Hell, I want the guy to see what it feels like to have a guy like you on his ass, you follow me, O'Neill?"

There was a moment's hesitation, but Charlie thought he could hear the onset of positive anticipation, maybe some pride in his specialized abilities, when he said, "Yeah, I gotcha, but you got my gun. What am I gonna do, threaten to slap him?"

"I put a gun in his mailbox for you. You get there before him, pick up the gun, wait for him inside his house. I made sure the door through the screen porch is open for you to get in."

"The place ain't wired?"

"Only his coin collection, which is mounted on the wall of

the study, and that's turned off. But don't start getting ideas. The real dough is hidden. If you had enough time, you might find it, but the simplest way is to convince the guy to show you where it is."

"Dogs?"

"No."

Charlie gave him directions how to get there, told him about the break in the trees where he could hide his car. By the time they had it straight, Billy's mood was noticeably improved.

He said, "You guys are a barrel of laughs, ya know it?"

"Yeah, Billy, I guess we are. Have fun."

Charlie went outside and stood on a trash can to reach the telephone wire. He cut it cleanly. He got into Rosy's Ferrari and drove out of Regar's driveway. He went only a hundred yards and backed into a driveway that provided some cover for the car. He turned on the VHF radio that he'd brought with him from *Squareknot* and wired into the cigarette lighter.

"Sailor calling Jeweler, come in."

"Sailor, this is Jeweler, everything okay?"

"All set. Stand by."

He left the radio on, watched the area of Regar's driveway, which he could see from his vantage point. He reached in his pocket and took out the torn halves of money that had been on Regar's desk. He wondered if Regar could convince O'Neill that they'd been stolen. If so, O'Neill would be looking for Charlie again. Of course, Charlie still had O'Neill's gun in his pocket. And that threat had seemed to give him pause on the phone. He'd left Coughlin's gun in Regar's mailbox. In court, it could end up convicting O'Neill for Jason's murder. Of course, if something went wrong, Charlie might have to explain how it had come into his possession. But he didn't think it would unfold that way, and the overwhelming anger and resentment he felt toward these men made it worth the risk to try his end-game moves.

Right on schedule, a car pulled into the trees not far from where Charlie was concealed. O'Neill got out and hurried up the driveway on foot after getting the gun from the mailbox.

In his mind's eye, Charlie followed him into the screen porch, inside the house, saw him investigating quickly, as Charlie himself had done, to be certain he was alone, then looking at the coins, which Charlie had replaced on the wall. The glass had broken in only two of the frames when Bead dropped them. O'Neill was probably breaking the frames one at a time now, putting the coins into his pockets. He would assume, as Charlie had, that they must be rare enough to be worth some money.

"Sailor, you there?"

"Yeah, Jeweler; what is it?"

"What do we do if we don't get the signal we want?"

"If I see O'Neill leave, I'll let you know. You take Rosy home with you, and wait to hear from me. I'll move the boat, and we'll call it a draw."

"What happens when Regar finds the . . . stuff in the toolshed?"

"First, I enjoy thinking he'll mess up his pants. After that, my guess is, he'll bury it. He won't know how, but he'll figure it's related. If he calls the cops, it's his problem. He can't connect it to us. What's he gonna do, explain to the cops what he's been doing with O'Neill and us?

"But don't sweat it. I think I know O'Neill well enough to predict it won't go that far."

In another minute, the black Ferrari came past and went up the drive. Charlie gave Regar a couple of minutes to be sure he was inside, then came out of his place of concealment. He used a flashlight to see that O'Neill's car was a blue Monte Carlo. Then he backed Rosy's car into Regar's driveway, went as far up as he could without danger of being heard. He got out and moved up close to the house.

He saw two possibilities. One would be very hard to watch, maybe impossible; maybe he would have to intervene. Regar would be tied to a chair, and O'Neill would use a knife. But Regar wouldn't be able to tell him where the pieces of money were . . . because they were in Charlie's pocket. Of course, O'Neill wouldn't believe that.

Charlie stood out of the light that fell from the study window and peered in. O'Neill pushed Regar into the room, and immediately Regar's hands slammed onto the desk where he knew the envelope should have been. The voices were muffled by the windows, but Charlie could see Regar's reaction in his eyes. O'Neill had the gun on him, shoved him again. Regar held his hands out, body language all mollification, and Charlie hoped O'Neill's overconfidence would tempt Regar into Charlie's trap. It was the cleaner way.

He talked to O'Neill as he moved around the desk. Charlie thought he could read his lips saying, "Okay, I'm getting it for you." His hand went into the drawer where he kept the forty-five. Charlie had put it back. Regar talked to O'Neill with animation, a smile of supplication dancing once across his features, playing at defeat. His other hand was making motions at O'Neill, distracting him as his hand came out of the drawer full.

Yes, I was right, Charlie thought. The doctor would have been too slick for him. O'Neill would have lost in the first round. Regar had pulled the trigger, heard the click of the empty chamber. He might even have had time to look down aghast and see Charlie's calling card—the piece of quarter-inch line around the barrel, tied in a square knot—and recognized what it was. Surgeons are into knots, so he might have made the instantaneous connection to the name of a boat he'd taken a picture of and a man he'd tried to kill. For an instant, Charlie hoped, he might have realized that the man had won, had turned his own murderer against him, before O'Neill fired, blowing him against the far wall.

Charlie saw the gaping chest wound and the inert form and sprinted across the yard. He got into Rosy's Ferrari, turned on the accessory power, said into the radio, "Jeweler, you there?"

"Go ahead, Sailor."

"Make the phone call; the car is a Monte Carlo, this year's model, dark blue."

"Roger Wilco."

Charlie shook his head. Roger Wilco. The old guy thinks

he's Broderick Crawford. He let the Ferrari coast down the drive, started it when he got to the street, got the hell out of there. It took a major effort to stay anywhere close to the speed limit.

Michael heard the telephone voice say, "Police station, Mc-Dowell speaking."

"Hello, I'd like to report something suspicious."

"Who's calling, please?"

"This is Mr. Williamson, Two Ninety-two Ridge Drive." Charlie had read the name from a mailbox, next to a driveway that was close to Regar's, on a piece of land that would command respect. "Twenty minutes ago, as I was entering the Quick Mart on Route One A, a man asked me directions to Water Street. I immediately recognized him as someone I'd seen on television, but I didn't place him at first. I gave him directions, then he asked if I happened to know where Dr. Regar's house was."

"Yeah?"

"Well, it happens that I do know that house. I've been to parties at his home, so I gave him the directions. He thanked me and left.

"Only a moment ago did I realize who the man was. It was the fellow who was in that celebrated trial down in Boston, for killing his landlady with a tire iron. The police who arrested him got in trouble for roughing him up."

"You mean Billy O'Neill?"

"Yeah, that's the name! Doggone, I couldn't think of it, but I'm positive that's who it was.

"Anyway, when I realized who it was, I was concerned. I decided to call Dr. Regar and make sure everything was okay. And you know what?"

"What?"

"The phone's out of order . . . like maybe somebody cut the wire. You don't suppose this O'Neill character is over there doing something awful, do you? I mean, the news reports made him sound like an extremely unsavory type of chap."

Michael waited the few seconds it took the man to pull himself from the boredom of night-desk duty to a state of alarm.

"What kind of car was he driving?"

"Hmm, let's see . . . yes, it was a late-model Monte Carlo; in the streetlights I couldn't be sure of the color, but I think it was dark blue."

"Thank you for your call, Mr. Williamson. We'll check it out."

McDowell was fairly new on the job. He used the phone to cover his ass. He woke his chief out of a sound sleep. Five minutes later, he picked the man up at his front door, and they headed for their rendezvous at Regar's driveway with the town's three radio-dispatched cruisers, who'd been told to use flashers if they needed them, but no goddamned sirens. Before they reached the drive, they came upon one of the cruisers pulled over. The cop hurried out of the trees when he saw them, leaned over to say into the window, "Dark blue Monte Carlo; pulled back in the woods. If I hadn't been looking for it, I'd a never noticed."

Billy O'Neill stood in the middle of Regar's study cursing. He'd turned the place upside down, still hadn't found the pieces of torn money, of course, since they weren't there. That's what Charlie had expected him to do.

When he heard the siren blaring up the driveway, saw the flashing lights in the front yard, he bolted for the back, which is what the chief expected him to do.

He was halfway out the door of the screen porch when the hand-held spotlight blinded him, and his gun hand came up instinctively. In the next two or three seconds his body absorbed about a pound and a half of lead from the guns of the police, who remembered quite clearly the vilification of their brothers in blue who'd arrested him before. Before the echo of the barrage had died down, McDowell stepped briskly forward, picked up Billy's gun, held it in Billy's limp hand, pulled the trigger twice, for powder burns, just to be sure.

One of the policemen standing in the shadows said softly,

"Police. Drop the gun and put up your hands, or we'll shoot."
A nervous laugh came from another part of the shadows.

They had looked in the window before they flushed O'Neill,
so they already knew Regar was dead. The chief said, "Somebody get back on the desk at the station, call the state police."
He shook his head and spoke to nobody in particular as he
nudged O'Neill's lifeless form with his toe. "At least this time
Billy O'Neill won't walk, and the rest a them crazies from
Boston will think twice about fuckin' around in my town."

When the state police got there, and somebody looked in
the shed, they found Coughlin and Bead. The chief was a
little embarrassed to have two more dead bodies than he'd reported. But after they radioed for a computer check on their
identification and found out who they were dealing with, one
of the staties said under his breath, so only the chief could
hear, "Hey, don't count teeth in a gift horse, Paul. We may
not know why or how, but you got yourself a fuckin' hat
trick here."

24

Lew told the police that his assailant was a small man, and that he had been alone. It took the heat off a red Ferrari and a beautiful woman with a damaged face. Not that the heat was very intense anyway. Charlie figured mere attempts got a lot less police effort than successful murders, and Lew improved rapidly.

There were other loose ends. Frank Singleton could have read a paper, seen the crime wave among his Ferrari customers, put two and two together, and called the police. But Charlie didn't think abstractions like justice and civic duty weighed heavily in Frank's mind, certainly not enough to risk censure for his own part.

The fence who bought Jason's Ferrari, the taxi driver who took Rosy and Coughlin to the dock, the usher Rosy tipped to seat her beside Jason at the track—if one or more of them stepped forward when they saw pictures in the paper of the dead, then Rosy could have become very much a part of their investigations. But most of those people had skeletons of their own to keep covered, and the man on the street isn't known for his willingness to step forward and participate in an outbreak of violent death.

Charlie did leave a forwarding address at the dock. He

figured if something they hadn't thought of led the police to them, they'd just have to hire a lawyer and hope for the best. Being a fugitive was no answer.

He never told Rosy the details of what he'd done to Regar and O'Neill; that had been his choice, and he wouldn't ask her to share the rap, if it came to that. He told her only that they were no longer a source of worry. Strictly speaking, that wasn't true. He worried that he'd gone too far, that he might have more meanness in him than he'd ever wanted to face.

For a couple of months, every knock at the door caused a quickening of the pulse. But after that, Charlie figured the cops hadn't been too concerned about finding answers for the unexplained.

The police had a mixed bag of resolutions and question marks. Since the questions weren't easy to answer, the tendency was to accept the face value of a bunch of dead troublemakers. Regar, while considered a victim, lost some points in the sympathy vote when they found his bizarre leather outfit and the unexplained cash, the cash that Coughlin and Bead had amassed, and which Charlie had stashed in one of the doctor's old black bags. There was idle speculation that his links to the bad element may not have been strictly the luck of the draw.

The phone call from "Mr. Williamson," in fact, indicated O'Neill had some prior link to Regar. That became suspect when Williamson denied having made the call. It gave them a snakebitten feeling. But it was easy to rationalize that the caller was some equally solid citizen who just didn't want to be involved, so he'd used Williamson's name and address to get quick action.

The gun found in Dr. Regar's hand had killed Coughlin and Bead; the gun in O'Neill's hand was later found to have killed, in addition to Regar, Jason Richards. In some ways, the circles were closed. But no scenario the police could fabricate seemed to explain the obvious clean-up of both crime scenes. Among themselves, they speculated that there were other people involved. With the press, they admitted only that an investigation was ongoing to determine exactly what had transpired.

The apparent escape from the police was little consolation for a while for Rosy. The horror stayed with her, and Charlie had to tell her many times that the bad guys were all dead, and hold her, rock her back to sleep in his arms.

Unexplainably, she was fixated on the idea of going to Tortola, as they'd discussed the night before she was abducted, but Charlie was afraid of taking her on a lonely sea voyage. It would be too easy for a despondent person just to step off the stern. He'd rented a small house that had its own dock where he could keep *Squareknot*, on the Annisquam River on Cape Ann, close enough for Michael and Lew and Lucy, the only people with whom she could be open about her ordeal, to visit regularly and help her back to a sense of security.

It gave her a broad base of support, which is what he thought she needed. Michael's inquisition was more gruff than Charlie's, his curses more vociferous. Lew, recuperating from injuries physically, though certainly not mentally, more serious than her own, gave her a fellow victim, an outlet for empathy. Lucy and she spoke of women things, mother-and-daughter subjects. It was the first time she'd ever had that type of thing with a woman she trusted, a woman of experience who knew how to be thankful for the good things in her life, how not to dwell on the bad.

By mid-September, she seemed to Charlie to be mostly back to her old form. That being a form still characterized by a certain reserve, he wasn't too sure whether it was good or bad. Every now and then, a detail of her ordeal would rise to the surface, and she'd tell him about it in a tone that screened out a lot of the emotion involved. He began to think of it as being like the physical mechanism with which a body sloughs off splinters.

On a day sail out of the Annisquam, she told him the story of the man on the snowmobile, what he did to keep from dying, how that's what she'd been contemplating when he saw her with the knife on her wrist. He was horrified. She pointed out that her friend showed her a picture of the old sourdough that had appeared in the Anchorage paper the next day, photographed in his hospital bed, grinning without his dentures, holding the stump up for the cameraman. The caption read, I'M STILL ALIVE!

The wind picked up, and they were occupied for a while shortening sail.

When they were relaxed in the heeling cockpit again, making eight and a half knots on their return to the Annisquam entrance, she said, "I never did figure out why the old man didn't cut the rubber track of the snowmobile instead of his arm."

Charlie puzzled over it a moment, grinned lazily, resisted the impulse to laugh, said, "I guess, in a situation of extremity, it's hard to think of every option. One does what one can."

In a minute they both laughed softly, and Charlie said, "Jesus, I hope it never occurred to him that he could have done that."

After a while he said, "You never get any rest, Rosy, if you spend all your time trying to see around the good things to find the bad."

"You think that's what I do?"

"Maybe. What do you think?"

"Sometimes I think the good stuff is in danger of being overwhelmed. You have to wear blinders to keep it in focus."

A little while after that, she said, "Maybe I should go to law school."

"You want to be a lawyer?"

"Maybe a prosecutor."

He thought that was a healthy sign. She still had youth enough to mount a crusade. It also reminded him that this woman who had been so cruelly used was not without claws of her own.

Charlie had more or less decided that the ideal was beyond his reach, but that he was ready to embrace the okay, when he could find it. As for the Rusts and O'Neills, the Regars and Coughlins, he planned to stay out of their way, for as long and as much as they'd let him.

He doubted that would satisfy Rosy. In her twisted way, she'd been playing the masked avenger before she met him. While she stayed, though, she was an outstanding part of the okay he wanted to embrace. Stray cats come and go. If one can handle that, while they're around one feeds them cream, hoping to get close enough to hear the music of the purr.

It was nearly dark when they reached the dock. They spliced the main brace with rum-and-tonics liberally limed. She made a stick-to-your-ribs chef's salad while he mixed up his favorite envelope dressing. They heated some soup and crusty French bread he'd baked in *Squareknot*'s oven, opened a bottle of California white.

They dined in the cockpit with the lights of their little house on the Annisquam shining down on them. Lew and Lucy and Michael could be seen through the windows, sitting inside a warm glow of incandescent light, but they were pretending they hadn't noticed the boat's return.

After dinner, he poured each of them a shot of brandy, and with the sound of the moving water, occasional late-returning boats parading their green starboards, moaning the deep grumble of low RPMs, the rich smell of sea air under a billion stars, it had the makings of romantic, and Charlie could see it coming. He could tell that, if he sat very still, he was going to get in this gorgeous creature's knickers again, for the first time since "the incident," as Rosy referred to it. She leaned comfortably into his side, his arm around her protectively against the promise of winter that hovered on the waterfront on fall evenings in New England. After a while, he realized she was asleep.

"Me and my bright ideas," he murmured, "wasting all that energy on sailing."

He drank both brandies himself, thinking about the bruises on her mind, hoping they'd been isolated, wouldn't rot to the core. He believed there was good stuff underneath.

218

But as the brandy burned deeper, expending itself against the oncoming chill, some of his smugness slipped. Blinders, she'd said. Is that what keeps me going? he wondered.

The issue unresolved, he decided not to waste energy on it and carried her below with the utmost care. She came dreamily awake, kissed him in an inviting way, and he made gentle and knowing love to her into the night, basking in her repertoire of fireside purrs and full-moon yowls.

In the morning, before he opened his eyes, he gradually became aware that the warm weight on his chest was Rogers. He also was aware that his subconscious had kept at the issue of blinders while he slept; had, as so often happens, delivered him an answer he couldn't find in daylight.

Rosy was right. He told himself that was okay. A lot of great racehorses had needed them before he did. He found much to enjoy about life, as long as he didn't have to be picking at the scabs all the time.

Blinders were never a hundred percent effective, though. For example, without turning his head, he knew that she was gone.

ABOUT THE AUTHOR

Don Matheson was born in North Carolina in 1948 and grew up in Pennsylvania. He earned a degree in philosophy from Vanderbilt University in 1972, but he credits most of his education to working as a rigger on a derrick barge out of Morgan City, Louisiana, as a waiter in Aspen, Colorado, as a baker in Anchorage, Alaska, and as a truck driver in New York City. During a ten-year career in business, he lived in Atlanta, Dallas, Kansas City, and Boston. He now lives with his wife, Vickie, in East Hampton, New York, on Three Mile Harbor, the home port of *Squareknot* in Charlie Gamble's next adventure, on which Mr. Matheson is currently working.